YELLOW WATCH

Yellow Watch
journey of a Portuguese woman

a novel

Carmelinda Scian

MAWENZI
HOUSE

©2022 Carmelinda Scian

Except for purposes of review, no part of this book may be reproduced in any form without prior permission of the publisher.

We acknowledge the support of the Canada Council for the Arts for our publishing program. We also acknowledge support from the Government of Ontario through the Ontario Arts Council, and the support of the Government of Canada through the Canada Book Fund.

Cover design by Sabrina Pignataro

Library and Archives Canada Cataloguing in Publication

Title: Yellow watch : journey of a Portuguese woman : a novel / Carmelinda Scian.
Names: Scian, Carmelinda, author.
Identifiers: Canadiana (print) 20220281750 | Canadiana (ebook) 20220281807 | ISBN 9781774150825
  (softcover) | ISBN 9781774150832 (EPUB) | ISBN 9781774150849 (PDF)
Subjects: LCGFT: Novels.
Classification: LCC PS8637.C596 Y45 2022 | DDC C813/.6—dc23

Printed and bound in Canada by Coach House Printing

Mawenzi House Publishers Ltd.
39 Woburn Avenue (B)
Toronto, Ontario M5M 1K5
Canada

www.mawenzihouse.com

*For Ronnie,
who will always be with me,
Christopher and Gregory*

In view of the fallibility of all human judgement, we cannot believe that we will always judge rightly. We might so easily be the victims of misjudgement.

                                                                C G JUNG

CONTENTS

A Pilgrimage to Atalaia	1
Lucinda's Bouquet	12
Strays	20
Hansel and Gretel	25
The Butterfly First	33
Catcher of Souls	41
A Dragonfly Dashed By My Face	52
Yellow Watch	60
The Bêbeda	77
Warlocks, Spells, and My Mother	88
You're Old Enough to Start Dancing	101
She Liked Dealing	111
Snow Drops	124
Zeus	132

Waylaid Pilgrim	140
And Still I Said Nothing	159
The Disappeared	168
A Black Kitten	177
Casa do Relógio	186
No Wire Nor Rope	203
Even the Lowly Squirrel Cares For Its Young	211
What Do We Know About Anyone?	222
River Crossings	232
Acknowledgements	239

A Pilgrimage to Atalaia

My father held the chicken's neck down on a flat rock in the middle of our patio. He'd talked to her softly, the chicken knowing him well; he'd been feeding her the best corn all year so she'd give us good eggs. The chicken's eyes were flitting and she clucked noisily, afraid, I could tell. The knife cut through and she ran around in circles, gaining speed until she collapsed not far from where her head lay. I wanted to cuddle "Princeza Cinza!"—the name I'd given her because of her feathers being the colour of ashes—but my mother warned me not to get the spewing blood all over my new white poplin dress. I'd be wearing it tomorrow on our annual pilgrimage to Atalaia.

I started to cry. My mother grabbed me by my shoulders. "You silly, silly child. Princeza Cinza knew all along it was going to die some day. That's what chickens do—they produce eggs and die. That's their purpose."

The morning was still thick and black when my mother woke me the next morning. We had to get to Atalaia before the sun came up to wash our faces in the holy fountain. I hurried to get dressed, wanting to be the first to arrive under the clock painted in the front of my grandparents' house, my mother's parents, next door. Many of us were going, including the shoemaker, whose house was to the left of my grandparents' house, his wife and teenage daughter, Beatriz, who, though older than me, sometimes still came to play.

"Why do we have to leave so early, Avó?" I'd asked my grandmother the night before.

"Santa Atalaia only blesses those who arrive early."

"Why?"

"They still haven't sinned much by then. It's on those she performs her miracles. She protects them against evil for the rest of the year."

"What evil, Avó?"

"Oh, all the bad things that happen to people; things they do to one another."

We soon departed, walking along a dirt road, the only road from Amendoeiro to Atalaia. My grandfather led the way but I could hardly see him in the dark. Everybody carried a bag or basket or a blanket. I carried the patched cloth purse Avó had made me with small pieces of material she kept in a large basket. The purse was heavy with all the pennies I'd saved all year from the ten cents allowance my mother gave me on Sundays. I'd buy five cents ice cream cones, instead of ten, or five cents worth of roasted chestnuts or roasted peanuts and save the other five to give to the lineup of beggars in Atalaia on the way to the fountain.

After an hour or so, the first rays of light pierced through the dark charcoal horizon, helping to light the way. But the woods along the road still loomed dark and deep.

A few times I thought of asking my grandfather to carry me on his shoulders, as he'd done the previous year. But I didn't want Beatriz to call me a foolish baby again. The other day, she'd shown up on my terrace, surprising me. I was pretending to be an angel—a crown of dandelions on my head, wings of corn husks. I told her I could fly over her house.

"I'll throw you down from here, my little angel, and see if you can fly." She started pushing me over the parapet. I yelled, "Help, help!"

"You foolish baby."

It was chilly under the canopy of thick eucalyptus and tall pines, the spongy floor of dead leaves still wet and smelling of mildew and rot. I was happy we'd arrived, my legs hurting so badly, nearly buckling over. The dampness in the air made me shiver.

The men got busy looking for a shady spot under the biggest trees, the woods already crowded with people. The women carefully checked out the tree trunks for smoothness, not wanting to get hurt when their behinds got hit against them. Last year, Avó was left with a bruise on her behind the size of an orange. She showed it to me; she couldn't sit for a long time. "The hardest thing," she said, "is not knowing when they're coming for you."

"Why are the women hit and not the men?" Beatriz now asked. Everyone knew she was smart. She was the only girl in Amendoeiro going to high school in Montijo and she wore glasses, a sign of intelligence.

"So they behave well all year," my father said. The men laughed.

"Who started it?"

"It's a tradition in Atalaia," my mother added.

"I know, but who started the tradition?"

Everyone thought for a minute, then turned toward my grandfather.

"Oh," he said. "It likely began when we ran around with tails and fur on our backs."

All the baskets and bags carrying the food and wine were closely placed against a tree and neatly covered with a blanket for protection against thieves. My grandfather opened a bottle of *aguardente*, filled up tiny glasses, and passed them around. "To kill the night's germs."

Avó gave me a taste. It burned my tongue. She gulped down the contents of her glass in one fast motion. "I don't know how men can drink this." She waved her hand back and forth in front of her mouth but asked for another glass.

We left for the holy fountain, a small distance away from the picnic woods.

Beggars had already formed unbroken lines on either side of the dirt road. Two rows of scarecrows in their ragged clothes and matted hair. Some were blind, others missing an arm or leg, leaning on crutches, bonny hands stretching out.

They must've come last night, I thought, to be already lined up. I reached into my purse.

"Not yet," Avó said. "First the washing."

The fountain was small, oval shaped, made of white cement, with a spout in front. The water ran into a cement basin, quickly filling up with sand carried over by all the feet.

A long lineup waited in front of the fountain. The sand around it, soaking wet, the air cool and damp even though the sun was rising and warming up the day.

I waited behind Avó; the rest of our group was ahead of us. Avó finished washing and drying her face with a towel she'd brought from home. I handed her my purse.

As I bent toward the water, a pigeon landed on the fountain, grey wings fluttering, beady, nervous eyes gazing at me. The eyes of Princeza Cinza, as my father held the knife to her neck.

I turned and buried my face in Avó's skirt.

"What's wrong? Go back there and wash your face." She grabbed my hands and tried to loosen my grip but I refused to move.

My mother, who'd been standing with the others a short distance away, came over.

"What's going on?"

"Something seems to have scared her. She doesn't want to go near the fountain."

My mother placed her hand on my neck, trying to pull me away. I started to cry.

"Oh, leave her alone," Avó said. "What sins does she have anyway?"

I woke with a start, unsure of where I was, something crawling over my face. The canopy of pines and eucalyptus rising above me made me realize I was in Atalaia. We'd all been lying down for a siesta after a lunch of cod fish cakes, tomato and cucumber salad, bread, and black olives. Princeza Cinza was saved for later.

I looked around. Most people were still sleeping on their blankets. My grandfather was snoring, his belly rising and lowering with each breath, his mouth open like an O. The shoemaker farted.

Gradually, people woke, the chatter grew, like an oncoming gust of wind. My grandfather began slicing a watermelon. Beatriz and her mother peeled large, red-cheeked peaches.

"You want one?" Beatriz's mother asked when she saw me looking. She dipped in her basket and handed me a tiny, sickly-looking fruit.

"No thank you. I'm not hungry."

My father snuck up behind my mother and grabbed her arms, while the shoemaker held on to her legs, panting, his shirt coming loose around his waist, exposing his fat belly.

They dragged my mother to the nearest pine tree, then swung her bottom hard against the tree trunk, counting in unison, loudly and slowly, "One, *bump*, two, *bump*, three, *bump*, four . . . " Seven times. My mother's dress caught on the bark, revealing her upper legs. I turned away from their whiteness. My mother laughed the whole time. But I could see she was upset—her mouth puckered the moment they dropped her back onto the blanket.

My father and the shoemaker laughed so hard, they began to cough and choke. My mother slowly got up, pulled down her skirt and ran her fingers through her new perm.

My uncle Rafael, my mother's younger and only brother, and Beatriz encircled me.

"Time for you my baby, time, time, time . . . for . . . you . . . !" they crooned together.

They swung my behind against the pine with great force; I stopped counting after three, biting my lower lip so as not to cry. I hadn't imagined how painful this would be. This was my first time.

Beatriz and Rafael dropped me on a heap of pine needles that scratched my arms and legs, my dress rolled up over my head, showing my pink underpants. The men clapped, including my grandfather. The shoemaker bent his moon face over me and made the sign of the cross with his white, fat hand,

"Now, you're baptized."

I stood up, turning my back to everyone, and wiped the scratches on my arms and legs with spit, tiny drops of blood emerging from some. I kept my head down to hide the tears; my white poplin dress was rumpled and soiled.

My mother walked over to me. She removed the pine needles from my hair, retied the bow at the back of my dress, wiped the drops of blood with a handkerchief.

"Let's go to the washroom," she said. "Maybe there's water."

Her voice was shaky. She picked up the new beige raffia bag she'd bought for the occasion. Avó joined us.

The new washroom was a little distance away. Last year we had to pee far into the woods to get away from the watching men.

"Good you didn't take that crappy peach," my mother said. "Those cheap foxes. They ate the good ones and gave you the worst."

"You can't fool Milita," Avó retorted. "She's like a hawk. Remember last Christmas when she asked the man selling the holly by the market why the berries were attached to the stems with pins? We got away quickly—he was coming after us and cursing us to hell."

I could smell the washrooms before we even approached. A long, deep hole had been dug in the ground and enclosed with tall canes, the top leaves curly and dry. One side was for women and one for men. A skinny woman with black, frizzy hair stood by the door wearing an apron and holding a broom. She continuously swept the footprints on the narrow dirt opening leading to the entrance. She charged us ten cents each and handed us a piece of newspaper. She told us she'd hit a man on the head with the broom earlier in the day. She'd caught him peeking through the canes. "The pig wanted to see the women's asses."

Inside were two planks placed across a deep hole. I never looked down and held my nose tightly. I kept thinking about what the woman had said.

We washed our hands in a large clay basin by the entrance, the water soapy and brownish from all the washers before us. That cost another ten cents. My mother wet her handkerchief and wiped the dirt and blood off my legs and arms.

We walked back to the group. My mother and Avó were silent the whole way.

At three o'clock we all left for the Procession. Throngs of people walked toward the large white church on the hill, overlooking the town. It was said the church was to have been built at the bottom of the hill. But when the foundations began, the labourers would arrive each morning to find their tools mysteriously moved up to where the church now stands at the edge of the sacred grove. At the church's entrance was a large marble piazza with a long set of wide stairs leading down to the main street of town.

The piazza was already crammed with people when we arrived. We were lucky to find room at the bottom of the steps. Beatriz and I sat on the ground, my bottom still hurting from being hit against the tree trunk. The moment the first musical notes began, everyone leaned forward to have a peek. The band, dressed in light blue, came out first. The saint, wearing yellow and a white mantle over her head, was being carried by four men in dark suits on a pallet heaped with multicoloured flowers and ribbons. Walking down the stairs, one of the men slipped, the saint wobbled, almost toppling over. Everyone went, "*Ohhhhhh*." A woman yelled, "It's a miracle, the saint didn't fall and break." Two women dressed in black, standing near me, crossed themselves.

"It wouldn't matter if the statue broke," Beatriz whispered in my ear. "It's only plaster. The real saint is inside the church."

"That's not true. That's the real saint."

"You foolish baby."

As Santa Atalaia passed us, everyone followed behind, shoving one another in order to touch her. The procession wound around the two major streets of town. The crowd kept pushing. I wanted to ask Avó to lift me up, finding it hard to breathe. But Beatriz was walking beside me and I didn't want her to laugh at me again and call me a foolish baby.

On our way back up the church steps, Avó and I lost the others. We ended up in a large, crowded courtyard behind the church. Someone was playing an accordion, people were dancing. Avó grabbed me by the arms and started waltzing, bouncing me up and down. I'd never seen her dance before—didn't know she could. As we swirled around the courtyard, I saw horses tied up at the back, under a red tile roof. The horses smelled funny, as we neared them.

Beggars were sitting on bales of straw next to the horses. I recognized a couple to whom I'd given money in the morning. One was young, about Rafael's age, wore dark sunglasses with only one lens. His right arm was missing, the shirt sleeve hung empty, like a rag. He'd asked me my name and then had sang, "*Milita é valente . . .* " to the tune of our national anthem.

"Look, Avó, the beggars; they're eating."

"Yes child, Santa Atalaia provides. She's the protector of the suffering and the poor."

"So why doesn't she help them to see and walk?"

"She can't do that."

"Why not?"

"She can't change the world. Things are as they are: the poor are the poor and the sick are the sick. It's their fate."

Avó stopped dancing. We walked out. The procession rush was over. When we got back, my grandfather wasn't there.

"Did you see your father?" she asked my mother.

"He was behind us for a while. I thought he was with you and Milita."

Avó started walking back toward town. I followed her, knowing she was worried. I'd seen that frown before, seen it whenever my grandfather didn't show-up from work on time and had to be carried home from Antonio's Taberna at closing time.

When we passed the men's washroom, she called out, "José! José!" but no one answered.

An outdoor bar was set up not far from the washrooms. Strings of red and green banners swayed in the breeze above the barrels used as tables. A group of men stood arguing by the entrance. My grandfather wasn't there. One drunken man yelled, "*fodas, fodas,*" when he saw us, swaying his hips in a vulgar way. We hurried away.

Next we looked in the main tavern, the Vinho Santo, just below the hill where the church stood and across from where we'd watched the procession. We peered in from the door. The place was crowded, noisy, foggy with smoke. I wondered what kind of sacred wine they sold.

"There he is," Avó pointed to the bar, sounding relieved. "Go tell him it's time to eat."

The men stepped aside to let me to pass. There were no women. I could see my grandfather's back; I pulled at his arm.

"Dinner is ready, Grandpa."

"That's my *Neta*," he said to the man facing him. "Yap, my granddaughter is a Ferreira through and through. She takes after my side, strong and stubborn."

He swallowed the rest of the red wine in his glass and paid the bartender. Once outside, he lifted me onto his shoulders. Avó followed behind. As we passed the outdoor bar with the red and green banners he said, "The colours of our flag. Green is for hope, red for the spilled blood of our warriors. Always remember that Milita."

The sun was beginning to set, a full moon's shadow already peering down at us from the cloudless sky. The air was turning cool.

My mother and Beatriz were walking toward the fountain as we arrived. I could see their backs, twenty or so metres away.

"Where are they going?" I asked my father.

"To the fountain to wash your mother's bag."

"What happened to it?"

"Your mother didn't want to return to the smelly washrooms, so she went to pee behind some bushes and placed her bag on a pile of shit."

I kept looking toward the fountain, waiting for their return, knowing how upset my mother would be. She'd gone to Montijo especially to buy the raffia bag, the latest fashion.

Beatriz carried the dripping bag on their return now looking more like the big wet rats in the open sewer between my house and my grandparents' I sometimes saw.

"How could this happen to me?" my mother asked, eyes shifting from face to face, as she and Beatriz rejoined us. "A brand new bag . . . I have no luck. No luck."

Everyone tried comforting her. Avó said that once the bag got washed with soap it would be fine. My mother just shook her head. "No luck, I have no luck."

"Okay," my father announced. "Time to eat."

"Yap," the shoemaker said. "Before dark comes and the wild cats take over the woods."

"Lots of meowing this year," my father said. "I heard they're coming from everywhere."

"Avó, what wild cats will take over the woods?"

"Oh, never mind. Don't listen to them. Putas—bad women."

The food was set out on tablecloths spread over the blankets. A hushed buzz filled the air, as everyone sat down to eat.

My mother lifted the lid off the pan. The chicken lay with her legs up on a bed of rice, not looking anything like Princeza Cinza without her feathers and her head.

I turned away. Beatriz laughed, her laughter coming from behind me. I hadn't seen her approach. She locked my head tightly in her hands, forcing me to stare at Princeza Cinza.

"Some day, that'll be you. Your head will come off, off, off . . . "

Still laughing, she stood up and went to join her parents.

My mother handed each of us a plate with a piece of chicken, rice, and bread. I tried hard not to think of Princeza Cinza. I pushed the meat aside with my fork, determined not to eat it. But after I finished the rice and the bread I was still hungry.

I ate only the tiniest pieces at first. The meat was delicious. In the end I left nothing but the bones.

My mother walked to the pine branch where the raffia bag hung. But the sun had already set, the raffia remaining wet. She held the bag close to her nose.

"It's ruined," she said. "It'll always smell of shit and I'll always think of it. I'll never return to Atalaia."

What will happen to us without Saint Atalaia's blessings?

I gazed at Avó who was busy cutting up a cantaloupe for dessert. She didn't look my way.

Lucinda's Bouquet

Lucinda sat very straight on a chair in front of the small window in the tiny living room. She stared out, as though watching a stage or a movie screen. A dozen or so onlookers had already gathered outside by the time Ana and I arrived, our arms full of flowers. "White, the flowers must be white," Lucinda's mother had instructed. "Get plenty for a bouquet and for throwing. I want Lucinda lost in a shower of white."

We pushed our way forward to the front of the group.

Lucinda's dress was made of white organza and lace. The dress had a long, full skirt, a lace collar, and short puffy sleeves from which thin arms stuck out, reminding me of the dead branches of the sickly quince tree in my back garden. Her face was covered with a thin, short veil. Maria, the milkman's wife, standing next to me, thin face thrust forward, as though not believing what she was seeing, said, "Thank God someone is finally marrying the poor girl." She made the sign of the cross.

"But what's with white dress?" a woman dressed in mourning black beside her retorted.

Laughter.

A man behind Maria hollered, "Red, she should be wearing red."

I turned around. He had a fat, veiny face and was smoking a cigar. Another man said, "One less female for the *Casmurro* to feed." Lucinda's father's name was Manuel Pereira but people called him a curmudgeon because he was so ill-tempered. He'd been a foreman at my father's factory before his stroke two years ago. No one missed him when he left, my father said.

More laughter.

"Why are they laughing?" I whispered to Ana.

"Lucinda is wearing white."

"But she's a bride. Brides wear white."

"Yes, yes, I'll explain someday. We have to go in now—the ceremony will soon start."

I followed Ana to the front door of the whitewashed bungalow with a low red-tiled roof. The green paint on the door was parched and cracking.

The laughter and chatter behind us continued until we stepped inside.

The front door led directly into Lucinda's kitchen. It was dark inside. I could hear voices and feel movement but the faces weren't clear.

My excitement began to wane. I'd hardly slept all night and now I could hardly keep my eyes open. An emptiness was taking over, where a feeling of fullness had been. Last summer came to mind. My father spilled a glass of red wine down my new white organza dress trimmed with a large blue bow at the back. My mother often reminded me that the organza had been the most expensive the store had in stock. It was the first day of the *Festa de São Pedro*, June 29, when everyone in town had to be seen wearing something new. Later, I'd be changing into the dress for Lucinda's wedding, though the stain had never really disappeared, the dress never again felt as special.

It was early morning when Ana and I departed to the Pinhal, the pine and eucalyptus woods a distance away from my house. At that early hour, the sky had hung over us like a grey canopy but soon the sun began showing its face, lighting up the dirt road and the misty farms along the way. Dew filled the air, making the day chilly for May 1, *Labour Day*. My father said the holiday ought to be called *Unemployment Day*, since so many men were out of work. Two of the three cork factories in Montijo, where most of the men from our town were employed, had been shut down for months, and the one where my father worked, had reduced the work-week to three days. Strikes there had ended in terrible violence. Last month, one of the strike leaders was shot dead in front of the protesting men outside the factory gates. My father blamed all of our troubles on Salazar, our prime minister. "A son-of-a-bitch."

"We're lucky," Ana continued, "lucky that Lucinda's mother picked us to gather the flowers for Lucinda's bouquet. It means you and I will marry someday. It's a guarantee."

Ana was my second cousin, two years older, and already preparing for Communion. She knew things.

She knew Lucinda had long waited for her paramour with the Elvis pompadour, who'd left for Brazil to make his fortune years ago. He never returned or called for her. Rumours had it that he'd killed a man in a bar brawl and ended up in a prison camp in the Brazilian jungle. Others said he'd made up the story so Lucinda would stop writing letters he never answered. Ana knew Lucinda had had an abortion by the *Velha*, the old woman in Sarilhos, that nearly killed her. Lucinda grew thinner and paler and sadder afterwards. People stared and whispered, as she passed them on the street, not with meanness but pity. They called her The Jilted One. But last August a stranger, wearing a light blue suit and driving an Opel convertible the same colour, stopped at the Esso station in town facing the main highway. He was partly bald, portly, and sported a thick black moustache. He'd worn white shoes, one with a sole thicker than the other to camouflage his limp. Ana had seen him enter Antonio's Taberna that afternoon. I saw him later.

It wasn't often drivers bothered to get out of their cars when they stopped at the Esso station. A veil of dust blew up from the unpaved streets, even when it wasn't windy. In winter, rain sometimes lasted for days, turning the two main streets into bogs more fit for pigs. Lucinda helped Antonio's wife with cooking and serving meals to men with no families of their own to cook for them. She happened to be working the counter that day. She told everyone afterwards that the man wearing the light blue suit ordered a *Sagres* and told her he lived in Lisbon, was a widower, and had two grown sons. He returned a week later to propose marriage. Lucinda was twenty-seven.

As usual, there were rumours. Some people swore that he was a PIDE informer, a spy for Salazar's brutal dictatorship and his terrorizing secret police. That he'd come to Amendoeiro to spy on the factory workers after the last strike. His hands were uncalloused and his nails trimmed, and two of the last strike participants had disappeared in the night, since he'd appeared in town. Everyone knew PIDE paid its informers well. Some insisted that the man-in-the-light-blue-suit was not to be trusted but, at least, people stopped calling Lucinda The Jilted One.

Inside Lucinda's kitchen, my eyes grew accustomed to the darkness. The place was crowded with boxes, chairs, clothes, people. No one seemed to notice us. Some of Lucinda's sisters were yelling at one another, looking for things they seemed to have misplaced. There were many sisters. Lucinda fell somewhere in the middle and was the first to get married. The youngest sister, the one we called Simples, was standing in the middle of the kitchen, crying. She was about twelve or thirteen and looked like an overgrown small child. People began calling her simple after she repeated grade one so often the mother finally took her out of school. "No woman should have children after forty," my mother said whenever we encountered Simples on the street and she'd be talking to herself or laughing out loud. "This is what happens—you give birth to idiots."

Simples had a protruding chin, the yellow eyes of a cat, and curly hair the colour of rusty iron. Her hair was never combed and it stuck out of her head like coils. Sometimes boys mocked her when she passed them; some girls did too. They would bend over, scratch themselves and grunt like monkeys. I only did it once; Ana had urged me on. Afterwards, I asked God for forgiveness. Simples had started to cry.

Lucinda's mother, a thin, gaunt woman with small nervous eyes and greying hair pulled tightly back into a small bun, took the flowers from us. "Calla lilies," she said, "good, the flowers of the Virgin." She didn't thank us or ask us to sit down, or offer us anything to drink or eat. We were hungry, having left home before breakfast. We expected there'd be cakes and cookies and laughter, happy laughter, not the scornful laughter outside.

We stood watching Lucinda's mother place the flowers on the wooden round table. She separated the white calla lilies neighbours had given us, from the wild daisies we picked in the Pinhal. Then she took a pair of scissors and began decapitating the daisies, throwing them into a white basket. One of Lucinda's sisters, the one with the moon face everyone called Feia (though, with her long wavy hair, I'd never thought she was ugly) walked in humming a *fado* about a lost love. She was the eldest.

"Stop that, stop singing that sad song on this happy day," Lucinda's mother yelled, waving scissors in midair. "Stop it this minute. Don't bring any more bad luck into the house."

A muffled sigh came from a dark corner of the kitchen. It was then I saw Lucinda's father, siting on his wheelchair. The stroke had taken away his speech.

He stared at me—I was sure it was me and not Ana he was staring at—as though trying to tell me something. Maybe he remembered that my father had worked for him. His white moustache moved but no words came out. I felt sorry for him in spite of my father saying Casmurro was in with the government. Perhaps a spy.

Feia kept humming her *fado*, as if her mother hadn't said anything; Lucinda's mother kept cutting the heads off the daisies, lips pursed, silent; Simples kept crying; Ana and I kept waiting for some sweets or a drink.

We watched Feia arrange the calla lilies into a bouquet. She'd stretch out her arm holding the bouquet, gaze at it, then add another calla lily, as though Lucinda's wedding day and Feia's own life depended on the perfection of the bouquet. She tied it with a white satin ribbon.

Then she looked at Simples and said, "Baby, baby, why are you crying?"

"I don't want Lucinda to go. Who's gonna sleep with me?"

A sudden sadness seemed to sweep the kitchen, the way a chill enters a room.

"I will sleep with you," Feia said. "Let us be happy for Lucinda. She's the lucky one."

It was then Feia turned to face me. I wasn't sure she'd noticed us until this point.

"You take this to Lucinda," she said. "You're the youngest and the prettiest."

She handed me the bouquet and led me to the living room where Lucinda was sitting. Feia walked out and shut the door behind her.

The room was gloomy—the crowd outside the window had grown larger, blocking out the light. The sun had returned to its hiding place behind heavy clouds, as if not wanting to show its face again. It seemed a fiery storm was coming. I dreaded the month of May, dreaded the thunder and lightening it brought.

The room was quiet. The heart-stopping quiet of *madrugada*, the early dawn, as the last scraps of night fade away just before the roosters crow.

The only sound came from Lucinda's chattering teeth. This surprised me, considering the room felt stuffy, as if something had swallowed up the air.

Lucinda turned away from the window and faced me. She lifted up her veil.

Her face was pale, paler than her white organza dress, her eyelids were painted turquoise and thickly lined with charcoal, lips and cheeks, a cherry red. She reminded me of a rag doll Avó had made me and that I still played with when Ana wasn't around. Ana had long ago stopped playing with dolls.

"You beautiful child," Lucinda said. She began to cry, her sobs, deep and loud, her tears carving a smudgy line through the rouge. One tear stained the front of her dress, leaving a pink spot. She didn't seem to notice.

I wanted her to stop crying, wanted her to be happy on her wedding day. Joyful, she should be joyful, after the man in the light blue Opel rescued her from the town's pity.

But here I stood speechless, holding the calla lilies until her twiggy arms reached out for the bouquet. Her hands were trembling.

I opened the door and ran out of the room.

Lucinda walked out of the whitewashed chapel, that once had been a small cork factory on Main Street, and stood by the door. Her faded red lips were kissed by the man with the light blue Opel. Today he was dressed in a black suit and black shoes, one sole thicker than the other. The decapitated daisies were showered on them as they walked back to Lucinda's house, fifteen minutes away, the whole town following, including my mother and the groom's two grown sons who'd come to Amendoeiro for the first time. They didn't limp.

After the cod and shrimp cakes and cookies and cakes and small plates of rice pudding were passed around in Lucinda's patio and the port wine drunk in tiny glasses, even by Ana and me; after the clown, dancing and jeering to the music of the accordion player made us all laugh; and after everyone stood on the curb waving goodbye, as the light blue Opel convertible rode away to Montijo, where Lucinda would now be living, I asked Ana, "Why was Lucinda crying when I handed her the bouquet this morning?"

"What do you mean, Lucinda was crying?"

"Crying. She was crying. Tears ran down her cheeks, smudging her rouge and staining her dress."

"You silly, tch . . . tch . . . tch . . . " Ana clicked her tongue in mockery. "Brides aren't sad on their wedding day! They cry because they're happy. They can't believe their good luck."

Ana knew things. But I'd seen what I'd seen.

The next day I took a kitchen knife and carved out the red cheeks and lips and the turquoise eyelids out of my rag doll and buried them in my back garden. Then I threw the rest of her body parts onto the garbage dump.

"Good," my mother said, as she watched me. "It's time you grew up."

Strays

She bursts through the door as though hurled in by the hot wind. Hunched shoulders, scrawny, grey hair pulled back into a tight bun, pointy nose, long black dress worn for a baby daughter who'd died at birth long ago, she reminds me of a crow. She's carrying two metallic knitting needles, large tongs and scissors in her hand. My knees wobble. What is Crow going to do to my Aunt Luisa?

She waves at my mother but doesn't seem to see me, then hurries to Aunt Luisa, who's waiting in her bedroom.

My mother said I could help, so long as I didn't go nosing into the bedroom or yap all over town. "I don't fancy the police at my door or Father Batista showing up with his sermons."

"What's Crow doing to Aunt Luisa with those knitting needles?"

"She's not a crow. She's your grandmother's—Avó's cousin. She's family. Show some respect."

"*Sim, sim*, but what is she going to do to Aunt Luisa?"

"Oh, the baby came too early. People will talk."

Aunt Luisa and Rafael, my mother's younger brother, had been married for five months. It was a wedding that wasn't a wedding. One afternoon Aunt Luisa showed up in tears at my grandparents' house next door, where Rafael still lives. I'd never met her before; I thought she was pretty. The next day she and Rafael went to see Father Batista. Afterwards, there were small cakes and port wine, but no white dress or veil or guests or dancing.

"What will happen to the baby?" I ask.

"The baby! Don't you worry about the baby. He'll be in God's keeping."

My mother follows Crow into the bedroom, which is next to the kitchen, the house having only two rooms. As my mother opens the door, I peek in. Aunt Luisa is crying, while Crow holds up her bare legs. They're white, bloodless-looking, like the whites of an egg. The door shuts with a bang.

Thunder begins to roar in the distance. Avó (who's gone to visit a cousin in Palmela, not wanting to be around) believes the devil is more powerful than God, and will burn us to death one day. Thunder is his warning. I'm terrified of thunder. "Why will he burn us?" I once asked. "For all our sins." I've been praying every night ever since.

Now I say an Our Father and an Ave Maria. Maybe this is the end. Maybe the devil has grown tired of warning us.

My job is to bring in pails of water from the well in my grandparents' garden. The pail is heavy, and keeps bumping against my skinny legs, half of the water spills out, wetting my feet and shoes.

In the kitchen, I ladle water into a large pot over the kerosene stove on the small low cement counter and watch it boil for fifteen minutes. "It must be fifteen minutes to kill the germs," my mother said.

I keep my eyes fixed on the clock on the kitchen table. Above the clock hangs a large wooden crucifix. A tiny pear-shaped tear runs down Christ's cheek. I wonder if he's crying for us.

Steam fills the dark kitchen. There are no windows and my mother insisted on me keeping the door shut.

It's hard to see and breathe.

Crow reappears through the steamy fog, knitting needles and scissors held up, like a bouquet, as before. Grinning, she dips them into the boiling water, revealing her stained teeth. A tooth is missing. She's humming something I can't recognize.

She turns away from the stove, walks past me, shakes her head and clicks her tongue in disapproval. As she enters the bedroom, I hear her say, "The girl shouldn't be here."

Again I peek, my mother is rocking Aunt Luisa in her arms like a baby.

Piercing screams rend the air from behind the shut door. I cover my ears with my hands. I've never heard such howling, was never this close to such pain. Christ keeps crying. I'm sure his tear is further down on his cheek.

Eight pails of water, five boiling pots, four hours later, Luisa's screams dwindle to a wail. Tired, hungry, my shoes and feet soaking wet, I regret having offered to help. I want to go home, eat, put on dry socks and play with my doll.

Crow reemerges from the bedroom, a smell like throw-up follows her. Once more, she holds the knitting needles and scissors up high but this time there's blood on them. Her grin is wider. "Revenge," my mother would say later. "For the child God took away." I don't know what revenge against God means but I don't ask any further questions.

My mother comes out next. She carries a large pail covered with a bloody rag.

"I want to see Aunt Luisa," I say.

"Let her sleep."

I help my mother carry the pail to the open sewer running between my grandparents' house and ours. Water from the outdoor cement laundry tub, dishwater, rain, runs through it, forming a permanent puddle outside my garden gate. Once a cat drowned in it; it rotted until my father buried it.

Dusk descends; a drizzle begins to fall; the thunder moves closer.

"Good," my mother says, "rain will wash away everything."

She lifts the bloody rag from the pail. With the other hand, she makes the sign of the cross. I do too, not knowing why I'm doing it. In the darkening light, the pail's content looks like the blood of the pig my father killed last year. I help my mother lift the pail and tilt it so the contents can spill out. My mother starts crying. Drops of the dark blood fall on my legs.

"The baby, the baby!" I shout.

"Don't be silly, the baby is in heaven with God." She wipes my legs with her apron.

In the night, Aunt Luisa's screams silence the earth. Crow hovers over me with a grin as big as the moon. Then she flies away, behind the moon, large wings flapping over our house, over Amendoeiro, over the clouds, black skirt thrashing in the wind like a giant sail.

I wake up panting. Then I get out of bed and open the window. Dawn is breaking. The air is dense and sticky, the storm having failed to clear it. I dress and hurry to the garden to see what's left of the blood.

At the garden gate, the red puddle overflows with rain water. The rising sun shines on something white inside. A cloud of flies perform a mad dance above it. Just as I step outside the gate two stray dogs appear, fierce and famished. I hurry back behind the gate and quickly shut it.

One dog picks up the white *thing* with its teeth, the cloud of flies lifting up in unison. The other snatches it from him. They growl at each other, fangs out, drool and blood dripping from their mouths. They rip the white thing to shreds.

Is Jesus watching?

"Luisa was mumbling gibberish all night and was hot to the touch," Rafael says, as my mother and I walk in, the morning sun drying up any signs of last night's rain.

Dr Souza arrives late afternoon from Montijo. By the time the taxi lets him out on the highway, in front of Rafael's house, women from the neighbourhood had already gathered in the courtyard.

After taking Aunt Luisa's temperature, Dr Souza says, "Butchers," to no one in particular. We're all in the bedroom, except my father and grandfather, Avó having returned from her visit to her cousin the evening before. "You all ought to be in jail but I'm a Christian man."

He writes something on a pad and hands it to Rafael. "Soon," he says, "she must take this soon." As he departs, he raises his thick black eyebrows, and points at my mother and Avó, "The girl should not be here."

Aunt Luisa soon falls asleep, the pallor on her face making her look like a ghost.

"Let's go home and eat something," my mother says. "Rafael will watch over Luisa."

Outside, the neighbourhood women now overflow the courtyard. Most are old, dressed in black clothes and black headscarves, mourning for a lost husband or child. They blend with the descending dusk.

More Crows.

One of them is saying the rosary out loud while the others repeat the Our Fathers and Ave Marias after her.

"Will she live?" Someone grabs my mother's arm; my mother manages to free herself.

"Vultures and mad dogs," she whispers, as we walk away. "They've smelled death and can't get enough of it."

Hansel and Gretel

Father Marques stepped forward from behind the altar after finishing the Latin prayers and his furious swinging of the censer. The smoke from it nearly choked us. There was no altar boy. Tiny balls of perspiration had gathered on his face in spite of the morning chill. "Today I'm going to talk to you about the Christian life. Only those living with virtue, compassion, and charity can call themselves Christians." A streak of light streamed in from the small round window above the altar forming a halo around his head.

I was sitting in the front row with my cousin Ana. She'd already begun preparation for her First Holy Communion in June. It was now April.

"Taking what's not yours is a sin in the eyes of God," Father Marques continued, the pitch in his voice rising with each word. "Lying is a sin, envy is a sin, greed and not attending mass are sins. These trespasses anger God but cruelty angers Him most. He keeps a record of every single trespass. Remember that, every . . . single . . . trespass."

"You'll never get to heaven when you die if you don't go to church on Sundays," Ana had said after her first catechism lesson. "You don't want to go to hell and be burned alive or devoured by fiendish dogs, do you?"

Death and heaven and hell had never entered my mind before. Funerals marched by my house on the way to the cemetery in Montijo but these were someone else's great-grandparents or old aunts and uncles. Death or heaven or hell were not things my family talked about. They talked of work, the cost of food, how fast the pigs could get fattened so they could be sold at the open-air market in Pinhal Novo or killed and salted so we would have meat in winter. But the more Ana described hell's agonies, the more I was sure I wanted to go to heaven when I died.

It hadn't been easy convincing my mother. Only after Ana and I promised to go to the Pinhal to pick wild asparagus my mother would later fry with eggs, did she allow me to accompany Ana.

Something about ten year old girls dressed up as brides upset my mother. But then she didn't like most things about the Church, like the sound of Latin or the smell of incense and burning candles or kneeling down on wooden benches. She didn't believe in prayer, either. "There's no one up there listening, anyway," she'd say and shake her head, staring at you in disgust with the look she once had when she sliced a loaf of bread and found a mouse in it.

My whole family didn't trust priests. My father and grandfather called priests blood-suckers, who lived off the backs of the poor. They viewed religion the same way they did sport: an addiction that got you nowhere good but surely could land you somewhere bad. Father Marques was particularly disliked. About a year ago, he'd replaced old Father Batista, who'd been around since I was born and often fell asleep during confession. Even the two spinster sisters, whom the people called the Beatas, since they never missed Mass, had stayed home in protest.

Father Marques was too young, too handsome, smiled too much, not just for my family but for most people, even the Beatas. They'd commented, my mother said, on his pomaded hair, that made him look more like a *fadista* singing the *fado* on stage than a priest. He rode a red Vespa every Sunday from Montijo when he ought to have been walking like everyone else. "Who does he think he is?" people said. Then there were rumours. A girl had been seen riding on the back of his Vespa one night.

Father Marques now stopped talking and took a long breath, "Ahahah," his head tilting to one side, eyes fixed on the small congregation.

Today there were a few girls from Ana's class, two boys (also preparing for First Communion), five or six mothers, the Beatas, and Branca, the girl in charge of the collection plate, and her mother. They were both sitting on the other side of Ana. Branca was three years older than Ana, but already had big breasts making her look like a woman. She had bad skin.

Branca's mother had brought the white calla lilies now flanking the virgin on either side. She'd placed them there in vases before Father Marques arrived. A bee had buzzed around her new perm until Branca caught it with her sweater and stepped on it. The dead bee remained on the floor in front of the altar until Father Marques came in, picked it up by its wings, a look of horror on his face, and threw it outside.

The church was new in Amendoeiro. The narrow building on the unpaved Main Street had been a small cork factory before there was even the idea of a main street. A bell was hung from the tall, narrow chimney, the walls whitewashed, pews brought in from the church of Espírito Santo in Montijo, and a small Virgin Mary in a white mantle, holding Baby Jesus, was bought with money we raised in the bazaar one summer. The Virgin stood on a blue satin covered table serving as the altar.

Before we had a church, those wanting to attend mass had to walk the half-hour distance to Montijo, there being no buses on Sundays. Only the Beatas went.

But after Casa Rosa opened up at the entrance to the old dirt road behind our house—a safe enough distance from the centre of town—the Monsignor of Espírito Santo declared that Amendoeiro ought to have its own place of worship. Men visiting the brothel would be in immediate need of confession and absolution afterwards.

People laughed at first. "Does the Monsignor think we are children?" But soon people organized and donated to the bazaar and bought the Virgin. Everyone agreed that a church brought respectability to the slipshod group of dwellings passing for a town. Even my grandfather, who never stepped into the church, gave fifty escudos.

Father Marques stopped pacing and came to stand in front of me. I looked up slowly, afraid of catching his gaze. He took another deep breath, a drop of saliva dribbled from the corner of his mouth. He didn't seem to notice it.

"Gossip is evil." His eyes rested on me but I could tell he wasn't seeing me, he seemed to be staring past the church, past Amendoeiro. "Gossip is malice, it's the opposite of compassion and charity. Those engaging in it will burn in hell."

Mass ended.

Branca followed Father Marques into the room behind the black curtain to the right of the altar. She carried the collection plate. Ana and I waited outside to see Father Marques ride away in his red Vespa. It was a while before the Vespa emerged from the narrow lane beside the church, his black robes flying behind him in the wind.

"So what did the *fadista* have to say today?" my mother asked as Ana and I walked in. She had stewed lamb with potatoes and fresh peas for lunch. Ana would eat with us so we could go straight to the Pinhal afterwards. I told my mother what Father Marques had said about sin and hell.

"*Que merda!* What shitty nonsense. What does he know? Priests are men just like all the rest. I could tell you . . . " The dead-mouse-in-the-bread look was back on her face.

My father stepped in through the door; my mother never did finish telling us.

The Pinhal was a thirty-minute walk away. Not many people used the dirt road anymore after the new highway was built but it was a shorter route, cutting through fields, farms, and vineyards. Ana and I loved its emptiness. Well, mostly Ana, because sometimes the emptiness scared me. She called the emptiness "solitude." That's when the fairies came to her, she said, bringing good things. The fairies had never come to me. What I sometimes saw in the darkness of my bedroom, I couldn't share with anyone, not even Ana.

Ana talked the whole way. She was smart. She said that Little Red Riding Hood wouldn't have been eaten by the wolf if she'd been better acquainted with the woods. That was why Ana liked us going to the Pinhal. We needed to be prepared.

"Ana is a dreamer," my mother said. "Her head is high up in the clouds. Don't pay attention to what she says." But it was Ana who read me stories and fairy tales and taught me songs and proverbs and warned me that someday blood would run out of me like a water fountain. Then I'd be a woman, I'd know things, things she already knew but refused to share with me.

We passed scrub fields and oak trees, wheat and barley farms, the earth still smelling of winter wetness, the green plants already as tall as me. Soon the kernels would be full and be harvested. Clusters of red poppies, white daisies, and yellow buttercup stood in rows alongside the growing grains.

Ana said, "Taking asparagus from the Pinhal doesn't anger God. It's not stealing. God knows there's plenty and they'd go to waste if not picked."

It was as though she had read my thoughts. The moment Father Marques mentioned stealing this morning, I started worrying about our errand. Not that anyone had ever seen the owner of the Pinhal— he lived away in Lisbon or Sintra. This was why people felt free to picnic and stroll in it on Sundays, especially in summer. They took in the scent of pines and eucalyptus to fortify their lungs against tuberculosis. Everyone went.

Ana was right. Last September, my father brought home a large sack full of golden grapes in the middle of the night. In the morning I asked him if stealing grapes wasn't a sin. He laughed. "Oh child, God is too busy for such small things."

Now a flock of sparrows rose in front of us, their cries deafening.

"It's a wedding," Ana said. "See the two in front? They're the bride and groom."

I lifted my gaze but the birds had already gone and perched on the grapevines ahead.

"The ones following behind are their families and guests. Father Marques said that marriage is a sacrament like communion. Only after marriage can women and men come together and make babies. Before that, it's a sin to touch one another."

I was about to ask her what would happen to those who sinned, like the sister of a girl in my class who gave birth to a baby and she had no husband, but Ana was already pointing ahead to the Pinhal.

A group of boys stood at the entrance to the woods. This was a dirt path that ran around a large water hole and veered into the woods for a long while. I'd never gone to the end. The boys were throwing stones at the croaking frogs.

The moment we came into view, they yelled, "*fodas, fodas,*" moving their hips back and forth, back and forth.

"Keep walking," Ana said.

My face turned red.

It was darker and cooler inside the forest. I shivered. The air smelled of rot and dampness. Most Sundays, even in winter, we'd meet some neighbour or girl from school, but today the place seemed empty, except for the boys by the water hole.

The asparagus around the area where we usually played had already been picked. Ana walked further into the deep woods. I followed. She was sure we'd find plenty amidst the green undergrowth. She carried the basket. After a while, I could no longer hear the boys or the birds. The canopy of tall trees blanketed out the sun, suddenly turning the day into dusk.

Ana tore two branches from a pine tree and handed me one. "Just like Hansel and Gretel," she whispered, as though afraid to rile the gloominess with her voice. "We need to mark our path so we can find our way back." We carefully dropped a few needles every ten or so steps but after a while, we noticed that the ground was already covered with pine needles. We threw away our branches.

"Let's go home," I said, afraid of the long shadows and the silence around us.

But Ana persisted in looking for the asparagus.

She saw them first.

"Shh," she placed a finger over her lips and gently pushed me behind a thick pine.

Thirty metres or so ahead of us, we saw Father Marques' black robes blended with Branca's red dress. Her white thighs gleamed in the shadowy light. He kept pushing her against a tree, his hands covering her face, she giving out tiny, muffled cries.

"Is he hurting her?" I asked.

"You silly. Priests don't hurt people. Listen Milita," Ana's voice was shaky, different. "You heard what Father Marques said this morning about sin. Why would he hurt anyone? He's been chosen by God to do His holy work. Don't you tell anyone about what we've seen here today, okay? Not even your mother. We could be in serious trouble."

I started to cry.

"C'mon, I'll take you home. We'll leave the asparagus for another day."

It seemed that Ana and I hadn't been the only ones in the Pinhal that Sunday. The scandal spread quickly. Father Marques was sent away. An old, bald, glum priest replaced him. No one knew his name. They just called him Padre. Ana became a little Bride of Christ that June and continued attending mass. We never talked about what we'd witnessed in the Pinhal.

"Why aren't you going to Mass with Ana anymore?" my mother asked me at a later time. I told her I found it boring. This seemed to satisfy her.

People said they'd known all along that something terrible was going to happen one day. What could you expect from a priest who looked like a *fadista*? Branca went to Lisbon to live with an aunt. Rumours persisted about her for a long time. Some said she'd had a baby, others, that she'd gone into a brothel, still others that she was living with Father Marques in Lisbon. The milkman swore he'd seen them walking arm in arm in the Baixa.

One day a skinny fourteen-year-old from Minho, bleached orange hair and a thin moustache, joined Casa Rosa. The women talked of nothing else but the shame of a child *puta*, while the men lined up nightly outside Casa Rosa waiting their turn.

I ran into Branca three or four years later—she was visiting her parents. She was slimmer, wearing red high-heeled shoes with a matching purse, and a white silk blouse, her hair long, skin smooth and cleared. She stood out starkly from the shapeless women in our town in their cheap cotton dresses and old slippers.

The Butterfly First

I'd just sat down when I noticed her walking a short distance away on the dirt shoulder of the highway. It was midafternoon, hot, everyone lying down for a siesta. But I was anxious to start embroidering the pillowcases Avó had bought me this morning from a gypsy peddler passing through town. It was shady and cool in my grandparents' front patio and the highway, which ran along the railroad in front of their house, promised some distraction. I disliked my own house, tucked behind the shoemaker's house and at a right angle to my grandparents' property with only the dirt road to look at where nothing ever happened.

I didn't recognize her at first, a tiny figure clouded over by a thick layer of dust from a sudden gust of wind, her hair flying, her skirt billowing. The hot sun created a mirage of glistening water on the paved road in the distance. Not a car had passed by since I'd sat down. Even the stray cats and dogs were nowhere in sight, all likely asleep in some shady place.

I knew who she was as she got closer. Her name was Matilde. She was a year older than me but had been in my third-year class, having failed her first year. Both her parents had died of tuberculosis within a few months of one another and she'd moved in with an older married sister.

"Do you have an ice bag?" she called out, looking down at me from the raised highway. "I've asked everyone I've met and no one has one. The ice is melting fast."

It was then I noticed the black cloth bag hanging from her right hand, the water dripping down onto her dusty feet. She said her sister had given birth sometime in the night, a neighbour helping with the delivery. But by morning she had developed a high fever and infection was quickly spreading. This was why she needed the ice. She sounded fatigued, distant, older than her years. They hadn't called in a doctor; they couldn't afford one.

When I said that we didn't have an ice bag, her eyes became frantic, like the eyes of the trapped dogs the boys in the neighbourhood sometimes tied up and tortured for fun. She turned around quickly, without even a goodbye. I stared at her thin, already stooping back. Dust rose up with each step, the ice continuing to drip down her skirt and leg.

The design on the pillowcases was a bunch of violets with a yellow butterfly hovering above it. I decided to embroider the butterfly first. I saw the butterflies as tiny heavenly creatures, fluttering from flower to flower. "You're nine years old now," Avó had said when she handed me her gift. "You're too old to play with dolls; it's time to start working on your trousseau."

I wanted to be ready. Women and girls always talked of marriage, love, betrothal, men, whenever they got together, their conversations encircling me like signposts.

But after Matilde walked away, I carefully folded the pillowcases, tucking in the needle, thimble and thread, not feeling like embroidering anymore.

I stared at the road. One way, nothing, the other way, nothing. I stood up. Matilde was nowhere in sight. I started pacing the length of the patio, hardly containing myself, waiting for Avó to get up from her siesta.

"Do women die from childbirth?" I asked the moment I saw her.

"Sometimes," she said, her face contorting into a deep frown. "That's life, Milita. You ask too many questions." Then she brusquely turned around and walked back inside.

That evening, after dinner, I climbed to the rooftop of my house, as I often did in the summer. Only mine and my grandparents' houses had white stucco exteriors and terraces on top, a Moorish style my grandfather, who was a builder, had brought from our native province of Algarve. I liked peeking into people's gardens to watch what they were up to without them knowing they were being watched. It felt dishonest but I continued doing it.

It was nearly dark when I heard faint noises coming from the narrow passageway on the left side of our house. I quietly crossed the terrace and looked down. Beatriz, the shoemaker's daughter, had grown into a thin, pale woman; her fiancé, also thin and pale, sat on dining room chairs they'd brought to the lane for courting purposes, courting having to be done outdoors to prevent gossip. Her sweater was rolled up to her neck and he was groping her small white breasts with hungry hands. Then he opened his zipper and pulled out his penis, its shiny whiteness looking strange, frightening, embarrassing. I looked away, waited, then looked back. By now she was sitting across his lap, facing him, lips stuck together, his hands messing her hair. I crouched down low behind the parapet and waited, not sure what I waited for. Beatriz began making low whimpering noises, not unlike the cries made by the feral cats in the night during the mating season in that same lane.

I ran down the stairs, my heart beating fast, not caring if they heard me. That night I dreamt of giant cats making wild piercing sounds, one cat turned into Beatriz, her giant eyelids closing languidly, her long red tongue licking full magenta lips. I never said anything to anyone.

One afternoon later that year, I was home—school taking place only in the mornings—when Avó appeared at the door. She stood, stone faced, holding an empty, large brown potato sack. Her hair, normally neatly pinned up in a bun at the back of her head, hung wispily around her face.

"The damn cats are at it again," she said. "They ate the *bacalhau* I was soaking for tonight's dinner. I need you to help me catch them."

We hurried across my patio to her garden. The two cats, one black and one grey, had, periodically, snuck into her kitchen, and stolen the fish she'd cleaned and salted for the evening's meal. They were still licking their mouths when we arrived. Tiny chewed pieces of cod were scattered all over her patio. Avó went into her house and came out with two raw sardines that she swished in front of the cats' noses, luring them into the sack.

"Get the bricks Milita. Fast."

I threw in the two bricks she'd placed outside the door and we quickly tied up the sack. My heart was racing. It felt as though we were locking away all the balefulness in the world.

"Now you have to help me carry the sack to the river," Avó announced.

The river was forty minutes away. We turned the sack upside down, each of us holding one corner. Halfway to the river it began to drizzle but we'd walked too far to go back home for an umbrella. It began to rain harder. The bricks were heavy and the cats squirmed around in their frenzied struggle to get out, meowing desperately as if they knew what awaited them. The sack kept slipping, we kept grabbing at it, the burlap rubbing off the skin of our palms.

It was low tide when we got to the river, the water a mere grey trickle. We walked over the muddy banks, mud up to our ankles. Avó slipped and fell but managed to hold on to the sack. But the tie loosened and one of the cats pushed its paw through the opening and scratched Avó's hand. We threw the sack into the river. The water was so low it only partly submerged the sack.

Walking back, a terrible screeching followed us from the river, its echoes reverberating in our ears for a long time. Neither of us spoke.

Three days later, the scratch on Avó's hand had turned a luminous purple red, her hand swollen to twice its size. My grandfather took her to the hospital in Montijo for a tetanus shot.

"I'm cursed by God," Avó said when she arrived home, my mother and I waiting for their return. "Now the whole family will suffer. It's women who bring curses into the home. God doesn't forget that."

I ran into Matilde again one afternoon. School had started in October but she hadn't returned. I hadn't seen her since the day she asked me for an ice bag. I'd started helping Avó to carry baskets of pink, white, and burgundy mums and red dahlias, golden marigolds and white baby's breath from her garden that she sold to wealthy homes in Montijo. The baskets were heavy but I liked seeing the multicoloured bouquets. After all the flowers were sold, Avó would always buy me an ice cream cone from the street vendors in summer or roasted chestnuts in fall.

That day, after we made our rounds, we walked to the market to get fish and vegetables for Avó's dinner. Matilde stood at the main entrance, as if waiting for someone. I immediately asked her if she'd managed to find an ice bag that day.

"No. The ice had all melted by the time I got home. But a neighbour took my sister on his scooter to the hospital. She's okay, the baby is okay, but her husband's gone." She talked fast, as if repeating well memorized lines from a play.

"Gone where?" Avó asked.

"Gone. We don't know where he is."

Then she told us she was waiting for the market sellers to give her the cut-off heads of fish her sister would later boil and pour over stale bread. "Sometimes we're lucky to get a few vegetables and fruit left over at the end of the day."

Avó gave her a pink mum, from an unsold bouquet, and two potatoes.

"Why did her sister's husband leave?" I asked Avó, as we walked away.

"Oh, some men are like that. It's always the women who suffer."

I began to hate the ringlets my mother did for me every morning with an iron she would heat on the kerosene stove before I left for school. It took a half hour to do; I had to sit quiet and still.

"I want short hair," I said to my mother today.

"Never. You're not a boy—you're a girl! You have to dress and look like a girl."

"Never" with my mother meant I was never to mention my hair again.

That evening after dinner, I took a pair of scissors and hid them under my blouse. Once in my bedroom, I closed the door carefully so as not to arouse any suspicions. My mother didn't appreciate shut doors. I lay on my bed with my clothes on, scissors in hand, bloated with feelings I didn't understand. Night fell. A nebulous ray of light from the full moon floated through the window, allowing me to make out the outline of things. I threw myself from the bed and started snipping at my hair, chunks of it thudding softly around me on the floor.

I walked into the kitchen, ready to show my mother who was boss, my legs shaking uncontrollably.

But when I got there, everything was dark, the oil lamp not yet lit. Slowly I made out my mother and Avó standing in the middle of the floor. My mother was crying. Neither seemed to notice me. Only after I asked what had happened, did my mother say that my father hadn't come home from his shift work and might never come home again.

"But where is he, where is he?" I screamed. The thought that he might have abandoned us like Matilde's brother-in-law made my legs tremble even more.

Avó placed a finger over her lips and whispered, "He may have been arrested. There are troubles at the factory again."

"What troubles, Avó, what troubles?"

Neither of them answered. A few minutes later they walked out. I followed. Manuelito, now three, was sleeping. When we got to the unlit back road, I could hear a faint murmur. The light of the moon enabled me to make out a group of women huddled together, their children quietly surrounding them. Their husbands worked with my father.

A dog howled in the distance.

"Dogs howl at the moon," a gaunt woman, who always dressed in black in mourning for a lost child, said in a hushed voice to no one in particular. "They see things we can't. Awful things. Sometimes they see death."

"Why is everyone whispering?" I asked Avó.

"They're afraid of the PIDE. They come in the night and whisk away the men, never to be seen or heard from again."

Slowly, she explained that the factory workers had walked out in the morning to protest the death of a worker who had died the night before. The man had slipped and fallen into the cauldron where the sheets of cork were boiled. By the time they pulled him out, his body was crystal-white and ballooned to double its size. Unrecognizable. The men were now demanding better working conditions, more safety and compensation for the man's widow and his three children. I wondered why my father hadn't said anything to my mother about the accident last night. But then, my mother's nerves were bad.

The women and their children waited, dark figures blending with the night. I had long forgotten about my hair. The dog continued to howl. We were all turned toward the top of the road where the factory was located, waiting. Then someone noticed a shadow moving far in the distance under the pole with the electric light. It was someone on a bicycle.

"It's very bad," the man said when he arrived. His father was the night watchman. "No one is allowed to go inside the factory or to leave. Someone shot the foreman when he announced that all the workers were fired. Now the big bastards are involved. Major arrests are taking place. Go home. It's not safe to be seen in groups. Someone could be watching. The best you can do is pray and wait."

Pray and wait.

Avó and my mother huddled in the kitchen, my grandfather came to join them. No one said anything about my hair—I didn't think that they'd even noticed it. Avó told me to go to bed—there was school in the morning. I tried falling asleep, but the words *pray and wait* kept circling in my head like a carousel out of control.

I was still awake when my father returned. I ran into the kitchen. He said he was lucky to be let go. He was sure the factory would close, putting half of the town's men out of work.

Bad days ahead.

Back in my bedroom, I groped inside the dark armoire and found the pillowcases I'd hidden there, not touched since the day Matilde asked me for an ice bag; I always made excuses when Avó asked about them. I then found the scissors where I'd left them under my pillow.

First I cut up one pillowcase.

Then the other.

Catcher of Souls

The cart was wobbly, one wheel smaller than the other, the man and girl coming along the dirt road behind my house, hair blowing in the wind, the cart bulging over with their belongings. Two rolled up mattresses stuck out in front, two upturned chairs behind them, like two beetles on their backs, an iron washstand nearly falling over one side.

I stood watching from my garden as they entered the gate that opened onto the small courtyard of the unit they'd rented from my grandfather. It was one of two small units at the end of his property. The two units faced our garden. The girl glanced at me over the garden wall, but no smile or greeting. She wore a faded blue cotton dress and a sweater that was too short for her tall, lanky body in the chilly February afternoon. Her hands were trembling. As she turned to go inside, a tear at the back of her dress showed bare skin. She wasn't wearing underwear.

Her name was Solar. She was placed in my class even though she was two or three years older, a head taller than the rest of us in grade four. I'd never seen anyone like her, straight hair past her waist, milk-chocolate skin, eyes as green as a deep forest. She sat to my left. That first day, I watched her from the corner of my eye, as she stared out the window most of the time, even during lessons. At recess, she hardly spoke to anyone or joined in any of the games. She leaned against the whitewashed brick wall of the courtyard, watching us, yet not really watching, her gaze lost far beyond the school, far beyond us. We played hopscotch, even though most of us were getting too old for the game. But soon something changed. Under Solar's gaze, the game began to feel silly and childish. I refused to play. Before long, so did the other girls.

Senhora Correia, the only woman in high heels and matching skirts and sweaters walking the unpaved streets of Amendoeiro, came everyday from Lisbon by boat to teach us. She called out Solar's name one day and asked her who Afonso Henriques was. Solar kept her head down. When she looked up we all could see that she was crying. Senhora Correia said, "Our first king, Solar. Always remember that." Afterwards, she left Solar alone. The next day Solar didn't show up at school. I saw her on my way home, walking beside her father who was pushing his crooked cart filled with junk he sold in Amendoeiro and nearby towns.

His name was Antonio but soon everyone called him Tonto. This meant he walked wayward, was dizzy, a little crazy. He was taller than most people, hair blacker and longer, skin darker than Solar's. The threadbare pants he wore every day, that must've been grey once, were too short for his long legs and the red bandana around his neck was partly black from dirt. Barking stray dogs followed him up and down the streets announcing his presence. Behind his back people would point their index finger on their temples, turning them and nodding their heads to indicate that he was crazy. They laughed at him to his face. He laughed too, jerking his big head back, *ha, ha, ha.*

The first time I heard him laugh, I found it disturbing. His laugh was like that of the teary laughter of a clown. Beside him, Solar would stare out into the distance, never joining in.

"Last night the milkman waved a red rag in front of Tonto's face in

Antonio's Taberna," my father said at dinner, "while another man hid his cart. Tonto had already had a few glasses. He went into a rage. The more Tonto swore, the more the milkman waved the red rag, swaying it side to side like a matador."

My father laughed until he nearly choked on the fried mackerel he was eating.

I didn't think the story was funny.

A month or so later, a woman complained to her neighbour that her wallet went missing the moment Tonto and Solar departed from her door. Rumours spread quickly leading people to warn one another, "Watch out for the girl. She steals while the father keeps you occupied."

"Stay away from that *cigana*," my mother warned. "Gypsies are bad people, capable of anything. Anything. I wish your grandfather hadn't rented them the place."

Avó was nearby and said, "Blaming someone without proof is an invitation to Satan."

Avó believed in the devil, witchcraft, curses, spells, the evil-eye, the deadly power of envy and hate, more than she believed in God. In her opinion, God was too weak against the badness of people. "If someone stares at you, make a *figa*." She'd thrust her thumb between her curved index and middle fingers to remind me of how it was done. I was the only girl in Amendoeiro with a gold *figa* hanging from a chain around my neck instead of a crucifix.

The morning after the story of the missing wallet spread through town, Solar wasn't at school. I glimpsed her as she hurried in and out of her door later that afternoon. I'd kept looking for her over the garden wall, wanting to let her know I didn't believe the gossip.

After school each day, I returned to the garden whenever my mother went shopping or visiting friends and looked for Solar but she hardly left the house. Then one day, the summer holidays already begun, our eyes met, as she was coming out of her door. An instant, a flash. Enough to see her shame, her hurt, her loneliness. Solar had never returned to school.

Two weeks into the summer holidays and my mother had brought home a crocheting needle, a spool of white thread, and a lace pattern for an appliqué on a nightgown.

"It's time to stop wasting away your life and think of your future. Other girls your age are already building up their trousseaus. Don't do what you did to the pillow cases Avó bought you last year. I swear, there's something wrong with you."

Sitting on the small bench under the shade of the quince tree one afternoon, crocheting needle and white thread in hand, I noticed Solar on the other side of the garden wall. I waved to her to come over.

"Sit, Solar." I pointed to the narrow space beside me. "Do you know how to crochet?"

"No."

"Your mother didn't teach you?"

"I don't have a mother."

There were rumours. Some said Solar's mother was a French whore who'd left Tonto days after Solar was born. Others, that she was a wild Basque and Tonto had killed her when she fooled around with another man, this being the reason he kept running from town to town. He had a temper. He'd punched a man to a bloody pulp in Antonio's Taberna one night. The man had called him a thief or a liar or a gypsy, the story changed with each telling. Afterwards, my father told us, men cleared away when he walked in. They stopped waving red rags in front of him or hiding his cart.

Solar's leg touched mine. She was trembling, though July's scorching sun was already showering us with locusts and turning the wheat and barley fields to dust. I handed her the crocheting needle and thread, placed my hands over hers and showed her how it was done.

She smelled of almonds.

Solar returned the following afternoon and the next until she came over whenever she saw me in the garden and Tonto didn't need her. I did most of the talking. When I asked about her life—her mother— she went silent.

Chore-filled mornings and siestas (my mother insisted we take them) became unbearable, time passing slowly. I was eager to be with Solar. In the night, she began to fill my dreams, her trembling leg touching me, green gaze gently stalking me, the smell of almonds lingering long after I'd awakened.

I began to wonder about Avó's warnings.

"Watch out for soul-catchers," she'd been cautioning me ever since I was a child. "They have no soul of their own and can snatch yours with one single look. They'll possess you and leave you yearning for them the rest of your life."

Once I asked, "Was your soul snatched away, Avó?"

She stared at me, restless eyes now fixed somewhere far away, "It was a boy I knew. We were young. He lived on the farm next to ours . . . Oh, never mind. Old stories are useless. "

She walked away.

I came to read Solar's moods the way a dog reads its owner's. If happy, she'd flash open the gate and hurry forward, often whistling some tune I didn't recognize. If not, the gate opened gingerly, her steps sluggish, sadness pouring out of her, as she lurched forward.

Today she let out a sigh as she sat down.

"What's wrong?"

Silence.

"I'm your friend, Solar, you can tell me anything."

She gently placed her hand on my cheek. "*My friend . . .* "

Her touch had the softness of rose petals.

"Time to help with supper."

My mother stood filling the door frame behind us; I hadn't heard her approach. Solar flung her hand away from my cheek and hurried away, disappearing quickly beyond the gate.

I followed my mother into the house; she shut the door with a bang.

"I don't want that girl coming over again, you hear? What was she doing touching you?"

I didn't answer, the tenderness of Solar's touch still in my keeping.

"You know *ciganos* are bad people. Riff-raff. Just riff-raff bringing trouble to the world."

The next day, I stayed away. I had to. I peeked through the half-opened shutters of my bedroom before lying down for the compulsory siesta. Solar stood waiting by the garden wall. I closed the shutters.

Afternoons grew long, heavy, angry. I stopped crocheting in spite of my mother's threats of *fixing* me into a proper girl. I spent most of my time in my room, peeking through the semi-shut shutters. Days passed. Solar vanished from the other side of the garden wall.

My mother out shopping one afternoon, I dashed out of my house and headed for Solar's door, carefully looking around to make sure no one saw me. I hadn't been with Solar for three weeks. I knew my mother would be a while; she stopped and talked to everyone she met on the road, lamenting about her heart problems, her bad nerves, and how terrible, how difficult, it was to raise Manuelito, going on five. She was sure he was sent into this world to punish her. Why this would be so, she never said.

Solar's kitchen was bare, smelling of sour milk and dampness though it was summer, but the floor was swept. Two rickety chairs flanked a small wooden table, the washstand in a corner, a rag hanging where a hand towel ought to be. I sat on one of the chairs, tense, afraid of what Solar might be thinking of my sudden and complete disappearance and terrified of my mother's early return. Solar sat across from me, back straight, eyes expectant, like a pilgrim before an altar.

"I don't remember my mother," she finally said. "*Dat* refuses to talk about her, whenever I ask him."

I relaxed. Solar wasn't angry with me, wasn't judging. Maybe she'd learned to expect nothing from those crossing her path.

"There's no one you can ask?"

"There's always just been *Dat* and me. The two of us lived in a cave once. I was small but I remember the wetness of the rocks, the dankness, my fear of the bats flying around in the night. Another time we slept in a big tent with others. We'd all crossed a large river, *Dat* carried me on his shoulders, we all running from the gunshots in the distance."

After that afternoon, I visited Solar whenever I could.

My grandfather began talking of eviction by the end of August. Tonto was three months behind in rent. Besides selling his scrap, he'd held odd jobs but these never lasted longer than a few weeks, sometimes days.

"Does the *cigano* think I'm a fool?" Money and pride went hand-in-hand for my grandfather. "I'll show the bastard who I am. I'll put him on the street where he belongs."

Avó reminded him of the girl.

Where would they go? I wondered. I began praying to God every night to get Tonto a job.

Days later, my father was picking lettuce that I was to wash and get ready for the day's dinner, when Tonto burst onto his courtyard riding a battered bicycle he'd recently acquired. My father said he'd likely stolen it.

"Got a job at the bodega in Montijo," he hollered, nearly falling off the bicycle. "I'll be washing wine barrels, glasses, floors, maybe even pour a glass or two."

He pointed at me. "Tell your grandfather not to worry about the rent. I'll soon have the money."

"The job won't last long," my father said, once Tonto went inside. "He'll drink more than he'll sell."

Three weeks later, a stranger walked into the bodega demanding Tonto pay a debt. The man refused to leave without his money, Tonto punched him, the man punched him back, Tonto pulled out a knife, the police was called. "Bad for business," the owner told everyone.

Tonto was back pushing his cart up and down Amendoeiro, the dirty red bandana back on his neck, Solar beside him, barking mongrels keeping them company.

The murder happened Saturday night as the bodega was closing, a few days after Tonto was fired. The news spread quickly, like a fungus in a dank place—no one had ever been murdered in Montijo or Amendoeiro. Murder was not a word in our vocabulary. People died when God decided they should.

By noon the next day, about midday, a black sedan appeared at the top of the dirt road. I was pretending to help my father feed the two hogs, while keeping my eyes on Solar's door—I hadn't seen her since the news of the murder at the bodega. Two policemen dressed in dark blue uniforms with gold lapels hurried out of the car, leaving it idling, doors ajar, dust falling on the boys who'd appeared at the sound of a motorcar. One policeman held a pair of handcuffs; the other a gun.

Tonto was in his courtyard repairing his cart, whistling his usual strange song. "Gypsy lore," my father had said with a smug smile, as if the song explained Tonto's foreignness, his life.

At the sight of the policemen, he bolted out of the gate, long legs dashing by them, at the speed of a duck out of water at the sound of thunder. I'd never seen anyone run that fast.

Neighbours quickly gathered around the idling sedan. My mother and grandparents too. Stories quickly buzzed. Two witnesses had come forward early in the morning. They swore they'd seen a tall man with long hair run out of the bodega late last night, as he was being chased by the tavern's owner who clasped his bulging intestines until he collapsed on the sidewalk in a pool of blood.

Even Avó said, "Who else could it be? Who else had a motive to kill the tavern owner? Such a good man."

The two policemen ran after Tonto, the chubby one behind the taller one with the gun.

We all followed. The August heat still lingered though September had arrived, the dust rising from the ground nearly chocking us. Solar, who'd sprung out of the house at the arrival of the policemen, ran ahead of everyone, screaming, "*Dat, Dat!*"

Tonto was near the whorehouse at the entrance to the dirt road, about two hundred metres or so ahead of us and maybe sixty metres ahead of the policemen, when a shot was fired.

Everyone stopped. Some turned back. The remainder of us stood waiting in silence, as if paralyzed, eyes on the three figures in the distance and the one running toward them, still screaming, "*Dat, Dat!*"

We watched Tonto fold over at first and then collapse forward into a whirl of dust.

The policemen ordered us all to go home. As we walked away, I turned around. Solar was lying over her father's body, the dust settling on them.

In the evening, Avó walked into our kitchen.

"The gypsy was bad. But we can't abandon the girl like some stray cat or dog."

"But why us?" my mother said, always afraid, always mistrusting of outcomes.

"Aren't we Christians?" Avó retorted. "We must do the right thing. I thought she could sleep with Milita tonight. Tomorrow, I'll speak to Padre about sending her to an orphanage." The padre had replaced Father Marques. He was bald, head shiny as glass, shoulders hunched, and a large crucifix always hung from his neck, appearing to pull him down.

My mother frowned but didn't argue.

Solar was sitting on her front door step when I approached, the fading rays of the sun making her appear darker, older, bare feet covered in dust. She slowly lifted up her head, green eyes red now, puffy, streaks of dried tears and dust, like sailor tattoos, across her empty face. She stared at me for a moment, as if unable to comprehend what I was doing there.

I extended my hand; she took it, still staring with unbelieving eyes.

She devoured the boiled cod and potatoes and fresh greens,

sprinkled with olive oil and lemon, my mother cooked for dinner, as greedily as the stray cats swallow the fish heads and guts my mother throws them in the morning, as she cleans and slats the fish for the day's dinner. Afterwards, Solar washed her face, hands, and feet in a basin supplied by my mother. She lent her a nightgown.

My mother walked out of the bedroom carrying the oil lamp, Solar and I under the covers in my single bed.

As the last glimmer of light vanished from the room, Solar slid her arm under my neck, and pulled me close.

Her lips touched mine.

She kissed me again, longer this time, lips moist, tongue seeking. A shiver, unlike anything I felt before, shot through me, my body a melting sea of tenderness, her hands hungrily reaching under my nightgown.

I knew what was happening could never to be mentioned to anyone, knew that *it* must be forgotten with the first rays of morning. But I couldn't tell her to stop.

The next morning, we'd just finished eating breakfast, consisting of a bowl of day-old bread in hot milk and sweetened coffee when Avó walked in.

"The padre already knew that Solar had slept here before I even entered."

Solar was sitting next to me at the kitchen table.

"He said he'll arrange for Solar to go to Casa Pia in Lisbon," Avó continued.

Casa Pia? Stories leaked out periodically, terrible stories of beatings and starvation, rapes and dead fetuses.

I couldn't look at Solar. Her eyes were supplicant, tears were rolling down her face. A stifling silence made us all afraid to look at one another. Solar had likely also heard of Casa Pia. Or, perhaps, it was just the idea of being locked up in an orphanage for the rest of her life.

Not a word of solace from my mother.

Or me.

The old padre appeared on our patio soon after. We all came out to meet him.

"My child," he reached his arms to Solar, voice hardly audible, nothing like Father Marques before him, whose every word had sounded like a warning sent directly from God.

Solar pulled away brusquely. "You're going to a blessed place, my child. Be happy. The sisters will take good care of you."

She took another step back, eyes wild now.

I looked away.

Soon she'd be gone, I thought, then I wouldn't have to think of her or think of Tonto. My secret would remain buried. But at the most unexpected times and places afterwards, she'd appear before me, that catcher of souls with eyes as green as a deep forest.

A Dragonfly Dashed By My Face

My mind was made up. Not like the times before when I'd told myself over and over to speak up, only to see my resolve leap out under my mother's stare. Today I'd do it, even if it meant getting a beating. The pain would be awful, as it was each time, making it impossible to keep those shameful tears from betraying me. But I'd endure. I always did. Afterwards my mother would likely come home with pretty packages of candy or chocolate or material for a new dress or a new pair of shoes. Her voice would be high-pitched, endearing, excited, "Look at what *Mãezinha* has for you!"

I'd woken earlier than usual. The light coming in through the hair cracks in the shutters was still a dim grey, the new-born day barely out of the darkness. The night had been hot and humid, the air thick and still and the walls of my small bedroom seemed to be pressing in on me. I stepped onto the cement floor; its coolness offered some relief.

I placed my ear to the wall dividing my bedroom from that of my parents'. No sound. This was my favourite time of day, before my mother and Manuelito got up. Most mornings my father had already left for his shift work at the cork factory in Montijo.

I walked to the window and carefully opened it. A whiff of hot air hurled me back, the day's heat already smothering. Temperatures reaching 40 C for weeks, already killing a few elderly people and many cows. Sparrows and robins, usually gathered in the quince tree in the middle of the garden, weren't there this morning.

My father had planted the tree soon after we'd moved into our new house, built with my grandfather's help who was a builder. My father had heard the quince tree brought good luck to marriage. The tree never grew very big. This summer, the leaves had all been burnt by the scorching sun but a few fruit had managed to hang on, ripening early. The fruit couldn't be eaten; something in it choked you. It was only good for compote. "What a useless tree," my mother said each summer when she picked the quinces. My father never said anything.

I leant my arms onto the window sill, bracing the heat, waiting for the birds to arrive. But the birds never came, probably remaining in their cool hiding places.

Sunlight began to break through the murky light, bringing everything into focus. It was as though the world was being formed right before my eyes.

I looked at the vineyard across the road from my house, the orange grove to the right, the row of tall eucalyptus to the left, the shimmering river in the distance. All I expected—I could count on this familiar landscape like a good friend.

In the orange grove, the haunted mansion's decaying red tile roof loomed over the trees. No one in town had ever been in it or even remembered when it had been built. It simply had become part of the landscape. Every night, soon after midnight, a man with a gaunt face and hunched shoulders was said to walk the grounds. He carried a lantern and wore a long black cape. The mansion faced the river. Fishermen had seen him trying to enter the front door several times. They'd heard the knocking from a distance. I'd seen the outside of the mansion only once when a friend of my parents took us for a ride in his small fishing boat. The mansion stood forlorn on the wild, rocky and empty river bank, its ornate design strange in a town of plain fronts. People feared the place. The oranges fell to the ground every year, going to waste. Not even thieves or beggars dared jump the high concrete wall around it in fear of meeting the man in the black cape.

The story was that two brothers who'd inherited the mansion, had been in love with the same woman, said to be a beauty. She'd married the older brother but then had run away with the younger one, the one with the wavy hair. The older brother invited the man with the cape to the grove, offering him forgiveness. Instead, he offered him death. No one had ever seen the living brother or knew anything about him. It was believed he'd been frightened to return, frightened of what might be waiting for him.

Growing up I'd felt sorry for the murderer. Wives were expected to be faithful, chaste, brothers to respect one another. But now I thought him a coward. If he'd decided to kill his brother, he should have the courage to live by his deed.

The grove's rusty iron portal was directly across Casa Rosa, the whorehouse, located at the beginning of the old dirt road behind my house. The iron portal was kept locked by a heavy, rusty iron chain with a padlock. One night, a drunk on a dare tried to break it, only to be flung back by two icy hands. He'd sobered instantly. That's what he told everybody.

This past Christmas, my mother had been helping her Aunt Isabel, who was a dressmaker, to finish her work in time for the holiday. It was late into the evening when we left her house. My father had been working his late shift, and the old road had been our only option to get home. The new asphalted highway, with lights and traffic, was only accessible by us walking through my grandparents' property, our house being behind and kitty corner to theirs. There was an entrance gate, with rusty hinges next to my grandparents' bedroom and my mother didn't want to wake my grandfather. He wasn't the type to be disturbed. The town, so small it wasn't even officially a town, gorged in gossip, something my grandfather, as the family patriarch, was terrified of. A woman coming home late, unaccompanied by a man, was fodder to speculation.

We hurried by the gates of the haunted mansion, without looking at it, afraid. A large crowd of men waited their turn outside Casa Rosa for the skinny new girl with orange bleached hair and a moustache from Minho.

The men whistled, meowed, barked, snorted, as we passed. One stepped in front of us, arms open, as if to embrace us. It was Dinis, the baker. He lowered his arms and turned around the moment he recognized us—we were his customers. We kept walking, heads down. Once we got to a safe distance I asked my mother why the men, who'd stood so close to the iron gate, weren't scared of the ghost.

"Oh, men. They're all pigs. Sex makes them forget everything else."

"But Dinis is married and has a family, his daughter is in my class."

"Most of those men are married. Listen, men marry virgins but like having whores in bed. That's enough now. You're still too young for this talk." She remained quiet the rest of the way.

I was thankful now that she was still sleeping. I closed the window and turned toward the old armoire with its undulating mirror. The distorted reflection of my skinny legs poking from underneath my thin cotton nightgown, my high forehead and sickly dark circles under my eyes made me glance down. I looked nothing like the beautiful blonde women in the French catalogues modelling dresses Aunt Isabel showed to her customers.

"Too bad you take after your father's side," my mother often said. "All the Faíscas are scrawny and have ugly high foreheads."

Never mind. I opened the rickety doors of the armoire with great care, not to make noise.

There—all my dresses. Some with bows and frills no longer fitted me, but my mother insisted on keeping them.

Today I'd choose a dress that would make me look pretty but grown-up. My mother would likely choose the blue organza with puffy sleeves that made me look like a baby. It was the most expensive. It'd taken one year of twenty escudos per month to pay for it. But I'd insist on the new white poplin with pink polka dots and scooped neck.

I placed my hands over my breasts. Only a few months ago, there were only two tiny nipples. I didn't doubt my mother would soon buy me a bra. She was always watching me, as though she feared my womanhood.

Today was the last day of school. Tomorrow, the girls in my class and I would become part of the adult world. We'd all be going into different apprenticeships and trades, except Lourdes, the doctor's daughter, of course. Everyone knew she'd be going to high school in Montijo and then university in Lisbon or Coimbra to become a doctor like her father.

We talked of nothing else—the adventure, the experience, the dreams of love, romance, marriage, children, waiting for us now that school was ending. The thrill of sex, that dark, unspoken mystery we could never talk about, hovered over us, making us giddy, silly, unnerved. We all knew that honest women weren't supposed to even think of it. Only whores liked sex and men didn't marry whores.

A strange restlessness had been keying up my movements, making my voice and my laughter shrill. My mother became even more watchful, especially, since my period arrived.

"Empty your potty before school," she said. "Don't expect me to do it."

I stepped back with a jolt. I hadn't heard her come into the room.

I picked up the chamber pot, heart thumping, thankful it was only piss. I carried the pot at arms' length all the way to the manure pile at the back of the garden, next to the shed, where my father kept rabbits and chickens. The manure was composed of food leftovers, weeds, plants, piss and shit. My father used it to fertilize his flowers and vegetables.

One day this past spring, my father had been hoeing his garden, his back hunched over the spade and turned away from the shed. I approached quietly, walking behind him. I knew that the hen (his best one) that he'd placed on eggs resting on a bed of straw, wasn't to be disturbed. He'd warned me often enough. But I wanted to see the baby chicks rise out of the eggs as they hatched. I opened the shed door one centimetre at a time, so the hen wouldn't notice. But to my surprise, the hen and chicks were already waiting by the door. They shot out once the door opened and ran straight to the shitty mound. It was as if they'd known all along of its existence.

I ran after them, trying to catch each one with my bare hands, but to no avail. They all escaped.

My father came closer. "What have you done?" he said, in his usual mild tone. I started to cry. It wasn't that I was afraid of him—he'd never hit me before or even threatened to do so. That was left to my mother. My tears came from a feeling I didn't quite understand. There was something disturbing, sad, strange, about the tiny newborn creatures getting mired in the stinking filth. I said this to my father. He laughed. "You silly girl, chicks like manure."

Now carrying the pot back to the house, I promised myself that someday I'd have a bathroom like Lourdes. No more smelly piss-pots and fly infested dung heaps.

Lourdes had invited me once to her home. I'd been mesmerized by the flush toilet, the fluffy pink towels, the little heart shaped pink soaps in a shiny glass dish, the white bathtub. Lourdes' house spoke of elegance, softness, kind words trimmed with sweet smiles. It was as if it was protected from anything bad or shameful, so different from my own world. Her life seemed legions away from the ugly gossip, the rough language around me, and Avó's talk of farts and the laughter that followed.

The moment I stepped into the kitchen, I smelled the hot milk and coffee my mother had poured over chunks of bread left over from dinner the night before. Breakfast was always the same. It was mostly just us, my father having left early for work and Manuelito still asleep.

"If I had more money," my mother said, "I'd make French toast or bake a pound cake." She said the same thing every day.

Once breakfast was finished, I returned to my bedroom. The blue organza dress waited for me on the bed next to a new pair of white sandals. I picked up the dress and rumpled it into a ball. Then I sat on the bed, bracing myself. I decided that I'd miss school.

"Hurry up," my mother hollered from the kitchen. "It's getting late."

I smoothed out the dress. The heat and humidity making it difficult to pull the nylon dress over my head. It was tight around my chest.

"When you walk by the whores, don't look in," my mother said, as I walked into the kitchen. "Remember, you'll suffer the consequences." She'd been warning me every morning. "What about the new sandals? Am I not a good mother?"

"They're nice, *obrigada*," I said. No kiss or embrace. We weren't a kissing family.

Outside, a dense haze hung in the air, making everything appear distorted. I crossed the road to the shady side provided by the wall of the orange grove.

A soft murmur, like the buzzing of bees, filled the air. I could see a group of people gathered near the brothel. The road was empty, except for the odd stray dog or cat. Lately, most people walked along the new paved highway.

A dragonfly dashed by my face; my heart skipped a beat. Their long wings had always scared me. Avó said that if you got close enough, you could hear them whisper tales of their lost fate and of their faraway land when they once were dragons. But I never had. Avó told many stories.

The dragonfly flew for awhile ahead of me, as if pointing the way. I tried to hit it with my satchel but missed.

I began to distinguish men's voices. Some were yelling, but I couldn't understand what they were saying.

I increased my pace. The dirt began to fill the fresh creases on my new white sandals, probably ruining them forever. The dust, the heat, the perspiration, the clinging dress, began to make me feel soiled.

As I got closer, I saw that women and children formed part of the crowd. I pushed my way to the front.

A man in a blue shirt drenched with perspiration held a stick about six or seven feet long. He prodded a black horse, trying to force it to enter a deep, dark narrow building, about five feet wide, on the south side of the brothel. I didn't know if the building or the horse belonged to the whores.

The crowd kept yelling, "Hit him! Hit him!" Some people lifted their arms high above their heads and punched the air to show how it ought to be done. But the harder the man hit the horse's rump and the more people screamed, the more the horse neighed and reared onto the crowd in a primal refusal to enter the black space.

The horse turned its head toward me. Its large, liquid eyes were wide open, frantic.

I knew the look.

"Hit him harder," a man bellowed behind me. He was so close I felt his warm breath on my neck. A shiver ran down my spine.

I turned around.

The man was unshaven and had long greasy black hair that hung over his forehead. Our gazes locked for a second. Then we both quickly looked away.

"Pretty," he murmured in a husky voice, his moist lips touching my right ear. People pressed tighter. I was sure I'd be late for school.

I felt something hard rubbing against my back. Then the man's warm hand reached under my skirt, moving slowly, tenderly, up my leg, his breath turning to gasps.

The horse kept rearing, neighing. I remained still, watching, time ticking away. I was sure I'd be late for school but it was the last day.

Yellow Watch

The matches were where I expected them to be, on the kitchen counter, near the kerosene stove. The box was slippery from the spilt grease of the cooking pans. It slipped from my fingers, nearly dropping onto the floor. I stood still for a moment. My father's snoring was the only sound shooting through the wall of the bedroom, next to the kitchen. I thanked God that neither he nor my mother had awakened from their siesta. Then I turned swiftly toward the kitchen door, leading to the patio, before I'd change my mind. *Yes, yes,* this time the junk pile would be gone.

My father had been laid off from the cork factory again since the beginning of last November. It was now August. The workers had been told that the shutdown would be temporary. No one was to blame this time; now there was a lack of foreign interest in cork. After a couple of months or so, the workers had gathered early one morning outside the factory's padlocked gates to protest. But by noon the PIDE appeared once again.

"There's always someone informing those bastards," my father had said later that evening behind closed doors. My mother, my grandparents, my brother Manuelito, who would be turning six in December, and I had gathered around him in our kitchen, the cabbage soup my mother had been cooking all afternoon, getting cold, as it waited in soup bowls on the kitchen table. My father's voice—hardly raised above a whisper—had a new edge to it, something between anger and fear, fear of being holed up and tortured in the infamous dark cold cells. Everyone was acquainted with the stories, the horrors taking place in the night, as fingernails were pulled out and electric shocks to testicles made men cry out for their mothers. Hellish screams were often heard by those living nearby.

"The leaders were all arrested," he continued. "The rest of us got sent home with the butt of a gun. The secret police pays well . . . " He paused, glaring somewhere beyond us, somewhere beyond the kitchen walls. "No shortage of bread for those pigs."

I recall looking around then. The two wooden shelves displaying colourful ceramic dishes and coffee cups (that had never been used), above my father's head—where he always sat—the rectangular table pushed up against the wall, the wicker chairs, the clay water container in the corner that kept the water from my grandfather's well cool even in summer, suddenly appeared changed. It was as though everything around me that had been familiar yesterday had suddenly become strange.

Since the layoffs, my father and more than half of the men in our town had been waiting. Everyone waited. The men waited in Antonio's Taberna on Main Street and in the Vinho Tinto on the highway, while their wives knelt on sore knees in our small chapel, praying feverishly for foreigners to once again need cork. Only my mother didn't go. She didn't believe that God cared or even knew of her existence. "When I was born," she'd say. "I missed the hand of God." I always imagined there being too many babies born the same day and God's large hands blessing all their heads, except my mother's.

My father had started going to the municipal garbage dump in Montijo soon after the layoffs began. The dump was located on the south bank of the river Tejo, the garbage being carried across the wide river on barges. It was said the Lisbonites were too fancy to smell their own garbage but those in Montijo and in our small town didn't mind. It gave men employment.

I'd only seen the dump from afar, once when my grandparents took me to the Lisbon zoo. As the boat crossed the river, the black mountains of garbage had loomed over the whitewashed town like a dark fortress.

Initially, my father had only brought home foodstuff that he'd later boil in a large cooking pot over a fire in the garden and fed to the two pigs that, once fattened, would be sold in the open-market in Pinhal Novo for a good profit. But in time, he began carting home other things that he planned to sell at some later point. Where and to whom, he didn't say. Maybe he didn't know.

The empty bottles, rope, metal, copper wire, burnt-out light bulbs (good for their copper bottoms), broken baskets and toys and old cooking pots and broken tools, a tricycle with two wheels, and a wheelbarrow with one handle and two rickety kitchen chairs began to form a tower of junk at the back of my garden.

At first this became merely an ugly, smelly site. Once, I'd been crouched behind the garden wall, throwing corn to the chickens, when I heard a woman say, "Let us cross the road. This place stinks." But after my visit to the dump that February day, the junk pile took on meanings beyond embarrassment, beyond things I couldn't even begin to comprehend. All I knew was that *it* had to go.

I now shook my head vigorously, trying to dislodge any remaining doubts that might stop me from carrying out my plan. As I reached the corner of the house, I shaded my eyes with my hand to protect them from the sun.

The wind was battering the orange, lemon and quince trees my father had planted nine years ago when he'd first built the house. The trees looked skeletal, like ravaged ghosts, their curled-up leaves, dry from the sweltering summer heat, dancing violently in the air. Only a few stunted quince fruit had managed to hold on.

God was again mad at the world. That was what Avó said whenever hot winds brought no rain. Avó knew everything. She knew that soon after such sweltering heat, everything would be covered with swarms of locusts I found terrifying.

I found the piece of newspaper I'd hidden behind the animal shed. I picked it up on the road a few days ago, no one reading newspapers in my family.

I lit a match; the wind snuffed it.

For a moment I wondered if the wind was trying to *tell me* something. As a child, Avó could read the wind. Farmers had come to see her from all around to learn whether the winds would bring rain. This was in Algarve, where we are from and had lived until my grandparents and parents had settled in Amendoeiro. After she grew up, Avó could no longer read the wind but she knew prayers to take away the evil-eye and other ailments.

I cupped my hand around the second match, forgetting about the wind—it had never spoken to me, anyway. Next I dropped the burning paper onto the pile of junk that stood between the manure mound, my father used to fertilize his vegetables, and the animal shed, where he kept the rabbits and chickens. The pigsty was directly across, by the opposing garden wall. The pigs were sleeping.

There! Done.

The painful vision, like an aching tooth that constantly reminds you of its rottenness, would *finally* disappear.

I'd always said no to my father whenever he'd asked me to join him on his trips to the municipal dump. School took place only in the mornings and so I was free in the afternoons. But there was something about other people's garbage that repulsed me. Fear and shame too, kept me away. What if someone I knew saw me there with my father?

"You never know what you may find," he'd say each time, trying to tempt me. A man had once found a gold ring, another, a Kodak camera that worked. Clothes had been washed and mended and worn by different pickers.

Then that February afternoon I said yes. There was something in my father's voice that day. A need, perhaps. That must've been it. He likely wanting to show the homeless men he'd met there that he was different from them, that he had a daughter, a family.

We'd left soon after I came home from school and eaten lunch. My mother had refused to come along, insisting that she had too many things to do. But I knew different. I knew that she loathed the dump and anything to do with it, even though she'd never said so in so many words.

Her humming around the house had been replaced by fretting and long sighs that sounded more like a plea to the God she didn't believe in. Laments about the vanishing savings that were kept in a black cloth bag in the clothes' chest had become a daily reminder of our family's misfortunes. Then there were the homeless men who came calling at supper time. My mother would hand me a bowl of cabbage soup to take to them—the cabbage, potatoes and carrots grown in our garden—or chickpeas or kidney beans with rice, depending on what she'd cooked that day. They'd sit on the old rocking chair in the patio devouring the meal in less time than it took me to turn around. Sometimes my father would join them for a glass of wine he'd bought from Antonio's Taberna until my mother would signal to him that it was time for them to go. After dinner, most days lately, she'd leave to go on her visits to friends and her Aunt Isabel, the dressmaker, where some of her friends congregated. She was staying away more and more.

My father and I had walked for nearly an hour along the dirt shoulder of the main highway connecting Amendoeiro with Montijo. As we were about to cross the railroad tracks, at the entrance to the gravel road leading to the dump, a train was approaching from the side, veering around the bend. Thick black smoke curled upwards, blending with the dark clouds hanging overhead, making the chilly grey February day, even chillier. A few passengers waved. I waved back with both hands. Waved and waved until the train was out of sight.

Dung was strewn all over the road spilled over from the trucks taking manure to farms all around Montijo. The air smelled foul. A loaded truck passed by; the driver honked; my father saluted him like a soldier. "We're like a tribe here," he said, happy to be recognized. The truck left in a cloud of black exhaust fumes, leaving behind a trail of dung.

At the end of the road was a small tavern. It had a low clay charcoal grey roof that must've been red once.

"C'mon, I'll get you something to drink," my father said, leading the way.

WE'RE ALL FUCKED was written on the wall next to the entrance. The letters shone bright yellow against the greenish smut covering the building. I lowered my eyes. There were two spindly rose bushes, one on either side of the door.

We entered.

It was dark inside, there being only a small window overlooking the main road. Dust and cobwebs covered the window pane. "Close the door!" a growly voice hollered. "Don't let out the smoke."

Laughter.

The place felt like a cave with its earthen floor and low ceiling. The dampness, the thick tobacco smoke, the garbage stench and vapours from the cooking cabbage, nearly chocked me.

As my eyes adjusted to the darkness, I discerned a group of men and a heavy woman sitting at a long table by the window. A slim young woman, with long frizzy black hair, wearing a flowery apron, stood beside them. She held a small tray. "What you need is a husband," the man with the growly voice said. "Stop wasting it girlie."

More laughter.

My father laughed too. Then he motioned for me to sit at the table next to them and called the young woman over.

Her face was covered with pimples. One eye was swollen and closed, reminding me of a red walnut. My father ordered a glass of red wine for himself and a hot chocolate for me. I was tired and cold after the long walk, my clothes partly wet from the light drizzle. As she turned to go, my father gently slapped her behind. She gave out a gruff giggle, "You . . . you stop it." She slapped his hand back. Then he slapped her behind again. It seemed they were playing a game I didn't know. She was the tavern owner's daughter, he explained once she'd walked away.

After a little while, the man with the growly voice came over to our table. He was burly and bald, looking to be about my father's age. His face, clothes and hands were streaked with black dirt and he smelled like the manure truck passing us earlier.

"Is this your daughter?"

"Yes siree, that's my girl."

The man turned to face me. "Looking for treasure, are you?" He gaped at me, forcing me to look away. Then he walked out.

"Pai, I finished my drink. Can we go now?"

Endearments like papa or mamma or dogs named Lulu were reserved for the rich in Montijo. No one dared using such terms in Amendoeiro for fear of being ridiculed.

My father ignored my request and ordered another glass of wine from Walnut Eye. After she brought the wine, she lingered at our table. He lit a cigarette, puffing smoke into her face. She slapped the air back and forth, giggling away like a silly child.

"What's the hurry?" he said. They both giggled some more.

The tavern had emptied by the time we left, the afternoon was nearly over.

I quickly looked around now after dropping the lit piece of newspaper on the mountain of junk. There was no one. Yet the eyes were everywhere—in the houses, the trees, the plants, the wind. I hurried away, eyes semi-shut, the wind whirling dust and debris around in an even madder race.

Then something furry brushed against my leg. I stumbled. The box of matches slipped out of my hands, the matches spilling everywhere.

As I bent down to pick up the matches, I saw the cat. It was curled up under the large rosemary bush, black as midnight, still, seemingly indifferent to anything going on around it. Its mustard-yellow eyes appeared to know things, mysterious things I didn't know or couldn't even fathom. Maybe it was because cats lived nine lives and so had witnessed so much. No one knew where the cat spent the nights but every morning it appeared at the moment my mother began gutting the fish for the day's dinner. She did this on the patio's counter to keep the house from smelling. The cat would sit on its haunches patiently waiting for the fish heads and guts she threw at it. Then it would slowly walk away, unafraid, as if what it had received was its due.

I quickly gathered the scattered matches under the yellow-watch.

Once back inside, my father's snoring still filled the house. I covered my mouth with my free hand to stifle my gasping breath, while listening for other sounds. What if my mother was awake? What would I say to her? But there were no other sounds. I approached the counter with the cooking stove, where the matches were always kept. For a moment I couldn't recall the precise location where I'd taken them from. Had they been right next to the stove or beside the coffee pot, closer to the wall? I decided to place them beside the stove. I was sure that that was where they'd been and tiptoed back to my bedroom.

As I lay down on the bed, I heard a knock on the front door.

"Antonio, Antonio, the animals are on fire!"

I sat up with a jolt. The voice belonged to Luis, one of my grandfather's tenants, whose unit faced my garden. I couldn't understand why he wasn't at work!

My father hurried out in his bare chest, shoes untied, awkwardly trying to button up his pants as he ran. My mother, Manuelito and I followed. A few neighbours had already gathered by the shed. Then more came, my grandparents too, likely awakened from their siesta by the stir, Avó's grey hair, usually held up in a neat bun at the back of her head, hung loosely over her shoulders.

My father opened the shed door. The chickens and rooster

scrammed out. I counted them. Thirteen. Good.

Then he dashed into the burning shed, trying to rescue the rabbits. They were kept on the upper part of the shed, above the chicken coop, their cage facing the shed's open area where the chickens and rooster roamed and slept. The door had a latch that was always closed, unless it was feeding time. There were six of them, two grey, one brown and three white. I followed closely behind my father; I could hear the rabbits bumping against the boards.

The flames hurled my father out in an instant. "It's hell in there." His face was a vermillion red, perspiration streaming down his brow. "The son-of-a-bitch wind is fanning the flames."

I started to scream, "Someone save the rabbits, please, please, please..."

"Let's form a line," my grandfather hollered. Men, women and older children quickly lined up. The line started with my father, who stood next to the burning shed, and it ended with my grandfather by his well, fifty metres or so away. My grandfather started hauling water in a pail attached to a rope. The water was then poured into a second pail that was being passed from hand to hand until it got to my father. But by the time the water reached him, half of it had spilled out.

I started running from the blazing fire to the well and back again, trying to get people to hurry. Manuelito ran behind me, hollering, *chooka choo, chooka choo, chooka choo*, pretending we were a train. Soon, two other small boys trailed behind us.

The flames were winning; the wind showed no mercy. The rabbits stopped moving around.

The shed frizzled away into cinders in spite of the water being thrown on it, the smell of burning wood, fur and flesh filling the air.

I tried imagining the horror of being burnt alive. My stomach churned. I gagged, throwing up in front of everyone.

Avó, who'd been shooing the chickens away from the falling cinders, came over. "What's the matter Milita? They're only rabbits, child."

"No, Avó, not just rabbits. They were my friends."

It was easy for Avó. For her, rabbits, cats, dogs, were mere animals. Just that, animals to be disposed, as she saw fit. I hadn't forgotten the screeching coming from the two cats she'd drowned in the trickle of water in the low tide. They'd often snuck into her kitchen and stolen the fish that she'd gutted and salted for the day's dinner. I'd helped her carry the sack with the petrified cats to the river.

I could see the rabbit's faces lined up along the cage's wire mesh, whenever I brought them grass. Sometimes I sang to them. Other times, I shared secrets I didn't dare tell anyone else.

Avó grabbed me by my shoulders, "Listen Milita, don't fret. God sees and knows everything. He'll punish those who did this. No one gets away with anything in this world." She returned to the chickens, not even noticing the tears welling up in my eyes.

I needed to be alone. Needed time to reflect on what Avó had just said.

I walked toward our patio, away from the line of people still passing those useless pails of water to my father.

The black cat was curled up, sleeping, on the rocking chair, its yellow eyes closed. I pushed it off before it sprinted away. It gaped at me, making my blood run cold, as it always did.

I nestled into the chair and shut my own eyes.

Why couldn't my father have been a shoemaker like my uncle Manuel, who put new soles on old boots and shoes? I wondered. Or fix oxcarts and bicycles, like my uncle José, or be a tailor like my friend Benita's father, or a builder like my grandfather? They were all still working. Only my father ended up a garbage picker.

"Garbage-eater, garbage-eater!" two girls that had been in school with me, called me as I walked by, the day after my visit to the dump. One of the girls must've seen me there or knew someone who had. The next day there were others, "Garbage-eater, garbage-eater!" they crooned, as I walked by on errands to the grocery or bakery for my mother, or on my way to Aunt Isabel where I was for a few hours everyday to learn dressmaking. It was always the girls. The boys, if they were present, would quietly look away.

I never told anyone at home about this and began dreading leaving the house. Now I began praying feverishly, rocking myself back and forth. *Please, please God . . . it was never meant to turn out this way. Never, never, never. Please, please, please forgive me . . .*

I should've asked my father to turn back the moment we'd walked through the dump's black iron gates that February day. But I couldn't disappoint him; he'd looked the happiest I'd seen him in a long while.

The drizzle had turned everything dank, making the stink overpowering, inescapable. I pinched my nose with my fingers.

My father turned to me, "You'll get used to it."

A sudden buzzing sound made me look up. Hundreds of crows and vultures blackened the sky, turning the late afternoon into night. It was as though all the colour and light in the world had been sucked out.

My father took his shovel and large pail from an area enclosed by a wire fence where there were many other shovels and pails. Then he led me toward the mound closest to the edge of the water where the freshest food for the pigs would be found. Scruffy, gaunt men were bent over, busy digging at the base of the mounds as we passed. Some were loading trucks. My father greeted them all.

He started digging the moment we arrived, scrutinizing each shovel-full so as not to miss anything of value. Maggots wriggled out of pieces of potatoes and carrots and chunks of kale and cabbage that had turned the colour of phlegm.

I twisted my head slightly to the side, afraid of what I might see.

One day a fetus had been found wrapped up in newspapers. Some people said it had been part of a witchcraft ritual because a leg had been torn off. Others said that it had been aborted by a nun, since a rosary had been laid on it.

I was thankful that today it was only food.

It was then I saw the burly bald man from the tavern. He was hurrying toward us, a wide grin spread across his face. He was holding a red object in his hand that glowed against the surrounding blackness like a harbour light in the night. As he got closer, I saw that it was a large ceramic penis complete with hairy testicles, the black curly pubic hair carefully drawn in vivid paint strokes. The pubic hair and testicles looked real, like the pubic hair and testicles of the fiancé of the shoemaker's daughter next door, as I secretly observed the two of them from my terrace, as they sat on chairs in the lane next to my house.

Now my eyes roved from the garbage heaps to the pickers, to the crows and vultures still keeping watch above, back to the garbage heaps, afraid to lay eyes again on what the man was holding. A sudden hot blush flooded my face.

"It's a cracked wine container," the man explained. "But it's still useable."

I couldn't imagine anyone wanting such a thing in their home.

He came closer. His teeth had yellowish-brown streaks at the edges and his breath smelled like the garbage. He brought his prized possession close to my face.

"They didn't teach you about this in school, did they little girl? Ha, ha, ha, ha!"

My father stood holding his shovel the whole time, watching, a ridiculous smile on his face, reminding me of the crazy man who roamed the streets of Amendoeiro.

Then the burly man walked away. He hadn't gone far before he began showing his *treasure* to others. I could hear their laughter. My father resumed his digging. When the pail was full, we departed for home.

"I'm sorry for what happened," he said, shattering the silence keeping us company. "This is not the time to make enemies. That man is in charge of renting out the shovels and pails."

I didn't reply. My father didn't say anything else either until we arrived home.

He never again asked me to join him.

I now placed my palms together and recited ten Hail Marys and ten Our Fathers, thoughtfully, unhurriedly, unlike the half-mumbled prayers I said every morning. I wanted God to know how bad I felt. Only the stinking junk was to have disappeared.

Then I thought that if Avó was right, that if God *knew* everything, He'd know I was innocent. I repeated the same prayers again for good measure and waited. I kept hearing the sound of the rabbit's bodies bumping against the boards in their desperation to get out. Tears began to drop on my folded hands resting on my lap.

I continued waiting, not sure exactly what it was I waited for or expected to happen. But surely God would send me a sign. *Something*, to let me know He understood my predicament.

Manuelito came over with the other two boys and asked me to again do the train. I sent them away, envying their childish oblivion.

In a while my tears dried up. I wiped my nose with the hem of my skirt and stood up.

Maybe it was too late for explanations.

By the end of October, the factory was still closed. My father had rebuilt the animal shed with wood he'd gotten at the dump. That was all he brought home now that the two hogs had been sold. He still went there occasionally, making me wonder if he went to see Walnut-Eye. But with the rabbits gone, I kept those fears to myself.

The profits from selling the pigs had been spent on a pair of new shoes and a new wool dress for winter for me, the ones from last year had become too short and tight across my chest. The rest of the money went to pay for the doctor and medicines for my brother's tapeworms.

Most of our clothing had become well-worn. Even my father's Sunday trousers and shirt were beginning to look threadbare. My mother had begun buying groceries, bread and fish on credit. The only meat we'd had in the last couple of months was a chicken my father killed when my mother had the flu so she'd get well with the chicken broth.

My grandfather had money but he didn't like parting with it. He'd given fifty escudos each to Manuelito and me for Easter but the money had disappeared before we'd even seen it.

One day that Autumn my mother announced that she wanted to plant dahlia bulbs so she could have flowers in spring. She'd never been interested in gardening or growing anything before—I'd never seen a vase with fresh-cut flowers in the house. Avó gave her some bulbs from her own vast garden next door.

My mother and I stood watching, as my father dug the small area of the yard reserved for flowers. There were marigolds (to keep the slugs away from the vegetables), sweet pea, a clump of white daisies, mint, and the rosemary bush. The rest of the garden was used to grow vegetables. My brother tried catching the dirt my father was throwing onto a heap with his toy pail.

It was a warm, sunny afternoon but dark clouds were quickly moving in. My father sped up his digging in order to get the bulbs in the soil before the rain.

A large cockroach landed on his hand. My mother started singing a popular song about a cockroach and an old shoe. My father whistled along. I forced myself to join in. It had been a long time since we'd done anything like this as a family. Lately, my mother was out most evenings, joining women at someone's home to sew, embroider, knit or crochet and talk. I'd be left home with my father and Manuelito. She'd cook our meals and leave, sometimes not even eating with us.

Singing along with my parents helped to hide my nervousness.

What if I had failed to pick up all the matches?

The day after the fire, my mother had commented on the misplacement of the matchbox. She kept insisting that someone must've moved it because she'd never place the matches so close to the stove. The heat could ignite them. My father insisted that he hadn't even approached the stove counter. I wasn't sure my mother believed him. I'd remained silent.

My father decided the rosemary bush needed trimming—it was

covering most of the area where the dahlias would be growing. He asked me to go in the house and fetch a knife.

The moment I stepped into the kitchen, I got down on my knees and said an Our Father and a Hail Mary. I'd started including the Virgin in my prayers, thinking that as the Mother of God she'd have more compassion toward women.

Please, please, let no matches be found.

Then I hurried back out with the knife.

As my father began hacking the full outer branches of the bush, leaving only the spindly, inner dry ones, I saw *them*. There were more than a dozen.

The red tips had grown brown from the sun and water but their long wooden stems were unmistakable. These were the matches used to light kerosene stoves and oil lamps.

My father picked up five or six, spread them across his palm.

"What's this?" Confusion darkened his hazel eyes.

He looked at my mother; she also looked puzzled.

Then my father's face changed. A look of comprehension softened his brow. He bobbed his head up and down, as if to say, *I get it*. Then he brought the hand holding the matches close to my face, leaving it there for a moment, a moment that felt more like a lifetime. I couldn't look up and face him.

"Remember the box of matches?" he said to my mother.

For weeks after the fire, my parents and grandparents had talked of nothing else. Who could've done such a terrible thing? Who could've been so wicked, so cruel? My parents couldn't imagine having such enemies. At times, my father even blamed himself. He'd enter into long explanations as to how something flammable that he might've brought home from the dump could've burst into flames in the summer heat. But as time passed, other things began to occupy their minds. It seemed that I was the only one for whom the events of that day kept recurring, every detail played in my head in endless repetition.

"Come inside," my mother ordered.

I followed her, happy to move away from under my father's darkened hazel stare. My legs trembled so badly I thought they would fold at the knees.

In the kitchen, my mother pointed to a chair. I sat. She remained standing. I stared down at her worn-out slippers made from cutting out the backs of old shoes.

"What kind of monster have I raised?" Her voice was surprisingly soft, quizzical. "I should give you a beating you'll never forget. Jesus knows you deserve it."

I squinted, clasping my hands tightly on my lap, preparing for the blows.

But the blows never came.

That night, whispers from my parents' bedroom went on longer than usual. I placed my ear close to the thin wall dividing our rooms.

"What was I to do?" my father kept saying. "Tell me, *what? What?* These are terrible times. The dump was all I had left. Things were never supposed to have turned out this way."

Then he reminded my mother how they were still better off than many people. They owned their own home and had vegetables from the garden and fresh eggs every morning.

My mother started to cry.

Then my father.

His jagged moans tore through the stillness of the night like a clap of thunder. I'd never heard my father cry before. I didn't know men cried.

I took the pillow and placed it over my head, covering my ears.

Maybe my mother was right, I thought. Maybe God had his favourites and the children and husbands of those forgotten by Him didn't merit His care.

I still could hear murmurs. I pressed the pillow tighter until there was only silence.

A year had passed since the factory closed. People had stopped talking about the layoffs.

Part of it was fear, the uncertainty of who could be listening and what could happen to them. The two strike leaders, one from Montijo and one from Amendoeiro, the uncle of my friend Amalia, had simply *disappeared* since their arrests, never to be seen or heard from by their families again. Some of those who'd helped organize the strike had been taken in *for questioning*. That was what they were told. But days later they came out telling hideous tales of torture. One, the son of the mailman, was left with a permanent limp.

The Bêbeda

No one knew where the Bêbeda came from. That August, the scorching sun was melting the tar on the main highway, creating ghostly puddles in the distance that sparkled like midnight diamonds. The Bêbeda walked into Antonio's Taberna dressed in a long-sleeved black dress and thick black stockings in spite of the heat. She introduced herself as Amelia Fortuna and ordered a gallon of red wine to be delivered to her lodgings across the street on Sundays, Tuesdays, and Fridays. A bit of soup, too, or fish stew, a few olives, a chunk of bread. Lone men sitting in the tavern, poor labourers without wives or families to cook for them, had watched and listened with forks and spoons suspended in midair. It wasn't often they'd seen or heard someone displaying such extravagance in our dusty town, especially a woman. The story spread quickly, people hungry for anything promising escape from lives wedged between the evanescence of their dreams and the reality of their meagreness. By evening everyone had heard about the Bêbeda—the drunkard—and laughed. Everyone laughed, even my grandfather. I'd never heard him laugh before. He was a serious man who believed that laughter was the devil's trap into immodesty. I wondered what everyone found funny about a drunken woman.

The Bêbeda was seen wearing her thick black stockings that peered from under long black dresses and skirts for the rest of the summer. To my mother's thinking—and my mother was always thinking—the Bêbeda had to be mourning the death of someone close, perhaps a husband or a child. But the Bêbeda never said. "A penance," my mother would remind everyone, as though she had access to information no one else had. "Woollen black stockings in the sweltering summer heat is either self-flagellation or insanity." My mother favoured the latter.

"Stay away from the Bêbeda," she warned me, finger pointing at my nose. "Who knows what she ran away from or what she might do." I heeded my mother's warnings. I had to.

But the following summer—I must've been seven or eight, old enough to be sent out on errands—the Bêbeda spoke to me for the first time. The last time, too—I was never close enough to her again to invite conversation. I never dared.

In those days no one in town had refrigerators. Every morning João the fisherman came selling fish caught during the night and Joaquim the milkman delivered milk to our door carried in a large aluminum jug from which he poured a litre into our blackened aluminum milk pot. Bread was purchased daily from the two bakeries, wine from Antonio's Taberna, and vegetables, fruit, and groceries from a small establishment with a store front during legal operational hours and a backdoor counter after it closed. Even the enforcing official was seen several times walking away from the backdoor counter in the dusk, but no one said anything. Governmental rules may have applied to the rest of the country but not to us. Especially not to our men.

The hamlet where we lived had no electricity. The five or six houses stood almost like an afterthought on the other side of the railroad tracks that ran parallel to the highway. Behind the five or six houses was an orange grove, the river, farms and vineyards, and, a distance away, the Pinhal, the pine and eucalyptus woods where everyone went on Sundays. Oil lamps lit up the night, food was cooked on kerosene stoves, and water (the same all over town) came from open wells where cats and, sometimes, unhappy souls, drowned.

The day the Bêbeda spoke to me, she was leaning against the counter at the greengrocer in the same housing complex owned by Vitoria, a distant cousin of my grandfather and the town's midwife. The complex included the Esso station, Bar Central, a bookstore, and a series of small, windowless two-room units behind the family's second-floor apartment. The Bêbeda lived in one of the two-room units. I asked the grocer for a cucumber and two green peppers my mother would later grill for supper, along with fresh sardines. The Bêbeda said, "Cucumbers are bad for digestion, *queridinha*. They shouldn't be eaten." I was taken aback by the way she pronounced each syllable fully and clearly, so different from the rest of us who spoke in half-pronounced words, as though in a hurry or, perhaps, too lazy to say the rest of a word.

She'd called me *queridinha!* This was all that mattered to me at the time. No one had ever called me "little darling" before. In a town of cork-factory workers like my father, bricklayers like my Uncle Rafael, shoemakers like my uncle Manuel, and unpaved streets, open sewers, whirling dust, stray cats and dogs, gossip, debt, scoundrels and whores, there was no place for endearments. No one was rich enough to escape laughter and derision afterwards.

Even at my young age, I recognized that the Bêbeda was a person of higher education and class. She didn't belong in Amendoeiro. Wasn't one of us.

She came close to me and reached out to touch my ringlets which my mother had made that morning using an iron she heated on the kerosene stove. My mother liked me well groomed, better than other girls, whose mothers didn't bother to curl their hair.

"You beautiful child," the Bêbeda said. "Do you like butterflies?"

I stepped back.

The Bêbeda's face was red-patched and bloated, like the stray cat my grandfather pulled out of his well one day, swollen to double its size, a grin on its stretched little mouth. The Bêbeda's arms drooped like a rag doll's, as though they'd long ago given up the doing. Her breath smelled of mildew and vinegar, the same smell as the rotting wine barrels Antonio threw out onto the street each September before making the new wine he served on November 1, *o Dia dos Santos*. All Saints Day, when all the dead were honoured. Her dark eyes didn't seem to belong to her face. They looked lost. Clear, eager, restless, they were the eyes of a frightened child. I remained at a distance, fearful of what she might do, as I remembered my mother's warnings.

I hurried out of the greengrocer with the brown-paper package without answering the Bêbeda's question as to whether I liked butterflies.

"Why does the Bêbeda drink?" I asked my mother, as I walked into the house and handed her the cucumber and peppers.

"She's a bêbeda, that's why she drinks. She was born that way. Or maybe she's cursed, who knows? The devil sometimes has his way."

"I thought only men drank?"

"Some women do too. Just stay away from her. She's dangerous."

My mother pivoted, turning her back, and so put an end to all my questions.

But everyday on my way home from school or on an errand or visits to my cousin Ana, I'd look out for the Bêbeda. I pitied her having no family or friends, couldn't imagine her aloneness. I had my grandparents next door, my uncle Rafael, who lived with them and played the banjo, other uncles and aunts in town, friends of my parents and mine dropping in any time of day.

"How come the Bêbeda has no family?" I asked my mother one day.

She said that Anastasio, the mailman, told her that letters came in every month in expensive beige envelopes from Lisbon and Sintra with money but no return address.

"He figures her family is rich, that the calligraphy on the envelopes is that of an aristocrat. Nothing like the scribbles he usually sees. He's sure they're likely ashamed of her—why they sent her here where no one knows her."

I didn't tell my mother I pitied the Bêbeda. I pitied her in the way I'd pitied the stray black cat caught by boys in the neighbourhood last summer. There were three of them. They tied a piece of newspaper to the cat's tail and lit it with a match. It was evening, night approaching, the cat leaped and screeched, leaped and screeched, the flames zigzagging in the humid air under the purple-black dome of the sky like fireworks. The cat stopped screeching and crashed onto the dirt road, like a spent firecracker. The smell of burned flesh and fur sent me indoors. I never told anyone what I'd witnessed; I was too ashamed. I'd watched and said nothing. Did nothing.

Now I'd do the right thing. I was sure of this. I'd tell the Bêbeda that I loved butterflies the next time I saw her. Talk to her as if she was one of us and not a drunkard. I'd be careful so my mother wouldn't find out.

I began seriously looking out for the Bêbeda. Some afternoons she'd be sitting at the rusty iron table in the side yard of Antonio's Taberna. She sat close to the climbing grapevines, entwined in them, as though trying to hide from view. I wouldn't dare enter that courtyard. Only drunks, often spewing out obscenities, and the filthy homeless greybearded man with the melon-sized growth on his throat sat there. Other times the Bêbeda passed by my house, along the dirt road behind it, alone and mumbling to herself. The dirt road led to the river and the salt marshes and I wondered where she was going, there being no other hamlet besides ours along the way. One time she was carrying a doll—or was it a kitten? It was hard to tell. She held it in her arms like a baby and was talking to it. Talking loud. Some believed she was possessed by evil spirits.

By evening, she'd be seen standing at the corner of Antonio's Taberna, even in winter, no shawl or sweater covering her slumped shoulders. "The wine in their veins keeps them warm," my mother said. "They don't feel the cold or pain. That's why they drink." The Bêbeda hurled slurred words at passersby, like carefully chosen stones, words no one understood, her arms animated then, reaching out, out, out . . . It was clear to me, she wanted people to stop and listen to her story. The story no one knew, but no one stopped.

Neither did I.

I'd walk by her quickly, even when my mother wasn't with me, staring straight ahead, as though my head was held in place by a medieval iron mask, pretending I didn't see or hear her.

Afterwards, I'd ask myself why I didn't stop. *Why? Why?* I felt like a caged animal trapped by thoughts I couldn't control, thoughts making me wish I was someone else. I wanted the Bêbeda to know I was different from the others, kind and valiant, unafraid of my mother's beatings. But next I'd think of the bruises, lasting for days, and I wasn't sure that talking to the Bêbeda was worth the pain.

Then there was my cousin Ana, twelve at the time, always reading.

"It's not the Bêbeda's fault she drinks," Ana said one day, as the Bêbeda appeared at the bottom of her street. "It's the In-cu-bo."

The afternoon sun had been fiery orange for weeks on end, killing animals and scorching farms, people's gardens, and those daring to walk under it. Ana and I were standing in the shade of her house, the street empty at that hour with most people indoors having a siesta. Even the stray cats and dogs were nowhere to be seen. The Bêbeda walked by, so close to us she almost touched us. She was bareheaded, disheveled and still wrapped in her mantle of black, stumbling with each step, eyes fixed somewhere beyond us, beyond Amendoeiro. She didn't seem to see us.

The swelling was gone from her face, leaving deep wrinkles and skeletal cheeks so caved in that they seemed ravaged by something other than human endeavour.

"The In-cu-bo comes in the night while you sleep," Ana continued, her round cheeks dropped to show the seriousness of her warnings. "It has sex with you, without you knowing it, and possesses your spirit. Never get too close to the Bêbeda. The In-cu-bo can easily jump from her to you."

Ana pronounced the word slowly, firmly, lips pursed, head nodding, making sure I understood the threat lurking above my head. I'd never heard the word.

I thought about the Bêbeda's ghostly face for the rest of that summer—her unwashed body, uncombed hair, foul smell, her behaviour. I'd once seen her fall in the middle of town, rolling in the dirt of the unpaved street in view of all. Laughter everywhere. Then one day, the school custodian, an acquaintance of my mother, told us the Bêbeda had squatted down and urinated in front of the school's gate. "Right there," she'd said. "She urinated right there by the entrance gate and the children about to come out."

I'd grown up seeing drunken men. My grandfather had had to be carried home at closing time from Antonio's Taberna by my father and my uncle Rafael several times through the years. No one questioned why he drank, why all men drank. No one laughed. Men drank, people said, when life became unbearable.

But women? Weren't women supposed to stay home looking after their families?

It was some time before I admitted to myself that fear of the incubus in the night or of my mother's beatings was not what was stopping me from telling the Bêbeda I loved butterflies.

The Bêbeda's speech grew more slurred each year. It was as though the words wanted to remain inside her, her story hiding so deeply, it couldn't come out. Couldn't be shared. Her body grew more slouched, drool running down her chin, teeth missing, her mourning-black clothes turning grey with dirt, her hair longer, whiter, more matted, filmy eyes staring ahead as though seeing but not seeing. Certainly not seeing what we saw. In time she became invisible to us, familiar but not noticed, like the stray cats and dogs roaming the streets. People stopped laughing at her or talking about her. Sometimes boys still taunted her, as she passed by, pulling at her skirt and hair and jeering, "*Bêbeda, Bêbeda, you live in a bodega.*" No one reprimanded the boys and neither did I, though I was older and ought to have known better.

The fall I was due to turn twelve, my mother was taking me to Amelia's store to buy me fabric for a new dress when we noticed the Bêbeda's black figure in the distance. It must've been November 1, Avó was roasting chestnuts that evening that we'd eat along with drinking Antonio's new wine in celebration of all the dead. Avó did this every year. My grandfather called it, christening the new wine.

The Bêbeda was standing in front of the whitewashed chapel. It began to drizzle; my mother opened her umbrella and I snuggled up to her. The Bêbeda had no umbrella. A gust of wind lifted up her long, black skirt, making her look like a scarecrow or an apparition in the distance. As we neared, we could hear her knocking on the chapel's wooden door and shouting in an unusually clear voice, "C'mon, c'mon you bastard, come out. You, you . . . Show your face, you Almighty nothing, you son-of-a-bitch, you . . . You . . . Why? Why?" She began to wail.

As we passed, she turned around to face us, her pale face blending with the grey day. She raised her arms and punched the rain or some spectre that only she could see.

I stopped. My mother yanked my arm, "Don't look. Keep walking." She quickened her pace. I followed.

"Why is the Bêbeda crying?"

"I told you she's crazy." But my mother's words didn't sound as threatening this time. It was as if something inside her had softened, the way the chunks of stale bread do when I pour sweetened hot milk over them for breakfast in the morning.

"Is she angry with Padre?" He was the old priest who'd replaced Father Marques, whom everyone called the fadista, who'd been sent away after the scandal with Branca in the Pinhal.

"No, she's mad at God."

I couldn't imagine anyone being mad at God when He loves us all.

But my mother did sometimes complain that God had forgotten her existence.

The rain grew heavier, pelting our umbrella, as if the Heavens were punishing the earth. Rivulets of mud began to cover the street. My feet were wet, shoes muddy. I started shivering.

"Can we go back home?" I kept thinking of the Bêbeda screaming at God in the rain.

"No. You-are-getting-a-new-dress."

The Bêbeda was found lying on the cold cement floor of her kitchen, face drowning in her own vomit, urine, and excrement two weeks later. She'd been dead for days before the smell wafting from underneath the door alerted Vitoria, the landlady. She told everyone afterwards that, at first, she'd thought the smell was coming from some dead rat in the open sewer running along the cement courtyard. This happened often in winter, she explained. Not seeing the Bêbeda in a few days was not surprising because she'd become a sort of hermit lately.

There was no funeral, no priest, no flower wreaths, fall chrysanthemums in peoples gardens saved for other graves. Vitoria told us that two gravediggers from Montijo came in a black car, wrapped up the body in canvas cloth, and took it to the municipal cemetery to be buried in the pauper's section. Everyone waited for those who sent money in expensive beige envelopes to show up.

No one did.

As Vitoria cleaned up the mess, she found a small metal picture frame composed of tiny coloured butterflies buried in the filth.

The damaged photograph showed only the outline of a small head. Everyone wanted to see it. Men and women came from all around. They wanted to know—to understand—who the Bêbeda was. Vitoria displayed the photograph at the greengrocer's counter, next to the scale, a place where the Bêbeda would sometimes linger and talk.

The old padre showed up one day and blessed the frame. Another day, the whores from Casa Rosa, at the top of the dirt road, came to look, leaving coins beside it for the destitute. Others followed, leaving money and prayers.

I saw the photograph later. I didn't pick it up, feeling, somehow, that it was impious to do so, the frame with the butterflies being, seemingly, the last thing the Bêbeda held in her hands. Ana saw it before I did. She said the Bêbeda's spirit lived in the butterflies; they'd fluttered while she held the frame.

Some said it was clearly the photograph of a child. A girl with curls. Others argued that it was a man wearing a soldier's pointed brown cap. I gazed at the photograph closely. All I could see was the shadow of a small head. Nothing was clear and the butterflies didn't flutter for me.

Vitoria placed the Bêbeda's possessions at the curbside, free for anyone to take. Sheets, towels, two long black skirts, a good iron bed, a wooden dresser, mugs, glasses, plates, forks. No one touched a thing. This, in a town of beggars and unemployed men, including my father, the three cork factories in Montijo, where most of the men in Amendoeiro worked, having again temporarily shut down due to a fall in international demand for cork. After a few weeks, Vitoria carted all the belongings to the municipal garbage dump in Montijo.

After the Bêbeda died, people were certain the Devil had taken possession of her soul. Possessed, they said, she was possessed. They swore this on their mother's and children's lives. It had to be. How else, they argued, could someone drown in their own vomit, urine, and excrement? How could this be the workings of God? It had to be the Devil. Taking home anything belonging to a heathen was to invite bad luck into your home.

The wives of the unemployed men lined up in front of João's fish stall, waiting, along with the stray cats, for the fish heads he threw away, as he cleaned the fish. Later, they'd boil the heads to make broth they poured over stale bread for supper. My mother still bought whole fish with the few savings my father kept in a black cloth bag hidden in the clothes chest.

The women made the sign of the cross at the mention of the Bêbeda's name—even my mother—and asked God for forgiveness. *Perdão de Deus.*

I was never sure what or who it was the women wanted forgiven. The Bêbeda's trespasses? The town's? Her family's? God, for His oversight?

Warlocks, Spells, and My Mother

The morning sun was already scorching as we stepped off the bus. The heat rose from the cobblestones in steamy, spirally waves, nearly burning our sandalled feet. Manuelito, who was not known for his docility, said nothing. I wasn't sure if he even knew why we were here, why he'd come along. I said nothing either. What could I say when my mother had already made up her mind that her life was out of control? Her suffering beyond human repair? She was convinced that her *cruz*, the cross she carried every day, ambushing her chances at happiness, was the result of sorcery. A spell cast by someone at an early stage of her life. Who and why, she had no idea but Manuelito's birth was part of her unescapable tragic fate. How else, she insisted, staring at you with her large, almond-shaped brown eyes, at twenty-nine her nerves were a wreck, over the edge. I imagined my mother's nerves like a speeding car spinning out of control over a cliff.

We were looking for a *bruxo* whose name and address we didn't know. All my mother knew was that the warlock lived in a house with black shutters, a black front door, and a black bat-weathervane on a dirt lane facing the Tejo. We'd never been to Alcochete. It didn't seem like a town of *bruxos,* incantations, and evil omens. A large cathedral with two high steeples rose toward heaven above the whitewashed houses with their red clay roofs and pots of colourful flowering geraniums on their doorsteps and windows. Red and green and yellow fishing boats, lined the beach along the wide river. The town was known for its religious festivals and processions. The streets were configured in circles and semi-circles around the cathedral, we often ending up where we'd started from or in dead ends. We'd ask passersby for directions but soon got lost. Everyone seemed to know about the *bruxo's* existence but his lane had no name and the house no number.

The heat intensified as the sun ascended. We stopped under every tree we encountered for a bit of relief. There weren't many trees; the salty air from the wide river stunted their growth. An hour or so later, we found a small, low-lying house, more like a large shack, with the black shutters and door and the bat-weathervane. The river had emptied by then. There were kilometres of black mud, and the hazy hills of Lisbon shone in the distance.

We were tired and thirsty, my mother complaining continually, that another minute of the searing sun and she'd end up looking like a peasant or the Gypsies caravanning through town.

The door opened before we knocked. A woman dressed in a long black dress, in obvious mourning, grey hair in two braids, a deeply wrinkled face and restless dark eyes, stood smiling. She appeared to be waiting for us. I figured she'd seen us crossing the street; how else to explain how she'd known that we were coming? Only Avó knew of our visit, not even my father, who'd left for work before we departed. "Don't say a word to your father," my mother had warned me. My father didn't believe in the devil or in God, seeing both as a waste of time. He believed that people ought to help themselves.

The woman at the door announced that she was the *bruxo's* sister. She gave us each a glass of water and then led us into a small room, a tiny window high on the whitewashed wall letting in only a glimmer of light.

"*Bom dia.*"

A female high-pitched voice—yet not the voice of a female—came from inside the room. Feverish laughter, like that of an over-excited child, followed.

I could hardly see, my eyes not yet adjusted to the darkness of the room. Slowly, the outline of a man sitting behind a small square table came into focus. His hair was white, hanging straight down over his hunched shoulders, making his large pale blue eyes appear colourless. He didn't seem to have eyelashes or eyebrows and his skin was a translucent white, fragile looking, like egg shells, as though he'd never been outside in the sun.

He stood up. He too was dressed in black, woollen pants and a long-sleeve sweater in spite of the summer heat. As he walked toward us, his large breasts swayed under his sweater. A large cross hung from his neck.

A cold chill ran down my spine, though perspiration was still flowing from my pores. I found myself staring at him, then blushing from embarrassment. I'd never seen anyone like him.

He politely shook our hands, even Manuelito's. Smiled. A thin red line encircled his pale eyes. We sat on wicker chairs that were lined up against the wall. He came to stand in front of Manuelito and stared at him for a long time.

The room grew tense.

My mother started folding and unfolding her hands and shifting her body on the squeaky wicker chair, her discomfort snaking around the small room, devouring the air.

The *bruxo* then took Manuelito's head in his fine white hands, nails long and pointy, like a woman's. He moved his head right, left, left, right, on and on, sometimes gaping at it, as though he was holding a globe and trying to locate an unknown place.

He began moaning, *Humh . . . Humh . . . Humh . . .* Manuelito remained surprisingly quiet and still. Unusual for him, who couldn't stay still for longer than five minutes.

"This boy was not conceived in love," the *bruxo* finally said. A voice so thin and shrill, it was as though it was coming from outside of him, outside the room, outside of Alcochete, outside of anything familiar to that point.

My mother stood up. "I need to go out. You stay."

She was breathing noisily, her right hand over her heart, a timed explosive—we never knowing when it was going to detonate. We lived in fear of its intentions. All my mother needed was to place her hand over her heart and our guilt grew. Contradictions ended, voices were lowered, my mother got her way.

The day my father came home, two years ago or so and told us that the cork factory was shutting down indefinitely, my mother's right hand covered her heart. She ended up in a hospital in Lisbon where she was told she'd been born with a faulty heart. An artery was missing. Afterwards, my mother's hand seemed to be permanently poised over her heart.

How would I now dare to ask her if *I'd been conceived in love?* Even my father never confronted her on anything, never reprimanded her when she beat me or Manuelito or hollered terrifying threats to us both. My father always recoiled inward, like a turtle retracting its head inside its shell when perceiving danger. That was my father, the non-hero.

Two Sundays ago, my mother sat at the kitchen table ready to eat dinner, still wearing her red polka-dot poplin dress that had taken a year and half to pay for in monthly installments of ten escudos. She'd spent the afternoon visiting her old friend Filipe in Moita, an hour away by bus. Everyone knew, including my father, that Filipe had been *crazy* about her, back in their teens when we all lived in Algarve. But Filipe's parents had been itinerant farmers, unlike my grandparents, who owned large parcels of land. So they rejected him. Filipe had moved to Moita soon after my parents and grandparents settled in Amendoeiro. He'd married a woman with long brown curly hair and almond-shaped brown eyes like my mother's. But she wasn't my mother. He and my mother had remained friends. She visited him twice a year. He came more often, sometimes cycling the three-hour distance just to come in and say hello.

That Sunday, I'd made a tomato and cucumber salad from the garden, my father grilled large fresh sardines my mother had bought from a local fisherman before leaving for Moita.

Sitting there in her Sunday best, a trace of red lipstick still blushing her lips, glass beads on her neck reflecting the light from the oil lamp, she looked like a rose growing among weeds, like someone not belonging to us.

A new, private silence encircled her. It was as if the mother and wife that cooked, washed, cleaned, had remained in Moita. This new silent woman kept us quiet, fear kidnapping our words and wills, food swallowed only half chewed.

Halfway through the meal, she blurted out, "Antonio, I've been thinking a lot lately." She hadn't yet picked up her fork. "There's only one thing that makes sense to me. Someone has cast a spell on me, it has to be, I'm sure of it now. Nothing else explains the *strangeness* in the boy and all my misfortunes, my bad heart, my sufferings. He's a mistake that's ruining my life." (Manuelito's birth had been the result of a broken condom, my mother claimed.)

My father continued eating; he lowered his head further, chin nearly touching his plate.

"I need to find someone to remove this spell."

My father still said nothing.

I looked over at Manuelito, wondering if he understood what my mother was saying. She'd never called him a *mistake* before. He was gulping his food so he could hurry out to play with Benfica, the dog he'd carried home a year ago in his small hand, the new-born golden puppy the size of a large peach.

He and other neighbourhood boys had watched a neighbour's bitch give birth to a litter. Manuelito helped himself to one before the neighbour drowned the rest. The neighbour couldn't afford to feed more than one dog and the neighbourhood was already littered with strays. To my surprise, my mother allowed Manuelito to keep the puppy, as long as it didn't go into the house.

Manuelito named the puppy, Benfica, after his favourite soccer club. The dog slept under the outdoor cement staircase that led to the terrace. The place was full of junk, garbage, spiders, cobwebs and frightening cockroaches the size of a thumb. I was scared to even approach the entrance but Manuelito would often be found lying down beside Benfica. I couldn't imagine loving anything that much.

The *bruxo*'s sister brought him a pair of scissors. He gently cut a lock of hair from the back of Manuelito's head and trimmed two of his nails. Then he handed the hair and nail trimmings to his sister, who placed both inside a black pouch. They walked out, leaving Manuelito and me alone, my mother still outside.

Manuelito started kicking one of the table's legs and wouldn't stop. I wanted to join my mother, the room stifling now. A cave of nightmares.

I didn't.

Then I heard her ask for another glass of water and she returned to her seat.

She was crying.

I wanted to hug her, offer some comfort, but my mother wasn't one for affections. I didn't recall her ever kissing or hugging me or Manuelito.

I thought of what my friend Lourdes had said the other day. Her father kissed her mother on the lips every morning before leaving for work and in the evening when he returned. He called his wife *Queridinha*, little darling. I'd never even seen my parents kiss or touch one another in any loving way or heard them utter words of affection.

"Why don't we all go to Moita?" my mother had asked my father before leaving that Sunday, "It's been years since you've come."

I was praying he'd say yes so we all could do something as a family, like my friend Lourdes, whose parents took her to Troia Beach by train every summer. I'd never been there.

My father shrugged his shoulders and rubbed his hands on his patched trousers. "A man has to feed his family." He'd rather hoe his vegetables, tend to his chickens, rabbits, and pigs, but my mother was free to go wherever and whenever she pleased. Two years after the terrible fire that had burnt the six rabbits alive, he'd rebuilt the shed and acquired more animals. I was beginning to think that he liked being left alone.

Whisperings, like frenzied prayers or chants, now began drifting in from another room. Manuelito stopped kicking the table. My mother turned ghostly white, as if a hundred leeches had drained her blood. My heart began to pound.

The *bruxo* returned, carrying a package wrapped in brown paper and tied with string.

"You should've brought the boy earlier, " he said, handing my mother the package. "We've been waiting for him. Wrap a piece of his clothing around this package and place it in the middle of a crossroads on Friday at midnight. Remember, it must be Friday—the highest day of the *mistérios dolorosos*. Whatever you do, don't open the package."

He walked away and shut the door.

My mother paid his sister. There was no set fee; everyone paid what they could. I kept thinking of what the *bruxo* had said. How did he know?

We sat on an old bench under a pine tree waiting for the bus to take us back to Amendoeiro. My mother gave Manuelito and me a boiled egg and a chunk of bread she'd brought from home. She wasn't hungry. Manuelito threw half of his egg and bread at a mongrel circling nearby. My mother whacked the back of his head. "Food costs money." He whimpered.

I didn't recall Manuelito crying ever since he was an infant. Reprimands, hair and ears pulled, and smacks to his head by my mother, being forced to sit still on the floor in a corner of the kitchen. Five or ten minutes later, he'd pop up like a jack-in-the-box, as though determined to defy her. She'd spank him again; he never cried.

This led her to believe that whatever was wrong with him couldn't be fixed with regular beatings as with other children. Like me. So the threats would begin. She'd sell him to the gypsies caravanning through town; lock him up and starve him to death; tie him up in the hogs' pen so they'd eat him piece by piece.

Manuelito would stare at her with his large brown eyes—eyes like hers—that seemed to question her actions, as if she was the one in the wrong. Afterwards, my mother would lock herself in her bedroom, sometimes for days. The house grew messy, tense, the air prickly, my father and I not knowing where to hide, Manuelito not appearing to know the difference.

My mother remained quiet throughout the bus ride back. As we walked through the garden gate, Benfica jumped on Manuelito, barking joyfully. Manuelito picked him up and kissed him, talking and smiling profusely for the first time today.

My father was standing in the middle of the garden, holding a spade, which surprised us. We weren't expecting him until five o'clock. He explained that the factory gates had again been locked, an armed guard on either side when he arrived in the morning.

"Expect more layoffs." He hardly glanced at my mother as he spoke. It was fresh in all our minds how things hadn't gone well the last time the factory shut down. He never asked where we'd been. Maybe he knew.

The house was quiet for the next couple of days, my father hardly speaking about anything at all, my mother not leaving her bed.

I stared at the cuckoo clock in the kitchen, a wedding gift to my parents from Filipe. I was sure the minute hand on the cuckoo bird had stopped. How could Friday be still one day away? I imagined the freedom, the release, once the deed was done. My mother free from her spell. Our life, my life, normal, like the lives of others, like the life of Lourdes, the miasma of sadness hovering over our roof, our heads, our hearts, finally gone.

Yet when I thought of the crossroads on Friday at midnight, my blood ran cold. Then time seemed to race away. The crossroads, where spells were divined to make someone fall in or out of love, succeed or go astray, get sick or die, had always frightened me. Fernando, the baker, once told us how two cold hands had choked him as he'd walked the same crossroads where my mother and I would be going. Fernando had been too drunk to know where he was walking but he'd sobered up immediately.

The door to my mother's bedroom had remained shut for the third day. In the afternoon. I knocked, asked her if she'd like a cup of *cidreira* tea, as I'd done each day, to help her calm her nerves. Today she said yes.

I made her the tea and a buttered slice of bread.

I opened the door hesitantly.

She was staring at the ceiling, eyes wide open. I jumped back.

As I arched over her to check her breath, she mumbled, "That albino is a fraud. A scarecrow warlock. I'm gonna throw that package out and forget I ever went to see that shit."

This was the first time she'd mentioned the *bruxo* since our visit, the first time she'd said more than the word *no*, when I asked her if she wanted a cup of tea.

She drank the *cidreira* tea and ate the buttered bread, sitting up straight, leaning tall and dignified, like some injured queen.

The next morning, Friday, she got up, put on her red polka-dot dress, combed her hair, put on lipstick, went shopping, boiled kale and potatoes (from the garden) and chorizo for dinner, and sat down with us, never saying a word. She didn't even slap Manuelito when he took his sausage outside for Benfica.

All day I watched her closely to see if she'd throw away the package. She didn't.

After Manuelito and my father went to sleep, she said, "It's nearly time."

At eleven o'clock, she told me to fetch the package, which she'd hidden in the hutch in the dining room (that had never been used), keeping it safe from Benfica. Sometimes the dog snuck into the house if we weren't watching. He'd sniffed the package upon our arrival.

My mother wrapped Manuelito's red shirt around the package and tied it with string, as the *bruxo* had instructed. Manuelito had nearly drowned in that shirt, falling into the nearby river from the gunwale of a fishing boat he and another boy had climbed. Manuelito couldn't swim. A fisherman standing by threw him a plank and dragged him to shore.

As we stepped outside, my mother carefully closed the kitchen door, so as not to wake Manuelito or my father, who was already snoring. Benfica's raucous breath could be heard from under the stairs.

"Good," my mother whispered. "The dog's asleep."

The dirt road had no lights. No houses either once we left our hamlet behind, the road cutting through farms and fields. A full moon gleamed down, like some cosmic lantern, helping to light the way. All the creatures must be asleep, I thought, an eerie quiet blanketed everything.

We walked for twenty minutes or so in tremulous silence. An owl screeched overhead; my mother jumped back, dropping the package. As she bent down to pick it up, she screamed. I thought my heart would jump out of my chest. I turned around; Benfica was behind us.

"It's the shirt," she said. "The darn dog smelled it."

He had quietly trailed behind.

By the time we reached the crossroads, the moon was hiding behind a cloud. My mother tried placing the package at the centre of the four roads, but it was hard to see—all was darkness. We couldn't even see the *chorões*, the hottentot fig plants carpeting the embankments framing the dirt roads with their fatty dark green leaves and large pink flowers.

When the moon again showed its face, Benfica had the package between his teeth. It took two of us to yank it away from him. My mother again placed the package at the centre of the crossroads while I held Benfica.

As she dropped the package, Benfica lifted his head high and howled at the moon. In the distance, another dog joined in. Then another. The hair on my arms stood on end.

"Those might be wolves." My mother's voice sounded thin, hesitant, devoid of her usual authoritativeness. "The full moon brings them out."

We hurried home, never looking back, me still carrying Benfica in my arms in spite of his stale dog smell.

Benfica continued howling.

"What is the crazy dog sensing?" my mother asked. I wondered, too, and shuddered.

The next morning I woke late to an empty house. I learned from my grandparents that Benfica was missing and that my mother and Manuelito were searching the neighbourhood for him. My father had gone to meet with other workers about a possible strike, though the last one was still fresh in men's memories. Limps and scars, eternal witnesses to PIDE's brutality and Salazar's inhumanity, had become part of the town's history, its pulse.

The day was already hot. My grandparents and I sat under the shade of the grapevine and fuchsia bougainvillea canopy on their back patio waiting for my mother's and Manuelito's return. We drank lemonade made from lemons grown in my grandparents' garden. It was sour.

My mother and Manuelito returned without Benfica.

"Did you check the crossroads?" I said.

They hadn't.

We departed; Manuelito led the way.

As we approached the crossroads, my mother spotted Manuelito's red shirt lying on the side of the road.

Manuelito ran toward the shirt, now torn and dusty, the ripped brown paper bag close by.

We carefully searched for the pouch, looking even under the *chorões*. It was nowhere.

It was then I noticed wide tire grooves on the dirt road. They wavered onto the *chorões*, crushing the fatty leaves and pink flowers where the car or truck must've swerved.

Manuelito continued climbing the slope. When he reached the top, he shrieked.

We hurried up to him.

Two vultures circled the air. Four others were on the ground, wrinkled red heads busy pecking their prey, their hissing the only sound in the silent wheat field.

Manuelito ran toward the vultures; they lifted up in unison, madly flapping their wings.

Benfica's guts spilled out of his belly like sausage strings on a butcher block, a circle of maroon blood girdled him, almost like an afterthought, a decoration, a myriad of flies sucking up what the earth had not yet taken in.

Manuelito stopped about seven or eight feet from where the vultures had been feasting. He began to cry, lightly at first, then his sobs seemed to shake the very earth under my feet. I imagined I'd always remember *this* cry, *these* flies, *these* vultures, *this* moment.

I turned toward my mother. Arms raised high above her head, hands shaking up to heaven, she seemed to be having a conversation—an argument—with God, the God she didn't believe in. "I was right," she said, "that albino is a fraud. He hasn't broken the curse. It continues and continues and continues . . . "

She looked different. New creases seemed to be framing her eyes and mouth, making her look haggard, older.

I turned to face Manuelito, my back to my mother now, and put my arms around him, his small body convulsing against my chest.

"Why did Benfica die? Why, why?"

I had no answer. I just held him while my mother continued arguing with God.

She uttered a long, deep sigh. "It'll never leave me, this bad luck. Never, never."

The vultures returned, circling the area in spite of our presence. They cast a dark shadow over the field of wheat stalks, red poppies, yellow buttercups, and what was left of Benfica.

You're Old Enough to Start Dancing

Shadows of the setting sun splinter my mother's face into a thousand pieces. A kaleidoscope I fear peering into. "Hurry up," she hollers, the nothing-but-bad-luck look back on her face. She'd left it behind, smiling the whole boat ride in the early morning sun and cool summer breeze. I'm standing at the shore, letting the surf stroke my feet for the last time, the undertow sending a ripple of fear through me. Visions of a young burial in quicksand.

My mother signals to João, letting him know that it's time to leave. He's the fisherman she's hired to take the three of us—her, my cousin Ana, and me—to Moita Beach in his small fishing boat. He'd sat all day on a large rock nearby under the sizzling sun, fully clothed, his craggy skin like the tattered soles of old shoes. He ate his lunch of grilled sardines, tomato salad, bread and red wine (part of his fee) on that rock. He never went in the water.

Ana said, "Fishermen fear the sea. Water isn't play to them."

"Why doesn't he join us?" I asked my mother, as we sat under the shade of a pine to eat.

"Oh, let him be. What is there to talk about with a fisherman?"

João leads us through sand dunes and brushwood back to where his boat had been left in the morning. The walk now seeming longer, harder, tiny creatures feasting on my legs and arms.

My mother plods ahead right behind João, as though urging him forward. He carries the two straw bags with dirty plates, utensils, and towels; my mother carries the blanket. Ana follows behind her. I trail behind Ana at a small distance, stopping now and then for a last look at the beach. The distant pounding of the sea makes me feel forlorn and a little afraid. A lone seagull flies overhead, its cry like a child's plea for help. As we near the river, fog begins to hang above our heads, hiding what is left of the sun. A gust of wind blows sand into my eyes.

"Milita!" my mother yells, her voice drowning out the seagull's cries. She can't see me for the brushwood. "Don't be spiteful. Are you slowing us down on purpose?"

She worries about missing the evening dance.

As a small child, I found the weekly Sunday dances boring, falling asleep halfway, my father carrying me home on his shoulders. After he emigrated to Canada, nearly a year ago, and as I grew older, it's the glitter in my mother's eyes and the trill in her voice that makes me wish she wasn't my mother and that I could've stayed home. She romps around the dance floor with other women, skirts billowing, as though something inside her needs to come out right there and then. One day she said, "You're old enough to start dancing." She bought us a transistor radio last summer and nearly every evening for two months demonstrated the steps to a tango, a cha-cha, o baião, a waltz, on the kitchen's cement floor. When I didn't pay attention, she'd hit me on the head with her knuckles. Then, for my thirteenth birthday on December 1, she bought me a black garter belt and fancy nylon stockings I was supposed to wear to the dances on Sundays. But the garter belt was too big or my hips were too narrow, and the garter and nylon stockings slid down to my knees. She gave up after that.

I know why she fears missing the dance today, but I can't say it out loud. She wouldn't appreciate it. It's Eduardo, the blabbering idiot delivering bread to our house for the last year. He's sixteen—he and his family moved from Alcochete last year. His father repairs boats and has never worn shoes. Eduardo laughs at everything. A clown in street clothes. My mother laughs along with him. She invited him to come and play *Brisca* at our house in the evenings. I always feign tiredness around nine o'clock and escape to my room; their laughter continues, often, for hours. Sometimes there's only silence, yet I know he hasn't left, the door never having banged shut.

I try hard to fall asleep.

The dances are held in the town hall in the centre of town, right next to Ana's house. Everyone goes, except my grandparents—my grandfather thinks dancing is another orchestration by the devil to lead humanity astray. At the south end of the hall, directly across from the stage, is the bar where men stand smoking, eating peanuts, shells thrown onto the sawdust-covered cement floor, and drinking beer and wine poured from barrels.

In the summer, the dances move to an empty field in the northern reaches of town. A large wooden plank floor is laid down for dancing and a crude platform erected for the band.

Now João stops. We all stop. He turns slowly, as if unhinged by a set of pliers, a puzzled look on his dark, gaunt face. He lifts his right arm and points ahead, long hair blowing in the wind, oversized white shirt swelling like a sail, reminding me of the Old Testament prophets in the stained-glass windows of the Church of Espirito Santo in Montijo.

My eyes follow his stretched arm. The wide sparkling river of our morning ride is now a muddy creek. João's boat, painted red and green, swatches of paint peeling off, rests on a scanty patch of grass twenty metres or so from the water. The word *FÉ* is painted in large black letters across one side. Faith in what? I wondered this morning when I first saw it. In God? In our country? In *São Pedro*, the town's patron saint and protector of fishermen? Faith that his daily catch is sufficient to feed his wife and his many children?

"How you gonna get us home?" my mother says.

"I forgot about the damn tides. But don't worry, it'll be slower but I'll get you home."

"Slower? The dance starts at eight. It's now six. We'll never make it back home in time."

João proceeds toward the boat, ignoring my mother. We follow. No one speaks.

We throw our sandals and bags into the boat and help João drag it to the water. Soon we're sinking past our ankles in soft, black mud.

"This is ridiculous," my mother blurts out. "We'll take the bus home."

She tells Ana and me to gather our stuff from the boat and we walk away without saying goodbye to João.

After a few steps, Ana says to my mother, "Aren't you paying him?" Ana is always reading a book or magazine I never even heard of. She's the one who discovered Elvis Presley and Paul Anka. Her intelligence and knowledge endows her with the right to question my mother.

"Pay that fool? Look at the mess we're in!" My mother shakes her shoulders and head to show her annoyance at the question, at João, at the lateness, at the way the day is turning out.

I glance back. João is sitting in his boat and has gained some distance in the thin ribbon of water; he and the boat form a black outline against the sinking horizon. I fear he might not be able to find his way home in the descending darkness. I whisper a prayer for him.

We can barely find our way into town in the foggy dusk, trees and bush along the narrow path now appearing like demons reaching out for us.

In the bus, I sit next to my mother. Ana sits behind us.

"Stupid fool," my mother says. "How can a fisherman forget about the tides?"

I don't answer. My mother will be asking the same question, requiring no answer, for days and days, until the question acquires the rhythm of a wail, until everyone crossing her path has heard it, until the story becomes another reminder of her bad luck. Persistence is a quality she relishes but only in herself.

As a small child I had a poor appetite, daydreaming during meals, my throat shutting after a few mouthfuls. "Eat your food." My mother would stand over me.

The first hit came, her knuckles hard on my head. More followed until the repellent taste of whatever I was chewing blended with my tears. In fresh *fava* season, things got worse. I'd chew and chew the slimy boiled broad beans but I couldn't swallow them. Then the curses began: marriage, motherhood, children, her own childhood, bad luck, her bad heart. Threats followed: mammoth beatings, curfews, starvation, and abandonment to the gypsies. "You'll see what they'll feed you, if they'll feed you at all."

After a while, she'd grow tired or bored or disgusted with her own words. I never knew. But by the next *fava* season, the scene played itself out again, my mother always seeing herself as an injured queen in a drama not of her own making.

Looking out the bus window, I see black. My mother's head leans back on her seat, eyes shut now. I think of how she so carefully planned the day. Matching yellow sun dresses for both of us, yellow plastic thongs—a pair for Ana too—a new knitted blue bathing suit for me with a built-in bra for my small breasts, and the pound cake she'd taken to the baker's yesterday to be baked once his own bread was done. Now that my father's cheques arrive without fail on the first of every month in letters trimmed with blue and red stripes, nothing is out of way for us.

The letters accompanying the cheques are mostly funny, filled with new things. I read the letters, my mother finding reading troublesome. Twice my father sent photographs. In one, he's so bundled up in a big scarf, hat, boots, and a coat the size of a chicken coop, that we didn't recognize him at first. He's standing on a sidewalk covered with snow, surrounded by mounds of more snow, a skeletal tree behind him. We can't imagine what it would be like to live in such a cold, white world, can't imagine what he means by heated houses until spring and days on end without the sun. But some letters are sad. Rough bosses, back-breaking days building roads and skyscrapers in downtown Toronto, crowded rooming houses shared with other Portuguese immigrants to save money and ward off loneliness. These letters soon disappear from view.

The swaying bus makes me sleepy. *A Seagull flies higher and higher into the clouds . . .*

It's 9:30 when we walk through the door.

Feet washed, hair combed, my mother hands Ana and me a red lipstick.

"Put this on," she says, "Lucifer is asleep."

My mother has been calling my grandfather Lucifer since he scolded her for all her traipsing, as he calls it. He doesn't approve of lipstick, seeing it as a woman's invitation to trouble. But nothing stops my mother. "Just because your father is across the ocean doesn't mean I have to live like a widow," she says whenever she's upset with my grandfather.

Her grievances with him go back to childhood. She was four or five when, in a drunken rage at the barking of their new puppy, Sporting, my grandfather grabbed a shovel, dug a hole, and buried the puppy alive, my mother and Avó watching. This was back in Algarve, on their farm. I'd grown up hearing these stories whenever my mother was angry with my grandfather.

"I watched him do it," she'd said, "the son of a bitch had insisted. By the time Avó and I dug out the yelping puppy, he was shitting green. Sometimes I still can hear his cries."

The dark, empty streets make us tense. We walk abreast, in silence, staring straight ahead.

A dog barks; I jump.

"What's with you tonight?" my mother asks. "Afraid of everything?"

"I'm scared of dogs."

"Keep walking."

After fifteen minutes or so, we hear faint, musical sounds in the distance.

We speed up our pace.

The dance floor is packed with couples and women dancing with other women and children running in between. Zigzagging strings of glaring lights give the people an over-animated look. The bright red, green, and yellow banners below the lights form a garish canopy overhead.

My mother and Ana start hopping to the rhythm of a polka. There are no empty seats; I stand by the stage, watching them. A tango plays next. I can't see them for all the dancers. When my mother again emerges, she's dancing with Eduardo. They whirl by me laughing and waving.

My mother's head is thrown back and Eduardo's leg is shoved between hers. The image of my father in that chicken-coop coat in the snow seems to follow them.

A bolero plays next.

"*Olá bonita*, may I have this dance?" A tall boy with shaggy black hair and sea-green eyes extends his hand to me. He's older, about eighteen or nineteen. I've never seen him before or seen anyone as handsome. He holds me so close I can smell the *Tabu* on his face. It's as though we've always been dancing together. A Paso Doble plays next. The handsome stranger whirls me around the floor in a kind of crazy gallop, my feet hardly touching the floor.

It's then I see my mother and Ana standing on the sidelines.

My mother waves for me to come over; I wait until the song ends.

"You're as pretty as a daisy in springtime," the stranger says. "I was on my way to Lisbon; glad I stopped by."

I walk away in a kind of daze.

You're as pretty as a daisy in springtime . . .

"We're going home," the old nothing-but-bad-luck look back on my mother's face.

"But we just arrived!" I say.

"Do as I tell you." She starts walking toward the exit, next to the bar where the men stand on the sawdust-covered floor. Ana and I follow.

I give Ana a quizzical look.

"You shouldn't have danced with that stranger," she whispers. "To get even, Eduardo danced with his next door neighbour, whom your mother hates. You know how your mother is."

"But Eduardo is not my boyfriend!"

Ana throws up her hands and shrugs her shoulders.

As we near the bar, we lower our heads, trying to ignore the jeers from the men. I glance sideways hoping for a last look at the Lisbon traveller.

Instead, I see João!

He's bracing the narrow pathway, his shoddy appearance contrasting with the rest of the boys and men in their Sunday best and Brylcreemed hair. He stands erect, staring at us, arms at his sides, face hard as the rock he'd sat on all day. What does his stare hold? Anger? Retribution? The deadness in the eyes of beggars knocking at our door when asking for a piece of bread?

As we step onto the street, I say, "*Mãe* . . . the fisherman."

"I saw him. Just ignore the idiot."

"He made my blood curdle," Ana says. "You should've paid him."

"That's enough." My mother waves her hand in the air, as if shooing away a fly. She'll likely go and pay him tomorrow. She likes people to think well of her.

We walk Ana home, her house halfway between the dance and our house, which is on the other side of the railroad tracks. Faded notes from a mambo get swallowed by the night with each step. I find myself wondering if the green-eyed Lisbon boy is dancing with someone else.

A noisy silence wraps around my mother and me like a shroud, as we walk. The streets are deadly quiet now, the stray dogs likely asleep. I look up and search for Ursa Major, hoping for some deliverance in the stars. But she's hiding in the vast blackness.

The house is dark as we walk in—electricity not yet brought to our side of the railroad tracks. With a swift strike of a match my mother lights the oil lamp on the kitchen table. The dim light creates fantastic shadows on the walls, like grotesque portraits.

"Sit down." She points to a kitchen chair.

I sit; she remains standing.

"From now on Eduardo is your boyfriend, you hear? You can't dance or flirt with anyone else. It wouldn't be proper or decent . . . and you wouldn't want to upset him."

"I hate Eduardo. He's ugly and stupid." My heart is beating so fast I fear my mother can hear it. I don't look up.

"Don't talk back to me. I'm your mother. I know what's best for you. Eduardo will make you a good husband. Someone every woman would want. He's kind, affectionate, and funny."

"But I'm only fourteen. I'm too young to think of marriage."

I begin to cry. Dreams and visions of romance crash onto the dusty cement floor.

She turns away from me and opens the table drawer where the kitchen knives are kept, gaping into it for what seems a lifetime.

She picks up a long, bread knife.

My teeth begin to shatter.

She turns to face me, knife in hand. I begin shaking uncontrollably.

"Look up." My mother grabs my chin. "I said, look up."

Her eyes glitter with a brilliance I've never seen before.

"I'll kill you. I swear I will, if you don't do as I tell you."

I'd heard these words before, whenever I did something that upset her, which was often. But tonight each syllable bounces back from the glistening knife blade, her words lingering in the breathless air until she says, "Go to your room."

Sitting on my bed in the unlit room, long after the thumping of my heart stopped, I find myself wondering what might have passed through my mother's mind. Perhaps while staring at the knives, while trying to select the right one, she'd glimpsed at some half-forgotten spectre from her own childhood. Perhaps she'd heard Sporting's yelps. Or perhaps the day had been too much for her. I'd never know. She wasn't one for confessions.

A shaggy-haired boy with green eyes asked *me* to dance—*You're as pretty as a daisy in springtime* . . .

This much I know; this will always be mine.

She Liked Dealing

My mother is ironing. My mother is always ironing. She irons when she's angry or sad or bored, which is most of the time. Sometimes she irons in the kitchen. Today she's placed the ironing board in front of the TV in her bedroom. We have no living room. The TV is turned off. Every so often, she raises her head from the red blouse she's ironing and stares at the black screen as though she's immersed in the watching of some melodrama. Her lips are puckered, eyebrows furrowed. A familiar look. I'm standing at the bedroom door but it appears she hasn't seen me or heard me walk up. Or maybe she has.

I ran the three blocks from Ryerson Public School, up the stairs, two-by-two, to our second-floor flat on Kensington Avenue to watch American Bandstand at four o'clock. My father bought us the black-and-white the day after our arrival, three months ago.

"*Olá Mãe*," I say, pretending I don't notice her mood. I turn on the TV.

Silence.

Teens like me—yet not like me—fill the screen in a flash of light and sound, ecstatically gyrating to "Chantilly Lace." Jerry Lee Lewis pounds the piano, flipping back his waves at the eager audience.

I fling my school books on the threadbare brown corduroy sofa.

"It's A Man's World" plays next. I fight the old choking feeling of helplessness, a listlessness that makes me feel crumpled, like a discarded piece of paper. Entrapment in a familiar vault.

Today is the coldest day in February in fifteen years, the teacher said. I'd hurried out in the morning without gloves. Tears now wet my cheeks, as the warm air thaws my frozen fingers. My bladder feels as though it's about to burst, yet, here I stand, terrified to move in any direction or utter a word.

I watch the dancers, envying their freedom, their happiness, their blondness. Another winter flashes before me. Not the Canadian kind, where the distant sun fails to warm up the frozen earth for half of the year, yet there's warmth indoors. A damp Mediterranean one. One where rivulets of water stream down cement walls and mould grows in every corner of the house, even on the underside of your mattress. Sometimes your blood feels as though it's turning the same greenish colour.

I must've been six, Manuelito had just been born. My mother dragged me from my bed by my hair, forcing me to stand facing his crib in the kitchen, my parents' bedroom too small to accommodate it. That afternoon, while my mother did her laundry in my grandparents' outdoor cement tub next door, her hands purple from the frosty well water, Manuelito in Avó's care, I went into the house and shredded the crib's yellow rubber mattress cover with a pair of kitchen scissors. Yellow ribbons, like falling golden sun rays, lit up the cold grey day. I covered the shredded rubber sheet with the blue baby blanket. As my mother put Manuelito to sleep in the evening, she discovered what I'd done.

She picked up the scissors—I'd forgotten them under the mound of yellow ribbons.

She pointed the scissors at my face. "I'll cut you up in as many pieces as you cut the rubber sheet. Where do you figure I'll find the money to buy another one? Umh? How am I to keep the mattress dry in these winter days without the sun?"

I kept my eyes on my feet, which were growing numb from the cold cement floor, my patched cotton nightgown too thin to warm me, my face turning red with shame and guilt. I hadn't thought of the cost, hadn't thought of my father being out of work again for the last four months, the cork factory closed for lack of work. Hadn't thought of anything.

"Why did you do it?" My mother kept screaming. "Why, why, why?"

I didn't answer, didn't know why I'd done it. All I knew was that this howling *thing* called Manuelito was taking up all my mother's and Avó's time and care.

Years later, as I stand in this room across the ocean, facing my mother, my defrosting fingers feeling as though they are angry at me, my bladder nearly letting go, it's not the fear of my face being cut up I remember but the release of something warm, comforting, rushing down my trembling legs.

"Why haven't you written Eduardo?" my mother finally says, muffled words uttered through clenched teeth. "It's been six weeks."

"*Mãe*, I've got a lot of homework to do."

"Okay, okay. Write to him Saturday. There's no school, so no excuse. I'll mail the letter. It's rude, you know, not to answer your boyfriend's letters."

"Eduardo is not my boyfriend," I mumble, as I turn toward the door.

"What did you say?"

"Nothing."

I grab my books and coat from the sofa and slowly walk out of the room and down the hall to the bathroom.

My bedroom, which I share with Manuelito, is directly across from my parents' bedroom. As I return from the bathroom, I announce to my mother that I'm going to do my homework.

No answer.

I sit on my single bed. *American Bandstand* filters through the partially opened door, my mother has never been a fan of shut doors.

Through the dusty small window with strips of dry blue paint peeling off the frame, I see Manuelito playing hockey in the lane with other boys. Someone must've given him a broken hockey-stick. My mother never asks him where he's been or what he's been doing when he arrives home. Freedom he has as a male I can only dream of as a girl.

Darkness is falling fast. I should turn on the light and fill in the word-blanks in my *English For New Canadians* textbook given to us three newcomers on our first day of school. Miss White showed us a blue photo album to be awarded to the student learning to speak English the fastest. I want that album. Yet, I continue gazing at the dilapidated roofs and verandahs of potholed Kensington Avenue, which is perpetually enveloped in a damp grey darkness since we've arrived. It's as though the sun bypasses it in search of better places.

I kneel down on the small green chenille rug behind the bedroom door, where I can hide from my mother. The rug is part of the furnished flat my father rented for us. This close to the linoleum floor, I can see dust balls, rips, stains, and the wear-and-tear from those who were here before us.

I put my palms together. *Our Father Who art in heaven, hallowed be thy name . . .*

I stop. *What's the point?*

My mother will never let Eduardo go. Not after the whispers, the laughter, the long silences between them back in Amendoeiro. Not after Eduardo lay beside her on her bed, helping her to fall asleep, she said—they said—my father already in Canada, I in my room. This took place every night. From the first day Eduardo, only sixteen then, came to deliver bread to our house back in Amendoeiro, he became her muse, a magic carpet taking her to a land of amusement and forgetfulness. A land—it appeared—existing beyond my father, beyond any of us.

Soon he started showing up every evening after supper. As soon as we finished eating, my mother would remove the plates, put them onto the small cement kitchen counter to be washed outside the next morning. She'd then place the *Brisca* cards on the kitchen table, ready, waiting, anticipating the joy Eduardo brought as he walked through the door. She liked dealing.

Now, rosary in hand, I beg God to give him tuberculosis.

My father's unhurried footsteps echo on the stairwell. He's whistling a song from his boyhood about a boy peeing in the hay. The clock shows 5:30—he's never late. He walks home from his construction job at the new TD tower on King Street to save on car fare.

"Hello family," he calls out. After two years of being alone, he's happy to have us here, happy to have a hot meal waiting for him at the end of a hard working day, happy to be in a country where everything is possible, as he often reminds us.

During a typical dinner of boiled cod and potatoes, sprinkled with olive oil and lemon, he tells us again about his friend Medeiros who ate french fries and apple pie three days in a row when he first arrived in Toronto, those being the only English words he'd learned. My father laughs so hard he nearly chokes.

"French fries and apple pie, everyday."

"Not those stories again," my mother says, as she gets up from the kitchen table, loudly scraping the hardly eaten food on her plate into the garbage can. She turns away from the table and faces the kitchen sink.

My father finishes his meal in silence. Manuelito hurries outside to play with his new friends.

My mother stands by the kitchen sink and begins loudly washing dishes she seems intent on breaking. I stare at her square back as she hums the refrain of a *fado* over and over about a woman jilted by her lover. Her humming is like an incantation she hopes will save her from whatever it is she fears.

I think about my parents' marriage. My father *kidnapping* my mother one night following a Moorish tradition left over from the time when they colonized Algarve. My mother was sixteen and my father eighteen, their farms across from one another. My grandmother, my father's mother, prepared the bed with white embroidered sheets, a white satin bedspread, and a white cotton nightgown trimmed with white lace, waited for my mother on top of the nuptial bed. On the dresser, a vase of orange blossoms, a traditional symbol of virginity, anticipated the bride's deflowering. My mother never forgot such whiteness and often spoke of it. She never forgave my grandmother either, for what she called, "The raping of my innocence."

"It was Filipe I loved," my mother told everyone. "But after Antonio used me that night I had no choice but to marry him. My future was written."

Filipe showed up at our house late one evening, I must've been four or five. He was already living in Moita, a small town an hour away by bus, having moved from Algarve soon after my grandparents and parents settled in Amendoeiro. He had cycled the whole way.

My mother's voice woke me. "Antonio is at work and he won't be home until midnight."

"It's okay. I'll just come in for a quick visit. I need to see you badly."

"People talk, Filipe. Amendoeiro wags its tongue like a bitch in heat."

I appeared in the kitchen, rubbing the sleep from my eyes.

"Look," Filipe pointed at me, a wide grin on his face. "We're not alone. Milita is here!"

My mother sat at one end of the rectangular kitchen table that was pushed against the wall, Filipe sat at the other end. I sat in the middle, facing both.

"Close your eyes," he said. I did. He placed three small packets of chocolate squares wrapped in multicoloured foil in my hand. I only saw those little chocolates at Christmas.

My mother's arms moved up and down in frenzied movements. She talked fast, giggled, her voice excited, happy. She kept pushing her long, curly black hair away from her face.

It was summer. Through the day, moths and mosquitos had gotten through the red and green plastic beads hanging over the kitchen door to keep them out. They circled the oil lamp, round and round and round . . . I fell asleep.

When I woke, Filipe was gone; the chocolates were melting in my hand, my father was not yet home.

"Don't mention Filipe's visit to your father or to anyone," my mother said.

"Why?"

"Just don't."

I never did tell my father or anyone. I remember thinking at the time that the secret around Filipe's visit had something to do with the Christmas chocolates.

Now I continue staring at my mother's back. Her brusque movements, seemingly pointing to her thoughts the way longitudinal and latitudinal lines on a globe point to geographical zones.

It seems the more my father likes this new country, new life, its promising future, the more my mother hates it. She complains bitterly to anyone who'll listen about the dullness of the grey, cold days, the dark, unplastered brick houses, the tasteless fruit and vegetables, the old flat with its battered furniture and stained mattresses, the wringer washing machine stashed away in the sunless, cobwebbed basement, where the octopus coal furnace swallows up most of the space, the shared bathroom with strangers living on the third floor, and the people of all colours on the street, wearing funny clothes and speaking languages she can't understand. After three months, the electric iron is the only thing she likes. All she needs to do is plug it in and it heats up almost instantly. No burnt holes left on clothes as the coal iron did back home.

The April sun fills the kitchen with a festive air, as if determined to wake the earth from its long frozen winter slumber. We've finished eating a Sunday lunch of liver and onions sautéed in red wine and bay leaf, poured over boiled potatoes (my father's favourite) when my mother announces that she's learned of a Senhora Oliveira who works in Immigration.

My father pushes back his chair, shrugs his shoulders in his habitual, what-does-that-have-to-do-with-me manner, and smiles his enigmatic smile, pointing nowhere.

My mother hadn't mentioned Eduardo since that cold day in February. I was beginning to believe that God was listening to my prayers, that, perhaps, Eduardo did get tuberculosis.

I want to beg my father to stop my mother from talking to anyone in Immigration. I know what she's up to.

Stop her, please!

But my father quietly walks out of the kitchen and heads directly to their bedroom. He turns on the TV. *Bang! bang!* Gun shots from a Western ricochet off the kitchen walls.

"Get dressed," my mother yells over the noise, as she stands up from the table and begins to gather the dirty dishes. "It's Sunday, Senhora Oliveira should be home."

"*Mãe*," I have to raise my voice to be heard. I stand up. My legs tremble so badly I hold on to the kitchen table for support. "I'm not marrying Eduardo."

"What? You ... You ... You ungrateful gir ... " She hiccups, as she throws the dish she is holding onto the floor.

My heart is thudding so fast I can't catch my breath.

Fernanda, the landlady from downstairs, is suddenly standing at the kitchen door. Her yellow dress reflects the sunlight shining through the kitchen window, making her appear like a phantasm.

"What's wrong?" she asks.

"Nothing," my mother answers in a tone that sends Fernanda quickly back downstairs.

We easily locate Senhora Oliveira's house on Palmerston Avenue. She's a friendly but reserved woman, hair perfectly combed into a french roll, impeccable manners announcing her higher education and class. She leads us into her living room and offers us tea. My mother declines, to show our respect. It would be improper to do otherwise.

We sit on a new green velvet couch; Senhora Oliveira sits across from us on a matching chair. I'd never been inside a beautiful room like this. My mother talks fast, betraying her nervousness. She tells Senhora Oliveira about Eduardo, how he and I are in love and can't live without one another, how we want to marry as soon as possible.

Senhora Oliveira stares at me. "How old are you?"

"Fifteen."

"She's just a child. It's not legal in this country to marry that young."

"But Milita will turn sixteen in a few months and she and Eduardo want to be together. They love each other."

It's a lie, I want to shout. But the words fail to find their way through my smile.

"I'll write *Urgent* on the application," Senhora Oliveira says. "Canada is very good at reuniting families."

My mother stands up and so do I.

Senhora Oliveira accompanies us to the door.

Walking home, my mother is silent. The warm April sun is waning, inviting a cold wind that cuts through my cotton jacket. I shiver.

When we arrive at the flat, my father is still sitting on the threadbare brown corduroy sofa watching TV; Manuelito remains outside playing hockey in the lane with his broken stick. My mother walks up to the TV and turns it off. She stands in front of it, facing my father, like a teacher instructing her class. She proceeds to inform him that a written parental consent is needed in order for me to get married because I'm underage.

"That's Canadian law. Senhora Oliveira will bring us the necessary papers. Eduardo will have a church wedding in Amendoeiro with a bride who will stand in for Milita. It's called, a proxy wedding. That's how it works. After the wedding he can apply to Canadian Immigration to come here."

My mother departs to the kitchen to prepare dinner. I remain standing next to my father, who continues staring at the black screen, as though the cowboys are still shooting the hollering Indians on horses and says nothing.

I head to my bedroom and partly close the door. I sit on my bed, hardly breathing, the hatred for my father is so intense.

Back home in Amendoeiro, I used to pass a homeless man every morning on my way to school. He was always drunk, curled up asleep by the railroad banks across from Antonio's Taberna. Some winter mornings, his ragged clothes and matted long grey hair and beard would be covered in frost. He had a growth the size of a small melon on the right side of his throat, and a son, who'd set up a small fish stall at the edge of town, selling fish he caught in the night. In time the son managed to get a small house and a wife. Everyone knew the son never spoke to his father or helped him in any way, the father surviving by coins and food thrown at him by people. Neither my parents nor my grandparents or anyone I knew criticized the son for not helping the father. I always thought it cruel. Now I wonder what it was the father had done to the son in order to merit such abandonment.

I kneel again on the green chenille rug. This time I say three Ave Marias and three Our Fathers and plead with God to give Eduardo the disease people fear mentioning out loud.

After school the next day, I sit in my parents' bedroom by the large window facing Kensington, *English For New Canadians* on my lap. *American Bandstand* blasting, but I can neither watch nor listen. My mother is in the kitchen humming her *fado*.

I look out the window, waiting for my father to appear from the corner of Dundas and Kensington, swinging his black lunch pail, green Molson's cap askance on his head.

Today, he's late.

I wait.

Look and look and look.

There! Finally.

I quietly make my way down the stairs and wait for the key to turn in the front door. As my father steps in, I say, "*Pai*, you can't sign those papers. I can't marry Eduardo."

"Your mother knows best."

He walks away without even a glance my way.

"What kind of man are you?" I grab his arm. "You let her do whatever she wants."

His slap burns across my face; he'd never hit me before.

We face each other, two adversaries in a duel not of our own calling, my tears already forgotten. His eyes are pained and dappled with pity and shame. Something else is there, too. The panic I remember in the eyes of rabbits my father kept in cages back home when there was a noise or movement they didn't recognize. I turn away.

A glimpse of yellow moves away from the partly closed door to Fernanda's flat.

I climb the stairs; my father silently follows behind.

October rolls in with an artist's brush. The two spindly maple trees on Kensington's littered sidewalks are now a brilliant russet, the weeds pushing through the cracked cement are golden, like ripened wheat. I'm back at school, grade 8, though I'll be turning sixteen in December. In class, I feel conspicuous, a head taller than the rest. In the four months since our visit to Senhora Oliveira, my mother hasn't mentioned Eduardo and no letter has arrived from him. I'd written him, without my mother's knowledge, of course, telling him that I didn't love him, didn't want to marry him and didn't want to ever hear from him again. He never responded.

We're again sitting on the threadbare brown corduroy couch facing the TV, about to start watching *Bonanza*, as we do every Sunday, when my mother announces that we'll be moving soon. She's rented an unfurnished flat on Borden Street, with more space, more light, more trees on the street. She flashes an envelope trimmed with tiny green and red lines from her apron. "Eduardo is arriving three days before Christmas. We need to buy new furniture."

I run to the bathroom, my stomach churning. Not sure if it's the thought of Eduardo's arrival or my mother's secret correspondence with him that's heaving up the contents of my dinner from my stomach.

"Open the door, goddamn it." My mother hammers the bathroom door with her fists. "Act like an adult. You've signed the papers."

I don't answer and sit on the lid of the toilet. My mother is right, I did sign the papers. Senhora Oliveira had brought them to our house.

Still. And still . . . I foolishly hoped that my life hadn't been packaged away by those few scribbles on the white paper. *Still . . .* I continued praying to God . . . *Please God. Please, please, let Eduardo get cancer and die.*

I can hear my mother in the kitchen, which is next to the bathroom, sobbing and cursing her luck, her bad life, the wickedness of God. My father and Manuelito continue watching *Bonanza*, Little Joe's voice meeting me, as I walk to my bedroom.

I sit on my bed, the blue photo album (I'd won it!) on the dresser, facing me. I open the album with the determination of a sprinter crossing a finish line and yank out Eduardo's picture my mother had insisted I insert. I tear it into tiny pieces that fall on the bed like flecks of dust.

Then I flip open the prayer book on my night table. An angry Christ points at me. *The Pantocrator Chastizing His Sinful Flock*, Cefalú, Italy, is written underneath.

A sign.

I pick up my rosary and hold it tightly against my breast. Surely God is punishing me for my bad thoughts, my selfishness, my disloyalty. I kneel down again on the green chenille rug and ask God for forgiveness. *Our Father who art in heaven . . .* Halfway through I stop.

Please, please God, make the plane crash.

I shudder at my own words. *What am I saying? Please, please God forgive me.* I finish praying the rest of the rosary.

Eduardo walks through the steel swinging doors at Malton airport after midnight two months later. My parents, a Portuguese friend of theirs with a car, and I have been waiting for hours, the delayed plane offering me a ridiculous glimmer of hope.

He's wearing a light beige raincoat that drags along the floor, collar lifted high, Elvis style, dark sunglasses, and black patent leather shoes too big for his small feet, the long points curling up. He reminds me of a spy in a comedic film noir.

As he approaches, a grin is plastered across his pale face that seems to say, *I fooled you!*

"I ate all the food they gave me in the plane," he says. "All of it."

I'll never let this idiot touch me, I vouch to myself. This much is in my power.

Snow Drops

The first warm day of spring and ice melts off rooftops and sidewalks and birds fly out of their winter abodes, serenading the trash and muck on the city's streets with their electric song. It's four o'clock. I decide to walk the five blocks from Marvel Beauty School at the corner of Bloor and Walmer Road to our flat on Borden Street. Along the way, clumps of snowdrops shine in the sun in the small front gardens of the dark brownstone houses, their little white heads pushing through snow and ice, announcing the end of the long gloomy winter and arrival of warmer days and blue skies. Spring warriors admired for their determination.

I walk in through the front door; my mother is waiting for me at the top of the stairs. I *feel* her more than I see her because she hasn't bothered to turn on the light in the poorly lit hall. Her arms are crossed in a way that makes the birdsong in my head disappear.

"What kept you so long?" she says, as I climb the steps. "It's nearly five o'clock."

"It's a nice day so I decided to walk."

"You know I worry when you're not home in time. Hurry up. We need to talk before the men arrive."

In the kitchen, she motions to a chair. I sit, she remains standing, looking down at me. A familiar scene.

I try to appear calm, as though I have no idea why I'm being summoned. I imagine my mother glancing up all day long at the sunburst clock that we'd bought at Honest Ed's the day after our arrival and which hangs in our kitchen and four-o'clock never arriving. I imagine—no, I know—that my mother is determined to set things straight, set them according to plan. Her plan.

It's hot in the kitchen, the furnace still on in spite of the warm day, but I leave my wool jacket on. There's a sense of emergency—a shortness of time—in all that is hidden behind the words already spoken. Drops of perspiration fall onto my hands, as I clutch my black leather purse, a birthday gift from her. My mother likes me well dressed.

"What do you think you're doing?"

"What? What have I done?"

Manuelito is watching *Bugs Bunny* in my parents' bedroom. This flat is roomier than the one on Kensington Avenue but we still have only two bedrooms and a kitchen. No living room. Manuelito sleeps on a cot in the kitchen, the cot, sheets, blanket, and pillow folded every morning and hidden from view behind the kitchen door. Not by him, of course. My brother is ten and Portuguese boys don't do housework. It's a female responsibility.

The sound from the TV forces my mother to raise her voice.

"You've been married for four months but you refuse to let Eduardo touch you."

She's right. Eduardo arrived three days before Christmas, as planned, and I haven't even allowed him to kiss me. He's not the lover I've dreamed of, the one in songs, romances, movies, whose kiss lifts you to paradise and keeps you up there forevermore. No, no, he's not the green-eyed boy with the tousled black hair from Lisbon who once asked me to dance in Amendoeiro and told me that I was as-fresh-as-a-daisy-in-springtime. Chose me of all the girls!

I hide my shaking hands behind my purse, eyes low. *Always eyes low.*

"How do you know this?" It takes all my courage to utter these words.

"Eduardo was crying this morning. Imagine! A grown man crying like a baby. He said his wedding night was the saddest night of his life. I couldn't console him."

His wedding night! Is that what the fool calls the night he arrived from Portugal?

It was midnight by the time the delayed CP plane arrived in Toronto. By two am, Eduardo was standing beside the bed, buck-toothed, buttoned-down grey cotton pyjamas reminding me of old men I'd once seen in a hospital ward in Lisbon. I'd forgotten about his crooked nose. He'd accompanied us to Lisbon airport the day we departed, he and my mother hugging each other—sobbing—as we departed. They were like two broken-hearted lovers in a melodrama. "It won't be long," she promised. "I'll make sure of that."

A doll dressed in white lace with brown hair and eyes like mine decorated the bed, the doll and bed a wedding present from my mother. I pulled the blue flannel night gown further up my neck. The lacy silk white one my mother bought me in preparation for this night, still in the unopened box on the dresser. She'd placed it there.

"Come here, *minha noiva*, my bride." Eduardo came closer, spit flying from his buckteeth, spraying my face. "Our souls will be joined together tonight in heaven."

A Manual for Men on Their Wedding Night. These honeyed words had to have been memorized from the manual circulating Amendoeiro when I was a kid. Perhaps he still owned it. My cousin Ana found one. The black-and-white drawings were sequential, step by step from the groom undressing the bride to penetration. *Sweet words to be whispered in the bride's ear to ease the pain. Many delicacies to be enjoyed.*

"Listen, Eduardo." I took a step back from his short reaching arms. "I don't love you and I didn't choose you for my husband. Okay? My mother did. She wants you here, not me. I don't ever want you to touch me. You understand?"

He stared at me—dull ram eyes—turned around, got into bed, and faced the wall. As I switched off the light by the bedroom door, I heard muffled footsteps on the creaky hall floorboards. I feared opening the door.

By the time I got into bed, Eduardo was snoring.

The next morning, the alarm clock on the night table showed 8:30 am. I could hear Eduardo and my mother already in the kitchen.

I stood by the kitchen door still rubbing my eyes. A new buzz seemed to fill the bare light green walls needing painting. Except for the sun-burst clock, the grey metal table and grey plastic chairs, the gas stove, whose top had never been properly scrubbed, everything in the kitchen had been used by others before us. My mother was wearing her new red-flowered frilly apron, fuchsia lipstick on her smiling lips, two combs holding up the sides of her long curly hair. I'd never seen her look this groomed this early in the morning. I didn't recall her ever getting up to make my father breakfast, who leaves every morning at 6:30 for his construction job at the TD towers on King and Bay Streets. Manuelito was busy shooting the air in the hall with his toy gun. My mother hovered over Eduardo like a fly over syrup. Golden french toast—a food normally reserved for special mornings like Easter or Christmas—brimmed over the good white china platter brought from Portugal. "Coffee? Hot chocolate? Orange juice?" Her almond-shaped eyes glittered in the half light of the cloudy, cold morning piercing through the small dusty window. I wasn't sure whether she'd noticed me.

Soon I realized that I was not meant to be part of this golden french-toast celebration. I walked to the bathroom and soaked myself in the bathtub until the water turned cold.

That night, the next, and the next, Eduardo reached out for me in bed without the *sweet words*. "No," I said each time. He faced the wall and quickly fell asleep. There were times when I was sure that I heard the hall floorboards creak but by the time I dared to open the door, there was no one there and my parents' bedroom door was shut. Maybe I was imagining things.

"I don't want to be married," I now say to my mother's fluffy pink slippers that seem to be growing in size, filling up the kitchen, the flat, my life. She continues to stand over me.

I can't believe I found the courage to utter those six words. My blood is rushing through my veins, making me feel light-headed.

"Are you *stupid*? You *are* married. Eduardo is your husband. Get that through your skull. You've *signed* the papers to marry him and bring him over. No one forced you."

I had.

"Eduardo is an idiot and ugly. I hate him. I can't have sex with someone I don't love."

"You're *seca* like your father and his mother. Dry sticks incapable of even imagining affection or love. You're like them, selfish and unfeeling."

"If I have sex with Eduardo no other man will want me."

We're now both yelling. Manuelito raises the volume on the TV.

I'd grown up hearing the stories, seeing the sadness, the disillusionment, the empty resignation in women's doleful faces. Those who'd had to settle for whoever came along and married them—widowers or ageing bachelors—after being abandoned by boyfriends who'd *stolen* their virginity. Men were expected to be sexually experienced—know what to do with a woman, show they were knowledgeable in sexual matters. But women were to remain virgins until marriage, unspoiled, like fresh produce. My father's younger sister had to marry a widower with two grown sons—she only nineteen then—after her fiancé left her alone with her wedding plans. Her shame stuck to her unsmiling face like a veil for the rest of her life.

"Are you a whore?" My mother's left eyelid begins to twitch, as it does whenever she's upset. She raises her hand to slap me; I wince and duck to miss the blow. Her hand rests in midair, threatening.

"Eduardo is your husband. You are a married woman. Finished."

By the time my father arrives from work, my mother is already in bed. She has been alternating between gut-wrenching sighs,

Umh... Umh... Umh, and curses against the usual—her bad luck, bad marriage, God's indifference to her needs and her pleas. Her eyes bring to mind the pained eyes of our dog Benfica back home when boys in the neighbourhood threw stones at him. I stand by the bedside, unable to touch her or even offer words of comfort. She smells of dampness.

"*Olá,*" my father says, as he walks into the bedroom at 5:30. His calloused hands with black jagged fingernails hang loosely by his side, dirty work clothes frayed, the faded green Molson Canadian cap he got as gift when we lived on Kensington Avenue askance on his head, his handsome face partly covered in dust. He stands by the door, facing me, feet shuffling, as though ready to walk out at any moment. He doesn't ask why my mother is in bed. It's a familiar scene, like a *Bonanza* rerun. One of which he knows the plot well.

Eduardo arrives twenty minutes or so later from his part-time job at Simpson's cafeteria on Queen Street, where he cuts up pears, peaches, and oranges that he places in small stemmed glass bowls and tops with maraschino cherries. A friend of my parents found him the job. He brags every night about how much fruit he's eaten. The job doesn't pay much but at least he's gone from the flat by the time I get up in the morning. I'm thankful for that.

"Time to eat," my father announces the moment Eduardo appears at the door.

I raise the bedroom window and holler down for Manuelito to come in. He'd gone outside after my mother turned off the TV. He hasn't yet found friends on this new street, no boys to play street hockey with, as he did on Kensington. He entertains himself by teasing the next-door neighbour's German shepherd chained to the inside of the low green garden fence. The dog is barking; the dog is always barking. Sometimes I watch it chew its chain, chew and chew to no avail. I want to unleash him, let him run free to wherever he wishes to go.

We sit around the kitchen table; my mother remains in bed. I ladle out the thick cabbage soup with chorizo she'd made earlier in the day. The soup is delicious. We eat it with crusty bread. Silence descends over the table like a pall. Only my father's hungry slurping fills the kitchen.

What can we say or do when my mother's unhappiness fills every inch of the flat, spilling onto our yesterdays, staining our tomorrows, blotting out the elixir of our lives? Our wills?

The meal ends quickly. Eduardo gets up from the table and begins to ladle soup into a small bowl. He takes it to my mother and I follow with a glass of orange soda, her favourite. He carefully—gently—places a pillow behind her head, as though he's handling a newborn baby. Then he proceeds to feed her the soup, spoonful by spoonful, and the same old stories he tells her every night at dinner. How many pears he pared, how many he ate, how Susie, the waitress, sleeps with the cook, who's married with two children, how a customer burped at the lunch counter, another farted. My mother laughs hysterically, deep laughs, as if uprooting something hidden within her.

I leave the room.

Manuelito is shooting the birds in the hall wallpaper, aiming for their eyes. My father remains seated at the kitchen table counting his coins. He has started an antique coin collection, buying a coin every week from an antique coin shop on Queen Street. My mother gives him a small allowance after he hands her his paycheck every Friday.

The kitchen cleaned, I go into my bedroom; Eduardo remains with my mother. I shut the bedroom door, sit on the bed, and think about my mother's words.

Perhaps she's right.

Perhaps it's time to stop holding on to my virginity like some insurance policy against disaster. Men here seem to be different. Virginity doesn't seem to be the valued prize in marriage sought by men back home, not the raft carrying women along the river of decency to a land of happiness. It's time, I think, to stop pretending to myself and others that I didn't sign the marriage and immigration papers, that I'm a free sixteen-year-old like all other sixteen-year-olds.

Didn't the priest, the few times I went to the Portuguese church at Bathurst and Queen, remind us of the need to accept the things we can't change? That's what he'd said, "God wants us to accept the things we can't change. Didn't Christ accept His suffering and His death on the cross? Father, forgive them, for they do not know what they are doing."

I stare in the mirror on the dresser. *Who is that old woman staring back at me?*

"You can make love to me tonight," I say to Eduardo as he comes into the bedroom after my father sent him away from my mother's bedside. "But no kissing, no patting, no talking."

"Okay."

I place the doll, whose eyes look like mine and which I close, on the dresser and we get into bed. I turn off the lamp on the night table, not wanting to see Eduardo's face or for him to see the disgust on mine. I lift up my white cotton nightgown, the silk one my mother bought me still in the package hidden in the closet. I try hard not to think of the spit bubbles dripping at the corners of Eduardo's mouth when he gets excited.

No sweet delicacies, just the raw feeling of torn flesh. Afterwards, I feel like bruised fruit no one wants to buy. Eduardo's final grunt still in my ears, I hurry to the bathroom, lock the door, and soak in the tub. I scrub and scrub, trying to wash away the clammy feel of Eduardo's body and the memory of his groping hands, but nothing washes away. Rape with consent.

In the morning, I decide to tell the girls at Marvel School that my proxy husband has arrived from Portugal. I'll make up a story; I'm good at inventing them. I'd written *single* in the application form in January and didn't tell anyone I was married, not even the Brazilian girl who befriended me. How could I? She talks of dates and dancing and drinking at the Silver Rail on Yonge Street on Saturday nights.

I graduate in June still pretending I'm single, the gold band hidden in the black leather purse my mother bought me.

Zeus

The car not yet fully packed and my mother is already sitting in the back seat. It's Thanksgiving, our first long weekend with a car. My mother is smiling, like a child going on an outing of her own choice. She's wearing her new red sweater, matching lipstick, and new sunglasses, though daylight is barely dusting away the darkness. She'd bought me an identical sweater, insisting I wear it. Except for the tiny wrinkles framing her eyes, we look like twins. At thirty-five, her long, wavy dark hair still shines free from silver tinsel.

"For once I'd like to go somewhere without my mother," I'd whispered to Eduardo one night last week after everyone was in bed for the night. He'd managed to get his driver's licence, and yesterday he brought home the new yellow Ford. We've been married for two years and have hardly been alone, my parents and brother Manuelito still living with us. My mother's idea, of course. Dances at the Portuguese club on Augusta Avenue, movies, Sunday visits to other Portuguese immigrants my mother met, picnics, shopping, and my mother always dressed and ready to embark on our ventures even before we were. Staying home was never her choice. Out, out, she needed to be out, needed to be away from my father whenever possible, away from a marriage she'd never accepted. He made her nervous, anxious, depressed, sad, she said. Oh, she was sad . . . Always the same story of him not being her choice in marriage but that of her parents. Permission from us or my father or discussion as to whether she should join us in our outings had never taken place. It was understood—always understood—that whatever we did, wherever we went, she'd come along. At eighteen, the unspoken desires coursing through me are still packages waiting to be unwrapped, ribbons waiting to be cut. I move from day to day, busy doing, doing, eating, sleeping, talking without reflection.

Sundays aren't so bad. Picnics with friends on Centre Island in summer and walks in High Park and James Gardens in winter make me feel normal, like my life mirrors the lives of others.

But Mondays arrive too quickly, weeknights limping through without end. Mealtime is bad. Eduardo recounts his idiotic stories from work where he now packages glass doors and windows, my mother laughing even when he burps. My father looks lost in his new silences, as though he'd left us long ago and only his shadow sits across from us. Saturday nights, while other teenagers dance, go to movies, drive up and down Yonge Street honking their car horns to their freedom, we visit other Portuguese immigrants my mother collects. They are seduced by her friendliness, her unmatched generosity. Eduardo is always the entertainer. The clown. I die from embarrassment each time, seeing the smirks on people's faces, their eyes trying to avoid mine. Then later that night, there's sex. This is my final sacrifice of the week, the bargain made between Eduardo and I. A gift of my body, my face turned away, and the price I pay for being left alone for the remainder of the week.

North America's obsession with sex puzzles me. Last week, Gerard, from work, brought *The Happy Hooker* to the salon. He read parts of the book to the four of us in the back room between haircuts. We all giggled, shyly looking anywhere but at one another. Shocking! A woman so shameless and depraved. How could this be?

Growing up, I kept hearing that only men and whores enjoy sex, not decent women. Sex was regarded as a woman's wifely duty, part of the marriage arrangement, like cooking and cleaning. But that night, it was I who turned to Eduardo. I never kissed him, couldn't look at him in the morning, but I broke my own rule of no sex on any other night but Saturdays.

"We can't leave your mother home," Eduardo replied when I suggested we go north for the weekend and see the famous changing Fall colours.

I was sure he'd want us to be alone, just he and I for once. But I was wrong.

"I'm sick of my mother, sick of her control, her sacrifice, especially her sacrifice." Surprise gave way to anger. "Can't we go somewhere alone for once like other normal couples?"

"But she does everything for us. What do you do around the house? Umm? It'll break her heart, you know that. It might even kill her. Have you forgotten about her bad heart?"

Of course I hadn't. I'd been reminded of its ticking fragility ever since I was a child. A questioning of her rules, her punishments when I was a child, an alteration to her expectations, a wrong smile or tone of voice, and puff, my mother's heart could simply stop.

Ah, my mother's heart!

That faulty neon light ever flicking its red beams above my days, reminding me to be obedient, be good, keep things as they are, follow my mother's command and wishes. This included my proxy marriage to Eduardo when I was fifteen; he arrived in Toronto from Portugal exactly one year after we did. Living all together was part of the path she'd chosen for us all. My father and I trudged along it without veering left or right. Whether my father questions any of this—has ever questioned any of my mother's decisions or whims—he never says. I've never heard them argue about anything at all. Smiles, my father just smiles.

Manuelito, twelve now, remains defiant of my mother's threats, which she never carries through, anyway. Disciplining him requires effort, a spilling of her energy, her time, her focus. She's grown tired of it. Now I'm the sole focus of her preoccupation. Through me, her days and happiness are measured. If I behave according to her expectations, life is easy, the house quiet, calm, meals on the table on time—she's a good cook. When I don't, like the time Gerard from work came to visit, she'll spend days in bed, sighing and lamenting her bad luck. "How could you invite that stranger here? You're supposed to be spending your day off with me."

By the time we arrive in Owen Sound, the sun is begin to slide behind farmhouses, barns, cows, long shadows blanketing the fields like tenebrous ghosts.

The picnic at Wasaga Beach and the visit to the Collingwood caves took longer than anticipated. It's late. Every motel we approach has the *No Vacancy* red neon sign blinking at us, like some hellish warning. My mother has stopped talking. Not a good sign. We pass the town and there's nothing but a looming darkening forest. After about ten-fifteen minutes, a small motel appears. The broken neon sign announces *VACA*. A black pickup is parked outside the office door.

The sky grows suddenly dark, starless, the moon nowhere to be seen, as though hiding behind a black cosmic curtain.

As Eduardo and I walk out of the car—my mother remaining in the back seat—a chilly gust of wind blows a battered aluminum garbage can, which seemed to appear out of nowhere, across our way. I shiver.

We enter.

An unshaved man wearing a rumpled black t-shirt that barely covers his belly, noisily chews gum behind a small counter. He says, "You're lucky. Only two rooms left."

We're sure he's lying—there are no other vehicles in the parking lot besides the black pickup, but we don't say anything.

We return to the car. Half of my mother's face flickers in quavering red blotches from the red light emanating from the broken neon, the other half of her face is in darkness. Her good-times, beauty-queen face she'd worn all day is gone.

She refuses to sleep alone in her own room, fearful that a murderer or some vagrant may come in the night and kill her. "Milita, have you forgotten about my bad heart?"

Okay.

The motel man leers at us when we ask for the queen bedroom upon our return. As he turns around to get the key we read, *Farts Are Fun,* on the back of his t-shirt.

My mother and Eduardo sit on the orange chenille bedspread. A round brown stain at the centre of the spread screams at me. The room smells of mildew, tobacco, dust, other people's sweat. I remain standing, afraid to sit on the vinyl orange chair with its bursting large tear, yellow stuffing spilling out. What could be crawling inside?

We eat the tuna sandwiches left over from lunch. The bread is soggy and the tuna warm.

"Eduardo sleeps in the middle," my mother says, the moment we finish eating, as if she's been rehearsing her words in preparation for this moment. "His presence relaxes me."

I'd forgotten, time lulling memory. Forgotten how Eduardo had turned into a nightly lullaby for my mother, back in Amendoeiro. "He helps me fall asleep," she explained to my grandparents the morning the scandal flared. The gossip was new. Different from the rest. A married woman, mother of two, sleeping with a sixteen-year-old boy, while her husband worked across the ocean. The hot flames of malice refused to abate for a long time, infusing the dull lives of the people in the small, sleepy town with renewed vigour. Eduardo's father had come knocking at our door about three am looking for his son. Someone hidden in the shadows of the barely lit road heard the father chastizing the son for improper behaviour.

Afterwards, I tried convincing myself that my mother's and Eduardo's nightly routine was what she said it was, a mother and child's cuddle before sleep.

How could I think otherwise? My mother was *my mother*.

Home early from work one Saturday a few weeks ago, I heard Eduardo's and my mother's laughter before I even opened the front door. Eduardo did not work on Saturdays and my father was usually peddling his antique coins at Portuguese Billiards on College Street where everyone knew him. *Uma Casa Portuguesa,* a fado sung by Amalia Rodrigues—the record brought from Portugal—blasted the air. They didn't hear me come in. When I appeared at the kitchen door, they stood motionless, faces startled, impish smiles, like children when caught doing something forbidden. My mother sat on a chair in the middle of the kitchen in her black lacy bra, one arm lifted high, her white bareness making me wince. Eduardo held a razor; he was shaving her underarms.

I soon faked a headache and escaped to my bedroom. Lying on the bed, fully dressed, shoes still on, I wondered if my father saw what I did. His younger smiles had given way to silences, which had grown thicker since Eduardo's arrival two years earlier.

I wake in the night, the taste of warm tuna in my mouth, my stomach churning, temples throbbing. I hurry to the bathroom, close the door and bend over the toilet just in time.

As I walk back to bed, light from the broken neon streams through the opening in the dusty orange nylon curtains, enough that I can see clearly.

The sheets are tossed, my mother's nightgown is pushed up to her waist, her black panties are half rolled down, as though put on in a hurry. Eduardo is lying on his right side, my mother is spooning him, her left leg curled over his.

Did something happen while I slept?

I approach the bed carefully so as not to wake them, two sleeping puppies, hugging.

I sit on a corner of the orange vinyl chair, trying to avoid the large tear, and watch them, watch the incandescent whiteness of my mother's legs.

Eduardo snores softly, lips parted in a grin; my mother's chest heaves gently in peaceful rest. They look as though all obstacles to their happiness have been eliminated.

An article I recently read said that Plato believed human beings in their original forms were whole: two faces, four feet, four arms, four hands. But Zeus, fearing their power, split them in half. Ever since then, human beings have been doomed to seek the world over for their other half in order to feel whole again.

Perhaps the connection between Eduardo and my mother was decided long ago, long before they were even born, before the beginning of their own histories. Age difference and social roles too superficial to stop them, their bond beyond impropriety, beyond convention, surely beyond my father and me. I'd seen the attraction the first day Eduardo came to our house delivering bread. The next day, before Eduardo arrived, my mother put on lipstick and her red polka-dot dress, usually saved for Sundays. She laughed at every inanity he spewed out. There was something lewd in her laughter, embarrassing, shameful, making me want to run away.

But what did the philanderer Zeus know about shame? Hera waiting, like a good wife, for the creator-of-all-gods-and-men to arrive home from his rendezvous with his consorts. Perhaps the god, too, couldn't help himself.

I try to fall asleep on the torn orange chair. But an exhaustion that seems to go beyond this motel room, beyond this day, beyond my eighteen years, keeps my eyes from shutting. It rained shortly after we checked in and now a miasma of dampness, mildew, stale tobacco smell, and dust, fills the room. I shiver and sneeze but Eduardo and my mother don't stir. I place my corduroy jacket over my legs and put on my woollen cardigan.

My eyes are nearly shutting when I hear a gnawing noise and the sound of tiny feet scurrying on the vinyl floor behind the dresser. I lift my legs off the floor and roll myself into a fetal position, too frightened to discover what might be keeping me company.

No sounds are coming from the highway. I wonder what time it is but am too afraid to step onto the floor and check my watch on the night table. Another sleepless night. They've begun accumulating.

I wake. My mother is standing over me.

"What are you doing on that chair?" She's dressed, her new red sweater back on and matching lipstick. I can hear Eduardo in the bathroom flushing the toilet.

"I couldn't sleep with the dampness."

"What dampness? There's always something for you to complain about, isn't there?"

"It was warmer on the chair. I put on my wool sweater." I point to the red sweater.

"Don't tell anyone about tonight. You couldn't expect me to sleep by myself in this forsaken place you brought me to."

Why didn't you stay home then? I want to say.

I don't.

The one time I questioned my mother, a knife nipped my throat. A tiny scar still remains.

I wait for Eduardo to come out of the bathroom. He doesn't look at me as he opens the door. I say nothing, not even good morning.

The metal shower is old, rusty, but as the warm water falls gently over me, washing away the stale smell of the room, I know . . .

What is it I know?

I know that my mother has devoured my father but she will not devour me.

The drive back home is silent and chilly, yesterday's sun is hiding its face this morning. October has opened its door to winter. My mother sits in the front seat next to Eduardo, as though that's where she belongs, has always belonged. I lie across the back seat pretending to sleep.

She insists on keeping the car window half open, snow flurries brushing my cheeks. She needs to breathe, she says, her heart is short of oxygen.

I close my eyes and try to recall the colours of the changing leaves.

Waylaid Pilgrim

I: *Departure*

Eduardo yanks the ring off my finger and throws it out of the car window onto the late evening traffic on the QEW. The yellow Ford swerves, nearly hitting an oncoming vehicle. I scream, picturing our mutilated bodies melded into the mangled car parts. Death flirting with me just when I found love, just when the promise of tomorrow began to blot out my yesterdays, always there. I've despised the thin yellow band on my finger ever since Eduardo placed it there five years ago, but I think it wasteful to throw away gold.

"It's over," he says. "I can't go on living with a whore."

"Who are you calling a whore? I love Claudio. I do, I do."

"Honest married women don't have affairs with other men."

I turn to face him, but he doesn't look my way.

"Listen, Eduardo, just listen, will you? I love Claudio. Okay? I'm not a whore."

His indignation surprises me—I didn't know he had it in him. Didn't know he could feel such anger. It had never shown in all the time we were married.

"Don't upset me more than I already am," I continue. "My mother forced me to marry you, Okay? You know this, for heaven's sake. I love Claudio and sex isn't wrong between two people who love each other."

Eduardo doesn't reply. Eyes fixed on the red taillights ahead of him, hands tight on the steering wheel, he drives as though he's being beckoned somewhere he fears.

"Where should I take you?"

His tone is now less incriminating, almost affectionate, like a parent subduing an unruly but loved child.

"Niagara Falls," I blurt out, as if answering a question in *Jeopardy*, as if this answer has been waiting to be uttered for a long time. "Niagara Falls, yes, yes, a place far away from my mother."

The idea of fun-filled Falls, the gaudy amusements, the tawdry thrills, pink cotton candy, seems to make this unfolding drama less frightening. It makes walking away from Eduardo, my parents, Manuelito, less of a quagmire of uncertainty, of dread. It helps to tame the guilt, too, not toward my mother but my father and Manuelito—I loved them.

"Don't blame your mother," Eduardo says. "She adores you and cooks, cleans, washes, irons, and shops for you. She lives and would die for you, you know that, and now look what you've done to her. With her bad heart and bad nerves, this could kill her."

His voice is clear, assured, pedantic. He believes what he's saying.

"What? What I've done?" The pitch in my voice rises. "What are you saying, you imbecile! What about what *she's* done to me? Why do you always defend her?"

He shakes his head, slowly at first, then in a kind of convulsion of disbelief. "When do I defend her?"

"Always, you always defend her. It's like you're the son and I'm the outsider."

He turns and stares at me, confusion in his eyes, as though I'm insane, I'm like the disheveled woman who stands at the corner of Yonge and Dundas hailing Jesus to passersby.

I can't believe what I've just called him.

"Why Niagara Falls?" he asks. "Why so far? It's way past nine."

I say nothing. My chest is pounding. I touch my neck with my fingers. I can still feel my mother's clutching fingers around it. The flesh is tender there, likely already bruised.

We pass the Ford plant, the spray of city lights fading away behind us. The traffic eases along with the knot in my stomach, heartbeat slowing down, *down* . . . We could be going on a Sunday picnic, except my mother isn't in the back seat.

For a moment I almost miss her downcast face, wrinkles carved not by time (she's only thirty-eight) but by the belief that life is a thorn-infested journey and that God bestows good luck only on those he favours. She is not one of God's favourites. Round, thick-waisted, stooped shoulders, it's as though the weight of every waking hour won't let her be.

Along the dark highway, the odd light suddenly appears, like a falling star in the black canopy of the big sky.

The idea that I may never go home again starts to take hold. Dreams of escape (ever since I can remember) have filled my every day since Claudio's first kiss in the lunch room. It began as a dare, everyone already back upstairs working, me married to someone else and he engaged. A kind of joke, really. Perhaps for him the thrill of kissing someone new. For me, his kiss opened the door to a world I never knew before, didn't know could be.

Suddenly my mother's sad, censoring dark eyes, my father's chiseled smile, hiding what I think I know but he's never said, and Manuelito's young, restless face—all faces as familiar as my own—begin to blur in the miles between Mississauga and this unchartered territory.

Now I feel bad calling Eduardo an imbecile. He's never been unkind. The decisions to buy the new back-split in Mississauga, new furnishings, weekends away, not to have children, were entirely my own. I've been bored and embarrassed by his dime-store jokes, his carnivalesque witticisms, repelled by his short bowed legs, his long crooked nose, sickened by the sweaty lovemaking I permit only on Saturday nights, his grunts, the sticky wetness afterwards I can never fully wash away, the drool escaping his lips when he laughs, but he's never mistreated me. Thanks to him I'm here and not waiting to meet the undertaker.

The car lights glare on a road sign announcing *St Catharines*. Just past it, a motel with a red telephone booth. I motion to Eduardo to stop. He swerves into the motel's parking lot.

I scramble in my wallet for coins and Helma's telephone number that I've been carrying with me for a while.

Eduardo says nothing. His anger seems to have given way to a sort of giving up, a helplessness, an acceptance of things which he cannot control. It's as though he understands, has always understood, that this day, this moment, has been incubating ever since we met. I told him often enough that I didn't love him.

He waits in the car while I dial Helma's number.

What if Helma doesn't answer?

A cold chill runs down my spine. I look at my watch—10:30. She's likely asleep and might not chance driving this far in her beat-up 1965 Chevy with no heat and a hole in the floor. Cold weather warnings were announced all day after the morning snow turned to ice.

"Hello."

Tears well in my eyes. I tell Helma where I am; she tells me to wait.

She'd been urging me for months to leave Eduardo. "Don't *shpoil* your life like I've spoiled mine." Helma is German, a Marilyn Monroe type, white bleached blonde hair, porcelain skin, clear blue eyes. We've worked in the same hair salon for over a year. "Once you divorce your husband and are on your own, you and Claudio can date like normal people. Get to know one another." She never mentions Claudio's fiancée. "He told me that you're his dream girl."

Helma is twenty-six, five years older than me; she has two small boys. She used to love her husband, she says, but he can't cope with the smells and noises of married life and only sex keeps them together but even there he doesn't satisfy her. "Doesn't do what I want, what every woman wants, *you know.*" Her piercing blue eyes rummage my face, searching for I know not what. I'm not sure what it is that every woman wants. There was nothing I ever wanted Eduardo to do to me.

Back in the car, I tell him that Helma is coming to get me. He turns on the radio and hums along with Elvis, the Platters, Brenda Lee, commercials: "*Brylcreem, a little dab will do you . . .*"

The bright sign announcing Falls Hideaway Motel, Coloured TV, shuts off. A burly man in a fur-trimmed parka stands by the lit entrance to the office. He stares our way. Ours is the only car in the parking lot; there's a pickup truck next to the office. Then all the motel lights turn off. My eyes follow the man's lit cigarette to the truck. He drives away.

I quiver in the dark void engulfing me—the desolation and strangeness of the emptiness seeping through my veins. All is black except for the odd car speeding by.

What have I done?

Eduardo continues humming along with the radio and asks no questions.

I recall Claudio's hungry love-making in the salon's stockroom in the basement after everyone went home, the splendour of his velvet touch, his quick spasm—uhhhh—forever etched in my soul. Unreal now, a script from some sappy TV series. What if Helma is wrong? What if Claudio loves his fiancée, a pretty tall blonde with big breasts, a tiny waist, and adoration in her eyes whenever she visits the salon. Last week, back from vacationing in Cape Cod, they walked out holding hands, laughing, her long bronzed legs glowing below a white miniskirt.

I glance up at the bluish moon, distant, sliced, unfriendly, pale rays failing to warm the cold February sky, frigid stars begging for warmth. This must be what is meant by the dead of winter, this lack of warmth, of hope.

Eduardo restarts the engine; he'd turned it off to save on gas.

"You can tell my mother I won't be coming home again."

He turns to face me. Turns the radio down. Then moans like an injured animal, *ahum, ahum, ahum.* "What about me? Where am I going to get sex?" He begins to cry.

I hadn't counted on this. Hadn't counted on his need of me. Wasn't my mother's companionship, her fussing, her admiration of all he did and said, enough for him? They animated each other's worlds, filling it with amusement, sufficiency, ever since he'd appeared in our life—her life—he merely sixteen then.

I stare at the swallowing darkness around us, trying to make sense of things I can't fully grasp. I'm sure Eduardo will likely throw me out of the car and drive back home, leaving me alone in this forsaken place.

He doesn't.

Janet Leigh in *Psycho* comes to mind. She'd stolen money, so we're less sympathetic to her brutal end.

What have I taken? What will be my end?

Today I'd arrived home determined, my mind made up. Today was the day. I was ready for the bruising of my mother's anger, whatever form it would take. One year of knowing Claudio, that blue-eyed love running through me like a flooded river of dreams and ecstasy, propelled me forward toward this waiting precipice. I knew Eduardo, my parents, and Manuelito, would be shocked by my leaving. We'd all just moved into the new home six months ago, this immigrant dream still smelling of fresh mortar, fresh-cut wood, and pink towels matching pink bathtubs.

What did I think buying a new house would do?

My father lent me fifteen hundred dollars toward the down payment. Did I fear disappointing him? Was that the reason I kept staying? Or did I in some hidden corner of my soul not trust Claudio? What if... Yes, yes, what if all I meant to him was a quick spasm in the back of his green Dodge?

I walked up the short set of still unscratched golden stairs to my bedroom, as soon as our dinner of beans and rice with chorizo that my mother cooked was finished. My mother always did the cooking; I washed the dishes afterwards. She and Eduardo had remained sitting at the kitchen table, he telling her the same old stories from Marland Inc, where he continued to pack glass doors and windows. As usual, he talked and my mother listened. As I walked up the stairs, their laughter pummelled me like a despised curse. My father and Manuelito had already escaped to the family room to watch westerns on the new coloured TV. My mother had long ago stopped listening to anything he had to say; he'd long ago stopped talking. They were like two enemy soldiers at a no-man's-land in a protracted war—they had learned to tolerate each other's presence. He brought home a weekly paycheque; she kept house. She never forgave him for the robbing of her virginity at sixteen. He'd gulped his food and soon departed to his lair. A normal evening.

I called out, "Eduardo! Eduardo!"

"I'm leaving," I said, as soon as he appeared at the bedroom door. I talked fast—it seemed easier that way. I couldn't hear my own voice. "I'm in love with someone."

"Someone, who?"

"Someone."

"I need to know who. I'm your husband. I have a right to know."

"Claudio from work."

"How long has this been going on?"

"A while. I love him."

Eduardo turned away from me, stepped out onto the landing, and called out, "Mommy!"

He'd started calling my mother "Mommy" after she once spooned ice cream into his mouth like a baby. It became their private joke.

My mother's heavy footsteps echoed on the stairs. She'd gotten heavier and was panting by the time she appeared at the bedroom door.

I sat on the bed and started to cry.

"Milita has another man." Eduardo faced her, chin to chin, placing both hands on her shoulders, as if they were about to start dancing.

My mother briskly pushed him aside, then leaped toward me, her agility making me wince.

"You've done what?"

"I love Claudio, I do, I do, I . . . I love him . . . " My sobs grew louder, more frantic.

Love, surely . . . Surely, surely, love would pardon my transgressions in everyone's eyes, even my mother's. Surely it would. I saw love as a white dove carrying God's blessings and lifting me toward heavenly forgiveness.

I was wrong.

Before I uttered another word, my mother pushed me down flat onto the bed, leaning over me, face just above mine, breath smelling of the chorizo eaten and the red wine drunk at dinner. Her hands clasped my neck. I tried loosening her grip, tried yanking her hands away but her hold only grew tighter. Gasping for air, I sank my nails into her face but she wouldn't let go. She began hyperventilating, like a wild animal in a chase. There was something feral in her gaze and loud exhale.

By the time Eduardo and my father yanked her off me, I'd lost all my bearings.

"Come," Eduardo whispered, while my father still held on to my mother who fought him like some wild cat.

"Get your boots and coat."

I whisked away my purse too. We hurried down the stairs, Eduardo's arm wrapped around my waist, guiding me forward, away from the house and, unknowingly, from his life.

My mother, freed from my father's hold by then, wailed behind me, "The *puta* is in love, ha, ha."

I glanced back, as I walked out the front door. My mother stood still at the top of the stairs, fluffy pink slippers overhanging the landing, making her appear as though she was about to fly. "In love, ha, ha, ha," she kept yelling. "What do you know about love, you whore?"

Car beams light up the unlit parking lot.

"That's Helma," I say, picking up my purse from the car floor.

"You can have the new furniture but I'm keeping the Ford," Eduardo blurts out.

"Okay." He'd never asked for anything in the five years we were married.

I bang the car door shut behind me without looking back or saying goodbye.

In Helma's car, I turn sideways, as the car beams briefly light up the yellow Ford. Eduardo is staring straight ahead at the darkness, car lights turned off. His dark silhouette fades into the surrounding blackness, as Helma and I join the other late-night travellers on the QEW.

II: *Arrival*

The bright morning light shines through the window, waking me. There are no curtains. I touch the unfamiliar nightgown, the thin sheets and blue blanket, then breathe a sigh of relief. The reality of the night before comforts me like the first warm rays of the spring sun. From now on, what I do, who I befriend, how I live, will no longer be beaten down by my mother. Claudio will be with me, openly, anytime, anywhere.

Two small white faces stare at me through the semi-opened door. Helma's boys, two and four.

"Hi," I say. They run away. I've usurped their bed. They slept on the living room couch. I hear Helma telling them to pick up their knapsacks, then she appears at the bedroom door.

"Before I leave for work, you need to know a few things."

She's wearing her brown winter coat with a fur collar that's been shedding and has her old black purse in hand.

"I'll tell them at work that you're not feeling well. I think you should take the week off. We don't want your mother bursting into the salon and making a scene in front of the clients."

Her tone is authoritative, peppered with German efficiency. Last night's sweetness seems to have departed on the icy wings of the night.

She explains that I should only answer the telephone after it rings once, hangs up, then rings again. "It means that it's either me or Claudio. Don't open the door to anyone—it could be your mother."

The apartment door bangs shut.

The bedroom is small. There's a bed and an unpainted dresser, bare floor, and walls. Everywhere there are signs of tightly watched budgets.

I can't seem to get out of bed. I look up at the ceiling and try to make sense of the swirly shapes in the plaster. A large bird with an open beak, two beady eyes, floppy wings, and the hoofed feet of a pig stares down at me . . . It appears to be laughing. I close my eyes.

There's no pathway down the high, craggy mountain. I find myself wondering how I got here. The fog is thickening in the descending twilight. I can't see two feet ahead of me. But I know I have to get down, must get down, have to find a way to get down this mountain. The long cry of a bird startles me. Then another, and another. I wake and hurry to the telephone in the kitchen.

"Hello."

"Metro Police here. Officer Mackenzie speaking."

The officer is friendly, officious, suspicious. He sounds young. He asks if I'm okay.

"Yes, yes. I'm fine."

"Though you are twenty-one and of legal age, your family needs to know you are safe."

"Does my mother know where I am?"

"Your family has a right to know where you are and that you are safe."

He says goodbye and hangs up. I hurry to the front door, making sure it's locked, chain up. Then I sit by the telephone and wait for Claudio's call.

The telephone never rings again.

Helma comes in around six in the evening and immediately begins to cook dinner. The boys are rambunctious, hovering around her for attention, pulling at her skirt, *Mutter, Mutter*. I, too, hover around her, waiting for a word from Claudio, desperate to know why he hasn't called, my life seemingly dependent on the words I pray she will utter. She talks to the boys in German. I go into the living room and flip through an Eaton's catalogue on a side table.

Half an hour later, Helma hands me a plate with a small boiled potato, a small veal schnitzel, and a slice of buttered white bread.

I eat sitting on the couch, plate on the coffee table. The potato and schnitzel are delicious. Except for two Oreo cookies I had in my purse, I hadn't eaten all day, fearing taking the bit of food left in a nearly empty refrigerator. I take the plate back to the kitchen and wash it in the sink. Helma is busy feeding the boys. It's noisy. I remove myself to the bedroom.

The February dark comes early. I lay on the bed and don't bother to turn on the lights. Helma's husband, Ernie, comes in at seven pm. They talk in German. There's tension in their voices.

I feel like an impostor in this alien world of children, private rituals, quarrels, unfulfilled expectations. I wait for Ernie to leave on his nightly outings to the pool hall that she so often speaks of, never sure if she feels free by his absence or is upset by it.

I fall asleep before he returns.

The boys again wake me with their giggling at the bedroom door the next morning.

Helma takes them away without saying goodbye this time.

A mouldy greyness funnels through the dusty window, turning everything the colour of dirt. I wait for Claudio's call.

I sleep until noon. Take a hot bath, stay in until the water turns cold. I put on the damp underwear I'd washed the night before and the same black pants and sweater I'd run away in.

A piece of mouldy cheese in the refrigerator satisfies my hunger pains.

Everywhere on the TV is the same talk of the FLQ, Pierre Trudeau and the War Measures Act, Quebec's independence from Canada, the minister's dead body in the trunk of a car. I settle for *The Road Runner*. The three books on top of the TV are in German. I regret not throwing the half-read *Bodily Harm* into my purse before leaving. The afternoon crawls.

In the evening, after Helma prepares supper and feeds the boys, I manage to ask her about Claudio.

"We had no time to talk; you know how chaotic Fridays are."

"Does he know?"

"He knows."

He knows and hasn't called.

Lying on the bed that night, arms and legs listlessly open, I try hard not to think bad of Helma. Her change of mood confuses me, but then I think of her driving to Niagara Falls at that late hour on icy roads and forgive her mood.

I tell myself I ought to feel free, balloon-light with a plump future waiting for me to carve at my own discretion. Yet a blue dampness seems to invade the room. I pull the thin blanket over my head. I want to run out, leave this apartment behind, wipe away all thoughts of Eduardo, my mother, Claudio's rejection. But here I lie, moribund, as though pounded onto the mattress by the fists of a heavyweight, staring at the bird with hoofed feet. I feel wilted, aimless, lost, like a waylaid pilgrim who's been given the wrong map.

Claudio calls Sunday morning, "I'll come by this evening." That was all.

Helma and Ernie took the boys to visit his mother right after lunch. The day is long.

Six pm and Claudio is standing at the apartment door, arms dangling by his sides.

I'd imagined this moment over and over and over, planned every word I'd say, made notes, wrote and rewrote them. But a glimpse of his blue eyes and tousled black hair and my resolve dissipates like an ice sculpture under a hot sun.

We drive for a while, neither of us speaking, afraid of looking at one another.

"We'll go to Harvey's for a hamburger," he finally says. "The one on Keele."

"Okay."

We chew the hamburgers in tingling silence.

Hamburgers eaten, we both stare out through the windshield and watch the cars driving in and out, couples, families.

Then Claudio says, "I came over . . . " He stops. "Look, I came over tonight because I have to tell you something."

I wait, feeling naked by his threatening words, the icy language of the February moon.

"We need to stop seeing each other. For a while."

He keeps staring straight ahead. "My parents fear your husband might come after me and harm me in some way."

"But I—I just walked out on Eduardo," I mumble, trying to hold back the tears. "Walked out on my whole family. Gave them all up for you."

Then he faces me, eyes intense, liquid, resplendent in the filtering light from a light pole a few feet away from the car. He pulls me tight against him, his tongue seeking mine.

We drive back to the apartment in silence. In the darkness of the visitor's parking lot, we become gnarled in the back seat, he tumescent with desire.

Early Sunday afternoon, I'm sitting at Helma's dining room table, jotting down my thoughts in a notebook. It helps. It's nearly two pm and neither Helma nor Ernie have come out of their bedroom. The April sun is busy melting the icicles on the eavestroughs of the six-floor, redbrick building, hitting our fifth-floor verandah's glass sliding doors with a loud thump. I jump each time. It's as though nature is protesting against I know not what.

Helma's bedroom is directly across from mine—earlier I heard her crying but soon there was only the muffled sound of rustling sheets. The boys were boisterous this morning, like two unleashed puppies—I heard them from my bedroom but didn't feel it was right to intervene. Not my place. When I finally did come out, around eleven, cornflakes soaked in milk decorated the couch, the coffee table, and the floor. There's no carpet. I helped them clean up the mess before Helma got up.

She finally appears; Ernie remains in the bedroom, door shut. She'd never stayed in her room this late on a Sunday morning in the two months I've been here.

"Help yourself to whatever is in the fridge," she says, before even saying good morning. Her white bleached hair stands out from her head, face pink and swollen, reminding me of the dried apple dolls becoming popular lately. "I don't feel like cooking today. Ernie is taking the boys again to visit his mother. You and I have the afternoon to ourselves. We'll order pizza."

I hoped we'd go to the Coffee Mill on Yorkville for Viennese coffee and dessert, as we did one Sunday about a month ago. It was fun, both of us dressed in our new black leather miniskirts and shiny white boots. But it wasn't to be. Instead, we dusted and mopped—the apartment had not been properly cleaned since I'd moved in.

The icicles keep falling; I keep jumping each time.

She hardly speaks. It's as if the wiping and the dusting is consuming all her energy, her attention. I, too, say nothing. The air fills thorny. My mother comes to mind.

Once the apartment is cleaned, Helma dips into her jeans pocket and shows me a business card. "Ms Wolfe," she says. "You know her? My client? Did you know she's a lawyer?"

She talks fast. Though she's standing close to me she doesn't look at my face but keeps looking out through the large window. "She can help you get a divorce, you know, get all your *shtuff* back and advise you on the sale of the house and all. Don't you want your things back and get you life in order? Wouldn't that be good?"

I remain silent, still holding onto the dustcloth. I, too, can't look at Helma and stare at the dustcloth instead. Another icicle falls; we both jump.

"It's time, don't you think? Don't you think it's time for you to do what's best for you?"

She comes closer and hands me the card. This time she faces me, blue eyes eager, questioning. "If you sell the house, you and I can open our own beauty salon. Work for ourselves, you know. Don't you want that, ha? Be your own boss? I'll pay you back as soon as I have the money, of course. Of course I will. I'll pay back every penny. Every penny."

"How long have you been planning this?" I manage to say.

"Oh, a bit," her expression changes. She becomes pensive, eyes fixated somewhere beyond me, beyond the apartment, perhaps back to a childhood of misery and hunger in Austria in the clutches of the aftermath of the Second World War of which she'd shared a few details late one night. "I've had it. Work, work, work, and nothing to show for it. Always the same shit. Ernie gambles, you know. I have to get out of this crappy apartment, crappy marriage, crappy life. It's all just shit. I need to make some real money and you and I get along so well." She smiles, an invitation to join her on this yellow-brick road of her own divination.

Was this why she came to get me in Niagara Falls?

I push the thought away, then think of the time she burst into my bedroom about three weeks ago, rollers in her hair, a lacy red nylon negligee. It was late. Ernie hadn't yet returned from the pool hall.

"I can't sleep," she said.

I was awake too, reading *Notes to Myself*—she likely saw the ribbon of light underneath the door.

She sat at the edge of the bed, close to me. I put the book face down on the thin blankets. One shoulder of the red lacy night gown exposed her shoulder and part of a small white breast.

"There's a friend at the pool hall Ernie always talks to on the phone, you know." She speaks low so as not to wake the boys. "They talk for long periods of time. Long periods. Sometimes Ernie whispers so I don't hear what he's saying. He doesn't want me to know."

"What do you mean, he doesn't want you to know? Know what?"

"I think there's something between them. Something more than friendship."

I say nothing.

"Something, I know there's something. He talks to him nearly every day for a long time."

I didn't know what the *something* could be. If it was what I thought it was, in my opinion it didn't make sense since Ernie had fathered two children.

Then she said, "There's nothing wrong with people having sex with their own kind, you know. They understand each other better."

I didn't answer and began trying to reread the cover of my book upside down.

She ran her fingers through my hair; her touch rippled down my spine.

"Look at me," she said.

I kept reading my book's cover upside down.

She held my chin in her hand and forced me to look at her. Whatever it was that she saw in my face—my eyes—prompted her to quickly get off the bed, one of the rollers thudding onto the floor as she hurried out of the room.

I picked up *Notes to Myself*, read and reread the same line, my mind leading me to tunnels I didn't want to enter. It was nearly morning before my eyes shut, and Ernie was still away.

Now I put Ms Wolfe's card inside the pocket of my jeans. By the time we put away the broom, the mop, the cleaning rags, and the lemon oil, dusk was descending. I told her I wasn't hungry and went to my room.

III: *Limbo*

At the end of October, there's a telephone call for me at work.

It's my father.

I'm speechless. I hadn't heard from him or my brother or anyone from my past in the eight months since I'd left home.

My hands begin to tremble; I can hardly hold on to the receiver.

My father makes it easy. "Milita, I come Sunday, okay? Come to your place." Simple, direct, uncompromising, no needless emotions or explanations or accusations or apologies. A lump forms in my throat with the thought that he might be missing me. I try hard to hold back the tears and give him my new address. He says he has it. I'd moved into my own apartment in June in the same complex as Helma's. The lawyers had made arrangements with the superintendent for Eduardo and Manuelito to deliver the furniture and my belongings. They made it clear they didn't want to see me. I watched them carry the furniture from the yellow Ryder truck to the lobby by hiding behind a thick maple across the apartment's entrance. A part of me wanted to go and hug Manuelito but another part knew that he no longer was part of my new existence. And I wasn't going back.

Helma changed jobs soon after I announced I was getting my own place a floor below her. We rarely run into each other. I haven't seen her in weeks. She never calls. Neither do I.

My father arrives early. I look behind him as I open the apartment door, making sure that he's alone. I'm almost disappointed not to see my mother. Every night before sleep, I still look under the bed, behind doors, inside closets, in fear of my mother lying there in wait.

I embrace him, his body recedes, tightens, as always, as if human contact repulses him. I show him around the apartment, the black vinyl couches the salesman promised looked like leather, the coffee tables, the walnut dining room set from the new back-split, all too big for the smaller space now. My father tells me that it was my mother's idea to return all the furnishings I'd paid for, even the red bull and red candles for the coffee table, completing the Spanish decor. I was sure my mother wanted to shed the house of any trace of me, I had no hope of any love she might have for me.

My father follows me around the apartment, sporting his usual enigmatic smile—aloof and friendly, critical and accepting—his masquerade and his signature. I've come to read his smile as fragments of a life not fully lived or even understood, my mother's unhappiness having long ago snuffed out the flame of his own being. My father's smile offers no alms.

I make tea and sit across from him on the couch; he sits on the matching side chair. The air is tense. I swirl my fingers around the rim of the cup to hide my shaking hands.

"I won't stay long," he says five minutes after we'd sat down.

"Okay."

This man sitting across from me, this man who gave me life, has nothing to say to me or I to him. We smile. The wafers on the coffee table remain untouched and so does the tea.

"Your father is *seco* like his mother," my mother always said. "Dry, all the Faíscas are dry like sticks." She meant that they lack emotions, feelings, connectedness. I never understood her but now I find myself wondering if, perhaps, she was right.

I find myself wondering, too, why he came to see me. He asks no questions about my new life. I'd settle for some tawdry confession, like I've missed you, but it doesn't come.

The tea has turned cold, when he says: "I came to ask you for the fifteen hundred dollars I lent you. Remember?"

"Did you think I'd forget?" My new assertiveness surprises me. My body grows tense; I'm leaning forward, chin out. "It's not even a year since I left."

I pull myself back and try to relax my shoulders.

"I always meant to pay you back."

I recall the dishevelled woman in the subway last week. She looked to be in her thirties, long messy black hair, white gaunt face, dead grey eyes looking out but appearing not to see anyone. She walked the length of the subway car, head erect, staring straight ahead above our heads. "Don't trust anyone," she yelled. "They'll all let you down. All of them."

"Is that why you came to see me?" I say, my voice softer, not wanting to offend him.

He shrugs, smiles some more. A gift, like doling out candy to a child.

"We're thinking of buying a small bungalow with Eduardo. That's why we need the fifteen hundred dollars. Without you, we can't make the payments on the big house."

It saddens me that they can't afford to keep the house, everyone was so proud of its newness, its spaciousness, the weed-free lawns. But my life is no longer tied to theirs. The gates of Portuguese custom and tradition, that filial guilt holding me back for so long, opened when I met Claudio. Yes, yes, a love I'm no longer sure of, Claudio away in Italy for three weeks now. He went to find himself, he said. Not a letter or phone call to this day.

I fear the unfamiliarity—the aloneness—of this new life. *What if Claudio never calls me again. What if he's still seeing his girlfriend?* But I've tasted this new freedom, its promise of grassy green pathways and I can't go back.

I accompany my father to the elevator. He stands erect, stiff, arms hanging by his side as I kiss him goodbye.

"Does Manuelito ever mention me?" I ask, as my father enters the elevator.

"No."

"My mo . . ."

The elevator door shuts.

And Still I Said Nothing

I ripped the letter in half, then fourths, eighths, until tiny pieces of paper covered the small kitchen table like so many chips of dried white paint. Who did Claudio think he was? A satiated lord discarding his concubine? He'd gorged at the full table and then grew sick of the food and drink he'd so coveted. He in Italy for one month and I waiting for a letter, a call, a postcard, and growing tired of the early morning checks of the *empty* mailbox and the silent telephone, the walls surrounding me, seeming to whisper, *You fool.*

The green fruit bowl has been empty since his goodbye, and I unable to bear the sight of grapes, Claudio's favourite. Dionysus fruit, I, a Maenad, swirling and gyrating around my intoxicated god, clusters of the glistening fruit in my hand like a thyrsus. A temptation. What if I'd held a cooking pot, a broom, a scouring pad, a soiled diaper, a sickly baby in my hands? Would Claudio still want to watch me dance? Or would he be sickened by the sight of his ravished bride?

Lately there had been signs I'd refused to see, but the rumblings in the air, like the sound of distant thunder, were real. Azure eyes restless, wavering, time spent together growing shorter, more hurried. Always a reason, a relative waiting, a friend in need, tiredness, an early client the next day. Even in that fervid night before departing for Italy, he said, "I promised my father I'd be home early tonight. I'm only twenty-two and my father hasn't been happy with me walking in at all hours. It's not the Italian way, you know, not to respect one's parents."

And still I said nothing. Though I'd known for three weeks.

Twice I'd brought up the idea of marriage, children, settling down, two people building a life together. The first time, Claudio just smiled. No words. The second was at Nancy's wedding, a hairdresser at my salon. The wedding had been a rushed affair, her bun-in-the-oven showing under the white satin dress. I was embarrassed for her, embarrassed for women who didn't do the right thing. Ha, I now thought, how easy it is to criticize others.

"Aren't we happy?" Claudio had replied, as though he'd prepared for this moment, lines rehearsed, defences ready. "Aren't we having fun? Every married guy I know wishes he was single. My two sisters are divorced, both have been abandoned by their husbands, and are struggling to raise children on their own. My father gets drunk every Saturday so he can cope with the rest of the week. I never heard a kind word spoken between he and my mother."

Claudio and I had been seeing each other openly for over one year now, since I'd left my husband and walked out on my whole family. We had all been living together in a new back-split in Mississauga. Only my father came to visit me once months after I left. I thought he'd missed me. Perhaps he did. But at the end of the visit he reminded me of the fifteen hundred dollars he'd lent me for the down payment of the new house. Manuelito never even bothered to pick up the telephone and dial my number. He must've had it since my father did and they were still sharing the same roof. Claudio was all I had now. He was my family, my friend, my new universe. But in the letter, Claudio didn't even write words of love or "I miss you," or even a hint of commitment. The two pages described the swarms of pigeons in Venice, the raging lambrettas on narrow cobblestoned streets, the delicious food and cheap wine, the vineyards shining in the golden sun of the Tuscan hills, and, "I'll call you when I get back."

How could this be?

"You're like no other," he'd mumbled between gasps and muted explosions on that last night, his spent body framing mine long afterwards, a velvet cover, my nail marks on his back. "I'm a thirsty castaway and I can't drink enough of you."

When I was growing up, a homeless woman roamed the streets of Amendoeiro. We called her *Vagabunda*. She'd walk by slowly, always humming some discordant tune, her hazed gaze somewhere in the distance, never on you, she never turning her head one way or the other, all her belongings in a dirty grey cloth sack hanging over her back. No one knew her name or where she came from or where she slept at night, a true vagabond, unusual for a woman in those days. Tramps traversing the country were mostly males. She never spoke to anyone. Bakeries in town gave her old bread, a cookie or two, grocers, rotting vegetables and fruit. Avó would give her a few figs, apples, pears, and Muscat grapes from her own garden at harvest time (my grandparents had a large garden). My mother would offer *Vagabunda* a bowl of cabbage soup, or a plate of beans and rice, or chickpeas with rice whenever she wandered onto our patio. *Vagabunda* would quickly devour the food standing up and then walk away without an *obrigado* or the uttering of another word. Knowing her age was difficult, her hair was long and matted, her face unwashed, clothes ragged and filthy, a smell of sewage wafting from her as she walked by. One day, she was pregnant. The culprit was never found, never owed up to what he'd done. A woman heard screams one evening as she passed by an abandoned shack on the outskirts of town just behind the tall canes by the creek. She found *Vagabunda* yanking the baby out of her body, dirty hands dripping with blood. Others came to help. "*O desgraçado* died after inhaling his first breath," the woman told everyone the next morning. "The disgraced one was born to die," my mother repeated to us after the news had flooded the town, people restless for gossip, for anything out of the ordinary. "Born to die," was what my father said when a sickly chick from a poorly hatched egg had to be killed. No one ever blamed the man who impregnated *Vagabunda*. Men are men, women said, even my mother and Avó. They can't help themselves. It's up to women to be smart, protect their chastity, make the right choices, be on guard.

Had I been on guard? I caved in to Claudio's kisses, lips full, warm, fingers soft as cumulus clouds under my dress, something in me unfurling with each touch, giving in, desire overflowing like an over-filled cup. Was love for Claudio just the grasping, the unfathomable hunger, the release? Sometimes, he whisked me to the bedroom or the couch, the rug on the living room floor even before three words were spoken or my period ended. "It's okay, I can't wait." I took him, always took him, happy to be wanted, the green fruit bowl brimming with Dionysus fruit waiting for him, filled before his every visit, I dancing, whirling, toward his every desire.

What was I thinking? Did I imagine grapes to be the bewitching potions women fed philandering husbands back in Amendoeiro? Evenings after some late visit to family or friends when my mother and I passed the brothel at the entrance to the old road behind our house, we'd see crowds of men waiting outside, whistling and scream-ing obscenities as we walked by. I'd wonder why the magic potions, the chants, and the prayers of their wives, had failed. "Married men grow tired of their wives; domesticity dulls them," my mother always said. Was that what Claudio feared? The dullness of everyday until death-do-us-part?

The clock on the kitchen table showed 4:30, the white clock rising above the white mound of the torn letter like some monument to peace but no doves flew from it. The outdoor lights of the modest U-shaped, redbrick apartment complex on Lawrence and Keele flick-ered earlier than usual, lighting up the early darkness of the cold, rainy October afternoon. Fall had engulfed Toronto with a vengeance this year, as though pushed by a restless winter.

I switched on the lamp.

My reflection on the living room window didn't show any changes, no bun-in-the-oven yet protruding from under my mini brown woollen dress. Not yet, the doctor said, likely in four or five months. For now, only morning nausea and ghostly paleness.

Vagabunda's baby had been denied burial in the *Cimiterio de Misericordia* in Montijo by Father Batista, denied baptism too, the baby having no father, *Vagabunda* not married. Hierarchy in the kingdom of heaven. Selection in the empire of blessings. Did Jesus know? Where had the baby been buried? Who'd buried it? Had the stray dogs dug it up the way they'd dug up the chicken with fowl pox my father had once buried so as not to contaminate the rest of the flock?

Was that what Father Batista feared? The contamination of his blessed flock?

The stuffed grey raccoon Claudio gave me the night he left seemed to be smirking at me from the side table. No explanation, he'd just handed it to me, as he walked in. A sort of offering. A tiny black heart hung from the raccoon's mouth. I hadn't noticed the tiny black heart until now. Was it a coded message for broken-hearted lovers? A disguised Morse code for goodbye? I don't love you anymore; my heart has turned black. He'd won the raccoon at the Exhibition.

I placed the raccoon in a black shoebox, threw in bits of the letter, crumbled a few cookies and slices of bread on top, and added in a note, *Reflections on your life, October 15, 1976*. Then I sealed the box with tape and tears. He would return in a week; I'd mail it then.

His life? What about my life? I'd given up my family for Claudio the way penitent Catholics give up the thing they love most for Lent, a down payment for immortality. Sacrifice showered with salvation. I did it for love, the stuff of romances, poetry, movies, TV, songs, stories passed on from one generation to the next, all those who died for love or the absence of it. Oh, that elusive wanderer! Find love and your life will shine like a guiding star through the dark abyss of existence. Romeo and Juliet killed themselves for it. So did Emilia, that *triste* throwing herself into her father's well after her boyfriend found someone else. Amendoeiro talked of "sad" Emilia for years afterwards, a warning for young girls. "Be careful who you give your heart to." But how does one know? After the lips and tongues and spasms, how do we peek into the heart?

I turned on the TV, something to shut out the extreme quiet, to stifle the secret murmurs being whispered by the walls. A beautiful young woman appears, wet hair framing her angelic face—she has obviously just taken a bath or shower. She covers herself in Johnson & Johnson baby powder while crooning, *Baby Powder, Girly Power.*

Sex, babies . . . How would I manage? I knew a few women who'd had abortions. It was now legal in Canada. Helen, the receptionist at work had had three or four, one just this past winter. She was married, had three daughters, but she and her husband liked sex in the raw, as she explained. "No rubbers for him or pills for me."

"The abortion was *nothing*," she said. She came to work the next day. "Just a bit of discomfort like a bad menstrual pain."

One strike and Claudio's seed would stop growing, squashed like a cockroach under a shoe. Finished. Nothing. Or was it a cut that did it? A stabbing? A poking? A sucking? Was the fetus, or its mangled parts, buried or just thrown down the incinerator, flushed down the toilet?

Aunt Luisa nearly died back in Amendoeiro, blood gushing out of her like a geyser. The old woman, Avó's cousin, whom we called Crow because she always dressed in black, had done the clandestine deed. She'd run as fast as a mouse in the light when she heard the doctor was being summoned, her knitting needles and scissors still dripping with blood as she dashed by me toward the door.

"Oh, the days of knitting needles are long past," Helen said after I told her the story. "Different times now, your doctor does it for you. It's all very safe. A woman should be in control of her own body, don't you think? It should be her choice."

Her body, her choice. I wasn't so sure, the picture wasn't so clear for me. *Something* inside me was seeking to become, to exist. What was *its* choice?

Choice, choice, I was sick of the word.

Claudio had been back for two weeks and still hadn't called. Maybe he was still *finding himself, his* words when first announcing his trip to Italy. "I need to make up my mind about a few things, need to think." I knew that the *two things* were his ex-girlfriend—someone he was seeing before we became involved—and me. Or maybe he still continued to see her.

Then on the third Saturday, one week after I sent him the shoebox with the raccoon, there was a knock at the door. A stranger filled the door frame. No hugs or kisses or gifts—I didn't expect any. Claudio was holding the black shoebox in both hands. I blushed at its sight.

Tall, eyes bluer than I remembered, black hair messily falling over his chiselled tanned face, an air of travelled worldliness, of things experienced, drunk and tasted, his presence naming everything in the apartment, lighting up the starless November sky menacing the large window. He stood before me, a river of awkwardness and hurt separating and silencing us, fixing us in place on either side of its banks.

Claudio at my door!

Ah! This time I wasn't allowing my resolve to fold upon itself, as it had done before. Who did he think he was? Did he imagine he'd just show up and the hurt, the humiliation, the longing would wash away like winter ice in spring thaw? He'd stand at my door and I'd begin my usual dervish swirl and place a crown of grapes on his head? No. This time I knew what to say, knew what to do.

"Claudio," I would stare him in the eyes, unflinching, "You don't love me enough. I don't want to see you anymore."

I imagined him walking away, blue eyes yellow with sorrow and I'd be free from his nail-studded love. Yes, yes, a love that had only brought me sorrow and his seed growing in me.

Instead I said, "I'll make tea."

I turned toward the kitchen and Claudio walked across the living room, sitting on the Scandinavian red chair he always sat on. Hands shaking, heart beating, I managed to fill the kettle with water, my eyes two paint brushes colouring the tea kettle, the cup, the kitchen, my mind, in a grey shade of expectation and confusion.

Should I tell him tonight? What if he walks out and I never see him again?

Calm down, down, down, you're not putty to be molded as he sees fit, a door rug to be trampled on.

I'd manage. Surely I would. When I could no longer work and pay the rent I'd move into that home for single mothers on Euclid Avenue run by nuns. I'd seen young women come and go for years on my way to the bus stop. Maybe I'd give the baby up for adoption.

What? Push that thought away. Who'd raise it, love it, coddle it, nurse it, name it? My baby in the care of strangers? Never—I'd find a way.

The boiling kettle fogged up the small kitchen. I heard Claudio's footsteps by the stereo and the sound of a 45 dropping. Percy Sledge began shouting, *When a man loves a woman*. Claudio had given me the record for my twenty-first birthday.

I placed the two peppermint-tea-filled mugs on the coffee table next to the shoebox with the raccoon. Claudio had put it there, like a silent punishment, a reminder of my cruelty.

He turned to face me: our eyes locked. There was desire, pain, fear in his. Did I see repentance, too?

His embrace nearly knocked me backwards, his lips nearly swallowing mine, tongue seeking, the anger between us fading away as fast as fog in sunshine.

"Claudio, I have to tell you something."

"Can it wait?" He kissed me again, pulling me tight against his swelling sex.

When I caught my breath, I said, "I've known since before you left for Italy. It's over two months now. I didn't want to spoil your holiday."

He held me gently by the shoulders, puzzled eyes staring at my face. "What? You're not on the pill?"

I shook my head.

"Let us drink the tea."

He took off his coat and sat down. Placed another 45 on the record player.

Vagabunda stopped humming after the birth. She'd be seen meandering through the Pinhal, the pine and eucalyptus woods near Amendoeiro, any time of day or night, or walking along the muddy river, or sunning herself in wheat fields, arms out-stretched, face up to the sky, always alone. A living scarecrow. One day she was gone. No one knew where she went or what happened to her, soon she became an old story. Forgotten. But that September when Avó harvested her figs, apples, pears, and grapes, I couldn't eat any of it.

The Disappeared

The apartment is small, crowded, dusty, not matching the shiny silver Alfa Romeo they picked me up in. I need to open a window, let in some air, the Parisian morning unusually hot, but I remain seated. After all, I am the visitor.

"The flowers are lovely." I point to the large crystal vase on the coffee table overflowing with pink zinnias, blue asters, and baby's breath. I need to say something.

"I buy a bouquet every week," Ana says, "fresh flowers remind me of your Avó's beautiful garden. Don't you miss it? Amendoeiro was paradise."

"Paradise?" I say, but Ana is already on her way to the kitchen saying something about making café au lait and how Marcel, her husband, has stepped out to get fresh croissants.

I look around, take a deep breath. The turbulent flight and the smell of diesel fuel—bothering me ever since I can remember—made me queasy, the ground under my feet still feeling unsure.

The small living room is crowded. Overfilled. Too many paintings, doilies, photographs, figurines, knickknacks of every sort, dusty souvenirs, faded postcards stuck to the walls. It feels as though the air has been snuffed out. I'm finding it hard to breathe.

Once Ana wrote, "You Americans don't know how to live. You buy things instead of enjoying life. Stuff, stuff, and more stuff."

I didn't bother to explain that Canadians aren't Americans.

Ana's criticism of American materialism now begins to bother me. What does she call this dusty clutter?

She reappears holding a tray with three steaming mugs.

Marcel follows, carrying a paper bag with croissants. He hasn't stopped smiling since the airport. Tall, perfect white teeth, chiseled jaw, thick blond curls. Ana is much shorter, chubbier. She also keeps smiling but without the perfect teeth.

She was my favourite cousin growing up. Ana, always ahead of me, was the adventurer who discovered Elvis Presley and Rock 'n' Roll and drew grotesque pictures on my small blackboard when I was six to show me why my mother's belly kept growing, my father's penis engorged, my mother's legs spread apart. I erased the white chalk pictures the moment she left.

Now we each pick up a mug, pasted smiles on our faces, like first-time guests on the *Tonight Show*. She hands me a croissant on a paper napkin. Mine has a delicious almond filling and roasted almond slivers on top.

Marcel stands up, says something in French, smiles again, walks out. Ana says, "Now we can talk." She sits on a footstool facing me. "Oh yes, flowers and your Avó's garden. She loved flowers, didn't she? We had the best childhood. *Uma enfância encantada*."

"An enchanted childhood? In some ways, I guess."

"You guess?"

She brings the foot stool closer, shakes a finger at my face.

"Where do people care for one another today the way we did then? Umh? Amendoeiro was an extended family."

An extended family?

Has Ana forgotten the poverty, the gossip, the derision? The empty dull eyes, faded faces, and toothless mouths of the turned-up palms at the door begging for a piece of stale bread? The silent women beaten by husbands, swollen black eyes in the market-place telling all, Amendoeiro a town of secrets as open as the sky, and gossip, the fuel lighting up the mundane lives of a small town. Children abused in unspoken ways: my mother's beatings, my face often swollen with blotches of purple-blue for days, just to keep me obedient; men protected by laws that turned wives and children into chattels, like furniture.

I should thank Ana for the scrumptious croissants and café au lait but I say nothing; my hands are tightly wrapped around the empty mug.

This wasn't how I'd imagined our first moments together. Weren't we supposed to be laughing?

I must ask her about her son and daughter away at camp. Instead, I say, "What about Salazar?"

"Oh, the government?" Ana's head jerks back a little, a sneer rises across her lips.

I lean back. Try to relax my shoulders.

"*Oui*," Ana continues, her smile fading. "*Oui, oui*, the government was bad. But what did the government have to do with the people? With us? Uh? We had good times. Don't forget that."

She stands up, picks up the soiled paper napkins and empty mugs and wipes the crumbs off the coffee table in one easy sweep. "I better make lunch. We have to show you Paris. Too bad you're only staying one night."

I ought to help her, I tell myself, as she walks away. Yet I remain seated, something inside me refusing to obey what I know I should be doing. Then I stand up, but find myself involuntarily rearing, like the black horse I once saw by the whorehouse being beaten and forced to enter that dark, narrow space it feared to enter.

What is it I fear?

In the fifteen years since we've been apart, Ana has never once mentioned the PIDE, whose blood-curdling atrocities were spoken only in muffled tones behind shut doors. Everyone was terrified they'd be the next to be whisked away in the night. Bones broken, toenails yanked, electric shocks to the most vulnerable parts of the body, dogs unleashed on the unexpected and the terrified, few making it out alive. The few who did, reminders of what could happen to us all, struggled with mangled bodies and thrashing memories, whispering tales of horror until they, too, soon died.

In the day, everyone busied themselves with daily chores, pretending everything was normal, routine. Who could be trusted? Sometimes it was a neighbour who snitched, a best friend, a brother, even your own child—fear and mistrust entered every home. The reward was good. Soon those on PIDE's payroll stood out with their well-fed bodies, new clothes, shiny Vespas, suspected friendliness.

Os desaparecidos, we called those who went missing. The disappeared were never mentioned aloud again, not even by their families, no one was sure who could be listening. All that remained was some faded photograph of a father, a husband or son half-hidden in some dusty corner and the women and their children needing to be fed. The lucky ones, those with families who helped them, like Esmeralda, the Bar Central's wife whose parents helped her keep the bar operating, carried on with their lives. The less fortunate worked for little pay in the cork factories or cleaned houses for the rich in Montijo, or begged door to door for a piece of bread, a bowl of soup, or a promise of tomorrow, maybe tomorrow. If still young, women stood on street corners once the sun set, or joined Casa Rosa.

Has Ana forgotten? *How do you do it, Ana? How is it possible?*

The clatter of pots, plates, and cutlery echoes through the house, a reminder of sorts. I tell myself that I must help Ana.

Instead I walk to the window.

What is it I expect from her? Mea Culpa?

Is that it? Fifteen years apart, twenty-five years or so since that smouldering August afternoon in the white truck, and I, like a beggar at her door, wait with turned-up palms.

For what? An admission of guilt? A few crumbs of sympathy. That's it.

I push back the curtains. A veil of yellow dust sprinkles my hair.

The tiny garden, encircled by a low brick wall, is messy, grass and weeds taller than the struggling pink geraniums. I couldn't wait to see her again. Why this confusion?

I wonder if I am the only one carrying the fetters of memory from that afternoon.

But why do I *need* Ana to remember it too? Need her to admit. Admit . . . Admit . . . Admit that she was the one who took me there. How was she to know the game we'd been invited to play wasn't a game we recognized?

Stop it. Stop it now . . .

It was red, I'm sure the wine Adelia's brother had in the white truck that day was red.

Was the truck white? It had to have been, white is the colour I've remembered the most.

Stop it!

Ana calls me to lunch.

The roast lamb and potatoes finished, the Bordeaux drunk, Marcel telling stories of wine-making in French, Ana translating them into Portuguese. He drives us to Montmartre.

The square is crowded, cafes brimming with people, music, chatter, artists painting, sketching, someone playing a guitar, a girl singing Edith Piaf songs (a good imitation), the late-afternoon sun enveloping everything in a golden glow. I'm glad we've come.

We enter Sacré-Cœur. Marcel hurries to place a coin in the basilica's audio, selecting English, so I can learn its history, smiling, as he hands me the ear phones.

"This is a favourite church for weddings," Ana says. "Do you remember picking daisies for that bride's bouquet? The daughter of the man on the wheelchair. I forget her name."

"Lucinda."

"*Oui*, poor Lucinda, she was born unlucky, wasn't she? Having to marry that old bald man with a limp. Not many choices for women who'd lost their virginity in those days. But you wouldn't recognize Portugal today. Everything is so changed since they joined the EU. No one talks of what used to be. No one wants to revisit that dark time."

She gently grabs my shoulders, holds my eyes, "You too, Milita, let the past be the past. What good do bad memories do to anybody?"

We linger in the square. Ana and Marcel stop for another café au lait at a stand-up bar. I don't want anything.

The air grows cooler, the late-afternoon sun quickly begins its journey west, creating massive shadows over the cobblestone square. Artists are packing up; tourists departing.

As we walk toward the parked Alfa on a side street, a dark blue pickup truck idles at the corner, exhaust from the diesel fuel stacking the air.

"The old smell," I say. "European diesel is different from North America's." Ana shrugs and doesn't say anything.

How would she know? She's never been to North America.

I think of her words, let the past be the past. But the smell of diesel is a broken flood gate, unlocking a torrent of faces, feelings, smells, Ana's assurance that the game would be fun.

I must've been six and Ana eight, she was starting grade two (or was it three?) later that October.

"Hurry up," she'd said, holding my hand. "Adelia promised we'll have fun."

Adelia, serious, scholarly, wearing glasses, hair in a neat pony-tail, the only girl in Amendoeiro already in a private college across the river in Lisbon, now home for the summer. Everyone respected her because of her intelligence, respected the family for their money and goodwill, Adelia's mother was the town's midwife, never charging anyone for her services. Adelia's parents owned the Esso gas station at the entrance to Amendoeiro, where the white truck was parked. Adelia stood by the truck's door, waving Ana and me in with her thin arms.

We climbed the rickety small stepladder. It was dark inside. The smell of cow dung, piss, dust, and diesel fuel made me feel nauseated. It took a while before my eyes adjusted to the darkness. Then I saw the others, six or seven of them, sitting in a circle on the truck's floor, as if about to hear a story being read at a school outing. I recognized two girls, Ana's friends, and another girl, a neighbour who was younger than I, maybe four.

Adelia pointed to a spot where Ana and I ought to sit.

Someone pulled down the truck's door, leaving only a slit of light at the bottom.

"So many girls!" a man said. Slowly I made out a soldier standing in a dark corner. He held a bottle of wine in his hand and raised it to take a swallow.

"That's Adelia's brother," Ana said. "He has just returned from fighting in Angola."

I didn't remember him.

"Angola? Did someone say Angola? There's no more Angola. *Psst*, wiped off the map."

Ana stopped talking.

He took another swig. "*Olá!* captives, we're in for an afternoon of fun."

The soldier placed the bottle on the floor and unbuckled his belt. His trousers dropped to his feet. He had no underpants.

I lowered my eyes.

"Everyone take off their panties," he ordered, his voice less friendly.

"You liar," Adelia screamed. "That's not what you said the game was going to be."

She stood up and faced her brother. He slapped her; she started to cry.

"You'll all get the same treatment if you don't do as I say. I'm the *comandante-geral* now." Then something gleamed like a star in the night sky. "See this?" He circled the knife in front of each of our faces. "I'll kill you all if you don't do as I say."

A younger girl started crying and calling out for her mother.

Adelia tried opening the truck's door but the soldier pushed her; she fell face down onto the floor. "I can't see, I can't see. My glasses are broken."

Something warm ran down my legs. I too started to cry. Ana held my hand. "Don't worry, all will be fine—I'm praying to *Nossa Senhora D'Atalaia*. She's the protector of children."

All the girls were crying now and screaming for their mothers, except Ana. She was saying the Our Father and Ave Maria out-loud, the pitch in her voice rising above the cries.

"Shut up, just shut up," the soldier yelled. "Who the fuck is going to listen to your prayers? Who the fuck do you think is up there listening? Nothing. There's fucking nothing . . . "

Someone knocked on the truck's door.

"Who's there? What's going on? Open up, open up," a man said.

A girl yelled, "Help! Help! Save us, please, please save us."

The soldier bent down, placing his left hand over the girls' mouth while pointing the knife at his sister's neck, who'd remained crumpled on the floor like a rolled-up sowbug.

A woman's voice urged, "Get the truck open, c'mon, c'mon, get it open."

The truck's door began slowly to roll up, the sunlight making me squint.

Adelia's father and mother helped us down the rickety small ladder, including Adelia, who couldn't stop crying. The soldier quickly disappeared from view.

Once we were all out, Adelia's mother gave each of us ten *centavos* for an ice cream cone from Café Central next door. I wanted to go home and change my wet panties and soiled dress but was too ashamed to tell Ana what I'd done.

Adelia's brother left for Evora a week later. He and his parents passed by our house on the way to the train station—they'd used the less busy old dirt road behind my house, instead of the new highway. He carried a black suitcase. He was placed in a military hospital. Adelia left for college in October. I never saw her again. Ana moved to Paris eight years later and I, two years after, went to Toronto. The events of that afternoon, or Adelia, or her brother, were never discussed by Ana or me, or anyone else that I knew of. The story was never told.

"Please tell Marcel to stop the car," I cry out to Ana. We'd been driving around Paris for two hours after a dinner of couscous in a crowded Moroccan restaurant—the Bastille, Arc de Triumph, Eiffel Tower, Champs Élysées, the blinding cluster of lights, the heavy traffic, the smell of diesel, spins around and around piazzas, my stomach getting queasier with each turn. "Isn't Paris beautiful by night?" Ana kept asking; Marcel kept driving; I kept worrying about messing up the white leather seats of the new silver Alfa Romeo.

The car stops on a dark street. Everything I'd eaten all day flushes out.

Back in the car. Ana continues lamenting the ridiculous shortness of my stay. "Even one more day. There's so much to see, so much to talk about!"

"Tomorrow I'll meet my husband in Venice—it's his turn to visit his family."

And I've seen enough of Paris and talked enough, all my questions coming to a soundless close, like the quiet of a closed wicket at a theatre after the performance has started.

Of course, I don't say any of this to Ana.

Soon after Adelia's brother was institutionalized in Evora, stories of the atrocities he'd endured in Angola began circulating. He'd been taken prisoner by one rebel group and kept for months in a hole in the ground covered with a sheet of iron, a tiny aperture for air. Later he was captured by a competing rebel group of boy soldiers, tortured and nearly starved to death, he was only nineteen or twenty at the time. Before his ordeals, he'd been part of a raid on a compound where everyone was shot, cats, dogs, and two babies. The babies had cried.

A Black Kitten

My father calls me this morning—the second Monday in September. "Everything ready," he says. By "everything ready" he means that the two dozen eggs and potatoes, tomatoes, Romano beans, and corn have been harvested and placed in old cardboard boxes and reused plastic bags, ready for me to pick up. My yearly gift. No bow or Hallmark card or words of affection. Such frills are not his style. I didn't grow up in a household where such niceties were ever seen or heard. In my family, no one kissed or hugged. Practical. My family is practical. Food on the table, a bed to sleep on, good clothes to wear.

Twenty years ago, after falling off a ladder at work on a construction site at King and Bay Streets and permanently injuring his left shoulder, my father built a shack on a neighbour's ten acres on the banks of Etobicoke Creek, where he spent most of his waking hours. My father used old timber and scrap metal from the neighbour's large junk heap. Inside the shack, he dug a pit where he burns wood in winter to keep himself and his animals warm. It seems that it's among his rabbits, chickens, and kittens that he feels at home, spending his days hidden from family and friends and society's grasp. He hardly speaks to anyone. A biblical hermit hiding in the wilderness. Except my father has no Bible; he never even held one.

The landowner gets vegetables and eggs in lieu of rent. A handshake reciprocity.

Me? I get a call on the second Monday of every September. "When, when can we come?" I always reply. But today I told him I'd let him know in a couple of days.

I stand in my kitchen, receiver in hand, bewildered at my own words. So curt and dismissive, when I've waited so long to hear his voice at the other end of the line!

Perhaps it's his dwindling visitations, the scarcity of his calls, the guarded responses. "How are you?" "Okay." "And everybody at home?" "Fine, just fine."

For the first few years after I left home, twelve years or so ago, he'd visit me at Easter and Christmas and call once a month. But gradually our communications dwindled to my yearly visit to the neighbour's plot of land at harvest time. How he met this neighbour he never fully explained, just that he would pay lower land taxes if the land was farmed. That's my father: his relationships are always at a distance. The scraps of communication with me were without my mother's knowledge, of course. She and I have not spoken since that February day when I ran away from her, ran away from my marriage to Eduardo—a marriage she'd arranged when I was fifteen—ran away from a life I had not yet lived.

"Everything ready." I think of my father's words. It's as though the vegetables and eggs he gives me once a year are the blood and bone binding us together.

Maybe they are.

This is all, Milita, all you get from me. Be satisfied.

Ever since I can remember, my mother called my father *seco*. Dry. He'd shrug and walk away whenever she accused him of being a loner. It's been years since he's visited his brother and sister in Portugal or even written to them. Whenever I ask him why, he answers, "Too late."

I always imagine a clock striking Time's last second.

I recall my father laughing with friends when I was a child. Every October, at harvest time, he would hire a long wagon driven by a set of four horses for the yearly picnic in Rio Frio. This was a large vineyard two hours away from Amendoeiro whose wealthy owner opened his doors every October for picnics on his pine and eucalyptus grounds and the free tasting of his new wine. Twenty or more of us on that wagon departing when night's wings still cradled the earth. My father would always sit at the front next to the driver telling stories and laughing until we arrived in the awakening dawn.

Gradually, he stopped joining us on our outings, claiming he was too busy looking after his vegetables and animals.

Has my mother been right all along? I never thought so. But now I think that perhaps my father is *seco*. Two meagre hours spent with me once a year seems to satisfy his fatherly needs. He never enquires about my sons or shows any interest in what I do.

Outside of time spent on the land, nothing seems to matter to him. Even his interest in antique coins has long disappeared.

Well... The coins disappeared.

I'd arrived home from work one evening to find the house empty. I was still married to Eduardo then and my parents and Manuelito were living with us in the house on Euclid. I couldn't imagine where everyone had gone, my mother usually at home when I arrived, busy preparing dinner. I checked the upstairs bedrooms. No one. As I came down the stairs, I began to hear whimpers that seemed to be rising from the basement. I hurried down.

My father stood under the basement stairs, a belt in his right hand. Eduardo and my mother held on to his left arm, as though trying to pull him away from something.

It was March, the fading evening light filtering through the small and dusty basement window was too feeble to light up the basement. A few seconds passed before I saw Manuelito lying on the basement floor, his body curled up like a sleeping dog, except he wasn't sleeping.

I turned on the light. Manuelito's grey sweater was rolled up to his neck, exposing his back which was smeared with blood.

My father shuffled by me toward the stairs, head down. I wasn't sure if he saw me. My mother and Eduardo carried Manuelito to the couch in the next room where the TV was. I followed. Blood drops stained the white cement floor, like abstract red blotches on a white canvas.

My mother walked by me toward the bathroom without even glancing my way. She came out with a wet towel and proceeded to wipe the blood from Manuelito's back. She was crying. I felt as though I was watching a silent drama unfolding on stage. Yet, the drama wasn't new. What was new was the feeling that I no longer wanted to be a spectator.

I walked out of the room; Eduardo followed.

"Your father found the lock broken on the small briefcase where he keeps his antique coins hidden under the stairwell," he whispered. "Manuelito has been trading coins, including two gold ones, for Superman and Spiderman comics, to other boys in the neighbourhood. I arrived just in time. Your father would've killed him. He kept hitting and hitting him with his belt, like some malfunctioning machine."

I walked away, saying nothing. *What could I have said?*

I looked for my father in the kitchen and living room, both now buried in darkness. He was likely in his bedroom on the second floor, denying himself supper as a sort of punishment. A penance. A sacrifice to the Devil, since, he doesn't believe in God. My father, of all people, the mild-mannered Antonio, the one who doesn't believe in spanking children. He'd never hit Manuelito before and only slapped me once when I was fifteen and for that I blamed my mother.

My father has never again mentioned the loss of the coins. Neither have I.

He's now standing by the rusty gate at the entrance to the land, as Claudio parks the car on the dead-end street next to the sound-barrier wall on the QEW. My father seems comfortable with Claudio. After all, we've been married for ten years.

"We're coming," I'd said, when he called back two days later.

His handsome face is caved in, his body thinner, more feeble-looking, than last year. He smiles, as usual, a politician's smile that divulges nothing.

What is it I expect him to divulge? That my mother is sorry for forcing me to marry Eduardo, who I didn't love? Sorry for trying to choke me when I announced that I was in love with Claudio?

As I kiss him, I feel the usual stiffening, the gentle pulling back. His arms hang limply at his side.

We descend the steep incline into the valley. The ancient Etobicoke Creek, originally named by the Ojibway—Wah-do-be-kaun (Where Alders Grow)—runs in the distance. A conservation area borders the creek on the other side.

My father takes us on our yearly walk to the creek through a densely weeded path. He walks as if he's lord of the trees, the flowers, the brush, the butterflies, the wide blue sky of this Arcadia below the unsuspecting rushing world of the QEW above. Cardinals, yellow finches, sparrows, swoop over our heads, serenading us. I pick Queen Anne's lace, goldenrod, blue cornflowers, purple willow aster, growing in profusion along the path. Each year I tenderly place these wildflowers in a vase and pray they will last one more day.

The water glitters in the dappled sunlight breaking through the trees. My father points to the slabs of shale in the middle of the creek where ducks usually gather. Today there aren't any. I can see my father's neck and back tensing as his eyes search the area. He clucks "*quack, quack, quack.*" The ducks soon veer around the bend into sight, their flapping wings filling the silence. He turns to us and nods in some acknowledgment we're supposed to understand.

We walk back toward the boxed and bagged vegetables waiting by the chicken wire fence that hems in a dozen or so chickens and the colourful rooster lording the coop. Claudio walks ahead of us. I follow at a slight distance, next to my father.

"Does anybody at home ever mention me?" I ask him in Portuguese.

"No." He smiles, as if I've just asked him if he wants a drink.

In all the years, I've never asked such a question.

We usually talk about his vegetables and animals, the weather, politics. He likes politics. Burdening him with personal questions he'll find painful is not my way. He's suffered enough living with my mother's unhappiness. But today something in me is pushing through.

"Someone saw Eduardo and mother going for a walk," I say.

"Who saw mother and Eduardo walking?"

"Someone I know that lives in your neighbourhood. She said they pass every afternoon by her house, arm in arm. Eduardo carries mother's oxygen tank."

"Your mother needs to walk every day after her heart attack."

"But you're her husband." My pitch is shrill, the words seeming to shoot out with a volition of their own. The birds seem to have abandoned us, likely flown to quieter places.

"It's you who's supposed to walk with her. You're her husband!"

Claudio turns around, a questioning look on his face. I wave my hand, letting him know that everything is okay. He proceeds to pick a ripened tomato and eats it.

"Why is Eduardo still living with you, anyway?" I'm a whiny child after losing at some game, a child needing coddling, though my voice is now softer. "I've been gone for over twelve years . . . Why doesn't he live his own life?"

My father shrugs and points to the patch of corn we're nearing.

"Good corn this year."

There, subject changed.

The hollowness of my words ricochet in my mind like a muted echo. Wisdom spoken in an empty room. It's years since my father's indifference—his silent giving up to my mother's decisions and actions that have shown that he, too, knows the nakedness of words.

It must've been clear to him where my mother's priorities rested the moment she, Manuelito, and I arrived in Toronto. Only days passing—suitcases not yet fully unpacked—and she already busy gathering information on proxy marriages and ways to bring Eduardo over.

My father now begins to peel back ears of corn to check them for maturity. Russets and yellows shine in the sun, inviting my gaze and my need to take home the corn he's unfolding.

"You know, Milita," my father says, gaze beyond me. "It's all bullshit." His voice is unfamiliar, guttural, sprung out from some hidden part of his being. Unguarded and unrehearsed. There's a touch of fear in it.

"Bullshit? What's bullshit? My wanting to see you more than once a year?"

"Ha," he chuckles. "It all comes to nothing, you know. All of it! All bullshit. At the end, there's nothing but sickness and suffering. Death waits for us at every corner, but we don't know it when we're young. You too, Milita. You'll see. You'll soon be old too."

A black kitten appears; it snugs up to my father's leg. He picks it up with both hands and gently strokes its fur. The kitten purrs, closing its tiny eyes, rubbing its head on my father's chest. It's as if the kitten wants more, expects more, is used to more. My father keeps stroking; the kitten keeps purring; I keep staring. Claudio waits patiently by the chicken wire fence.

My father turns slowly toward me, now holding my gaze. He has a carved grin on a face that seems like stone, putting an end to any other opinions or questions I might have. It's then I notice his patched dark blue cotton pants, the threadbare flannel shirt, and the faded green Molson Canadian baseball cap from the days when the brewery delivered a case of twenty-four every Saturday to our flat on Kensington Avenue. His clothes appear to be left over from his construction days fifteen years ago.

A lump swells in my throat and a tear sneaks down below my sunglasses. I casually brush it away. After all the money earned during his back-breaking days in construction work on roads and skyscrapers downtown Toronto, after the housing units built in Portugal as rental investment in preparation for his return (that never took place), after the savings carefully stashed away in his Royal Bank account, he's remained the same penniless boy growing up on that farm in Algarve where hunger hid behind every rock.

My father takes out his pocket knife from his pants pocket and proceeds to cut a few corn stalks I always use as fall decorations on my front porch. Claudio points to the dark clouds that have formed in the distance. He asks me to hurry or he'll be late for his golf game. Or perhaps he's had enough of a visit that hardly includes him.

"Come see the new chicks," my father says in English in his familiar cheerful voice. He leads us to a large platform he built using planks and pieces of corroded metal from the same junkyard heap he gathered materials to build the shack. The platform is rough and messy, resembling a scene from a tornado disaster. Yellow and russet corn cobs are spread over a large torn canvas so the corn can dry in the sun. Winter feed for the chickens, my father explains. Five or six golden chicks run around him in a sort of moving unit, eagerly pecking their way. He reaches into a barrel and gently throws them corn. He whistles. A lullaby the chicks seem to recognize.

"Sometimes coyotes and foxes kill a few," he says, grinning. "One year a coyote entered the shed and killed all the chickens and the rooster. It couldn't get to the rabbits high in their cages. I found the mangled bodies in the morning. Feathers, blood, guts, everywhere."

"Oh my God!" I place my hands over my face.

"Ha!" My father shrugs his shoulders again. "Life's not pretty, Milita. Get used to it."

His words keep the lump in my throat.

What papier-mâché doll does my father see when he looks at me? Does he know anything about me?

We reach the chicken wire fence. I help carry the corn stalks up to the car that's waiting on the dead-end street. My father and Claudio are ahead of me. My father is talking about the violent nature of history, a trickle of joy in his voice. How the strong kill the weak, like the coyotes and foxes kill chickens. "Portugal slaughtered the Moors, America the Indians, Germany the Jews . . . There's blood everywhere. We think we're civilized? Ha!" He spits.

I remain silent, too emotional to engage in conversation.

Claudio places everything in the car's trunk; my father watches from the rusty gate.

In the car, I roll down the window and look out. My father is waving goodbye, as if we've already gone over our allotted time. Perhaps he's impatient to return to *his* black kitten.

I call out, as I do each time, "When are you coming to visit us?"

He's locking the gate; I'm not sure he's heard me. But then he turns to face me and offers me another smile and another shrug.

Claudio calls out, "Christmas, come visit us at Christmas. I'll pick you up."

"I promise nothing," my father hollers back and waves. Smiling, always smiling, like a politician whose smile signifies nothing.

Claudio tries to take my hand but I gently push his away.

He drives away in silence. He knows me well, knows when I need to be left alone.

The longer I live the less I understand my father. Each year he becomes more closed, more removed from life—my life—a puzzle I need to try and stop solving.

Is it me? Am I the puzzle?

I won't come next year, I promise myself. Crumbs. All I get is crumbs.

Then I remember the tomatoes, the potatoes, beans, corn, and eggs in the car's trunk. I imagine my father thinking of me as he cultivates the earth, as he drops each seed onto the soil in spring, and waters it, and as he feeds the corn that he has grown and dried to the chickens.

Casa do Relógio

The Lisbon airport was crowded, messy, the two customs officials were rude until I placed a ten dollar bill in each of their hands, loudspeakers dispatched names and directions with military might, women yelled at children, dogs barked in cages, people pushed and shoved their luggage into me as I walked through the revolving steel doors. I'd forgotten the ways of the country. Men, women, and children, stood waiting for new arrivals behind a rope. I stared at the crowd trying to locate my uncle Rafael, who'd written to say he'd come to meet me. A thin, bald man, pasty faced, was frantically waving. It was Rafael, my mother's younger brother, recognition coming through the square, clenched jaw he'd inherited from his father, my grandfather, the one who believed that people who laughed too much couldn't be trusted.

"You're like me," my grandfather told me from the moment I could talk. "Strong and determined. No one pushes us around and nothing stops us from getting what we want. We're Ferreiras, strong, like iron." He went on to explain that that was why our veins were blue. He pointed to the veins in my arm, "See? Blue." I believed him until I came to realize that everyone's veins were the same colour.

I never heard him say this to Rafael, even though he carried the same name.

My grandfather's words served me well. Whenever I feared something, I'd tell myself, "You're a Ferreira," and pushed through, the bluster of life not easily discouraging me.

This was my second trip back home after twenty years. The first was ten years ago, after which Rafael's correspondence was reduced to a card at Christmas, except for a letter seven years ago, informing us of Avo's death (she'd suffered from diabetes) and a second one two years later—merely a note, really—telling me of my grandfather's unexpected death. I could never figure out why Rafael had stopped writing—this, from a man who'd once aspired to be a poet. Maybe having seen me that one time ten years ago sufficed to satisfy his *saudades* of me. Maybe I reminded him of things he'd rather forget. How was I to know? Then three months ago, a postcard, the kind you send when travelling, with a picture of a puppy, said, "Time for you to come see us. Time for us to see each other again and talk."

His request took me by surprise. Was he suddenly missing me? What could've happened that he wasn't mentioning in Christmas cards?

I needed to think about my visit, check with Claudio. Yet something in Rafael's words was calling me, a kind of plea was hiding in his scrawl and in the empty spaces on the card. Regardless of Claudio's decision, I knew I had to come.

"It's your family," he said, when I mentioned Rafael's invitation. "You go. You'll be freer without me."

"You haven't changed much," Rafael said, as he came closer. "I recognized you straight away. Always fashionable."

His checkered blue shirt was faded and thin from wear and so were the baggy grey woollen pants (and the season already hot) gathered in folds at his waist from a too-tight belt or too much weight loss. His two front teeth were missing.

I tried to embrace him—that was what relatives did after long absences. But he pulled back, as if an invisible wall had risen between us.

He picked up my suitcase and we walked out of the airport's big sliding doors, the morning sun already burning. He waved down a taxi that would drive us to Amendoeiro.

That's right, I thought, the Vasco da Gama Bridge had been built. Now we can *drive* to Amendoeiro.

"Only fifteen minutes to cross the river by car," Rafael gloated. "It's the longest bridge in Europe. Huge progress."

Growing up, visits to Lisbon were serious affairs, preparations beginning the day before, clothes ironed, shoes polished, hair washed and slowly dried in the sun, coffee pot filled and ready, excitement and trepidation running through our veins, the city big, unfamiliar, a maze of hurrying, unfriendly people, making us feel provincial no matter how well we dressed or how careful we were to pronounce our vowels. The ride across the wide Tejo took an hour, the ferryboat tickets expensive even for the lower deck, the upper deck reserved for the rich. Waiters in white jackets passed us on their way up, carrying trays of lavishly displayed ham and cheese sandwiches, sprigs of parsley on top. I imagined the splendour, the happiness, above those stairs. Once my grandparents took me to the Lisbon zoo and on our return my grandfather bought me a sandwich from the small bar at the back of the ferry, where men stood drinking cheap wine, eating lupini beans, and smoking rolled-up cigarettes, butts, peels, and spit ending up on the floor. The sandwich was smaller than the ones on the first class trays and without parsley, but it was good. The problem arose when the river turned rough, the ferryboat, a lost toy on unusually high waves, bouncing side to side, my stomach turning with the boat, the sandwich disembarking before I did. My first lesson that happiness doesn't reside in fancy ham and cheese sandwiches served by waiters in white jackets.

Vasco da Gama! For a moment I wondered what discoveries awaited me.

Rafael talked to the taxi driver the whole way about the high cost of living, the problems afflicting everyone since Portugal joined the EU. "It's not helping everyone," he said. "So far, the EU brought us nothing but inflation and drug-pushers. Everything costs double and parents are terrified of sending their children to school for fear they get accosted by druggies."

"*Sim, sim, homen*," the driver added. "Hey, man, I'm a car mechanic with a wife and a baby and have to drive this taxi on Sundays just to put food on the table."

I gazed into the front mirror to look at the driver's face. He was young, maybe not even twenty, curly hair falling over his eyes. He smiled when he saw me looking; he too had a tooth missing. It seemed progress had been born and died with the Vasco da Gama Bridge!

I looked out the taxi window. Everything appeared at once strange and familiar, shocking and endearing, like some rediscovered memento from some long-ago trauma. The cork factory where my father had worked across from the bullring, houses, gardens, streets, Antonio's Taberna, where I went everyday as a child to buy wine for the day's dinner, Vitoria's Esso station, all appeared smaller, shabbier, insignificant.

We arrived in a cloud of dust. The old road behind my house and Casa do Relógio, as my grandparents' house was known, where Rafael and Luisa now lived since my grandparents died, was still unpaved. Old tires, rusty cans, rotting wood, and barbed wire created a fence around Silveira's farm, directly across from my house, where we used to buy radishes, tomatoes, lettuce, and cucumbers in summer. Now all was fallow, tall grass, weeds, and red poppies, covering the once lush field like a blanket. Maybe Silveira and his wife had died and since they had no children the farm was abandoned. A group of gypsies had encamped there, under a large tree near the road. They seemed to be barbecuing, smoke filled the air, two horses roamed about. Were the gypsies squatting on the land? Barking dogs surrounded the taxi, still sending fear down my spine.

"Welcome home," Luisa said, as we got out of the taxi. She was waiting for us by the wooden gate, now warped and in need of paint, at the entrance to the garden. She was even heavier than ten years ago, hair thinner, large brown eyes lost in plump cheeks. Or maybe I'd forgotten. It had been years since they'd sent photographs.

Luisa led the way toward the house; I followed, Rafael was behind me. We passed a small vegetable and herb garden next to the manure pile, chickens roaming above it pecking for maggots and grubs. I held my nose. Oh, there was the well and the cement laundry tub where my mother had spent many of her days leaning over the washboard, hands red and covered in itchy welts from the cold water in winter. Newspapers and magazines, rags, pieces of rope and wire, a three-legged chair on its side, dirty plastic bags, even a discarded shoe curled up by rain and sun, littered the garden. Neither Luisa nor Rafael seemed to have noticed. The apple, apricot, and cherry trees I watched my grandfather plant were gone. Only the fig tree remained. Avô's grand flower garden was now only a memory.

As Casa do Relógio came into view, I stopped. The once imposing house built by my grandfather, the largest and only one like it in town with its Arabian terraces, stucco, and ornate pink chimney, a style brought with him from Algarve, now appeared ghostly, forsaken, a setting for a horror film, the white stucco as ashy as Rafael's face. I was finding it hard to breathe.

My grandfather had been a proud man, a man of ideas, action, and a rigid code of honour and discipline. He needed to stand out from the rest by his achievements and beliefs. "Work," he'd say, "saves a man's soul and lifts him high above the rabble." He was short, stocky with intense dark eyes, as if whoever and whatever he gazed at were in need of deep examination. Correction. He referred to himself as an orchid among geraniums. This was when he was sober, of course. When drunk, honour was not something he talked about or a blessing covering him.

I must've been four or five when my mother woke me one night, leaning over me.

"Hurry up. Get dressed."

I followed her to the railroad tracks running in front of Casa do Relógio and alongside the highway. It was winter, hard to see in the starless December sky. As we approached, I could hear voices but all was blurred in the looming darkness, except for the small area illuminated by the sole amber light pole on the highway, directly across the house. Avó stood in the shadows at a slight distance. I could hear her sniffling and sighing.

My grandfather stood in the middle of the tracks, directly under the soft light, shirt open, sleeves rolled up, in spite of the night's chill. He held his head high, chin up, arms open wide, as if talking to heaven. "I own the world," he yelled with all his might, making sure the world heard him. "I'm powerful. I can lift this railroad track right out of the ground with my bare hands."

My father, Rafael, and the shoemaker next door stood close to him. They'd managed to get him out of Antonio's Taberna at closing time, but had failed to get him home. That's when I was fetched. I always showed up before his rage shifted from the railroad tracks to his dog or his enemies (he had many) or the Church, the priests, or Avó. I was the last resort, a trump card used in the game of pacifying his drunkenness.

"I can do it, " my grandfather roared, both hands on the track. "See, see, it's rising."

My father placed me in front of him. "Look, look, here is your granddaughter."

My grandfather stared at me, blinked, wavered, slowly took my hand and quietly followed me home.

Now Rafael, Luisa, and I climbed the stairs to the terrace. The tall, ornate, Arabian-style chimney, decorated with pink bricks—a beacon announcing my grandfather's uniqueness and success (not merely to the town but to highway travellers and train riders going by)—was unfurling brick by brick, a heap of rubble at its bottom. I was dismayed. Rafael was a bricklayer!

I sighed.

"What's the matter?" he asked.

"So many dreams and plans lost in those bricks and mortar!"

He nodded, a sad grin appearing I hadn't noticed before.

We descended the narrow cement stairs and walked to the small courtyard in front of the house, where I sat as a child in summer to embroider and crochet. It was here that I began embroidering the pillowcases Avó had bought me from the gypsies caravanning through town. Only two of the green bushes, that once created a sculpted fence in front of the house, were still standing, skeletal brown branches cluttering the green ones. The Roman numerals on the clock painted on the front gable, giving the house its name, had faded. A relic without meaning.

The two hands on the clock had been on twelve. When I was old enough to tell time I'd asked my grandfather whether the time on the painted clock was noon or midnight. "It's up to you," he said. "You choose. Life is what you make it, Milita, remember that. You're in control."

Oh, I'd wanted to grow up like him, to be an orchid among geraniums, though I'd never seen an orchid, had no idea what it looked like.

It was noon by the time I unpacked and refreshed my hands and face in the cold water brought by Aunt Luisa in a porcelain basin. She pointed to the old outhouse when I asked for the toilet. They still had not built a proper bathroom, though electricity and running water had come to this side of the railroad tracks. I'd forgotten how flushing toilets and warm water could be such luxuries.

"You two talk," she said. "I'll make lunch."

Rafael and I sat next to each other on the back patio while Luisa went into the house.

The canopy of fuchsia bougainvillea and red Muscat grapes my grandfather planted when he first built the house still shaded the patio. We drank thick, sour red wine from Antonio's Taberna and ate large cracked green olives and small salted sardines on soda crackers.

Well, I ate.

Rafael said he didn't want to spoil his appetite but I thought his appetite had long ago left him, his thin body caved in as though it was being hollowed out from the inside. It was clear he wasn't well and I wondered if his need to see me was some kind of goodbye.

Some of the white gardenias surrounding the patio had survived, their velvety blossoms sparkled in the May sun, sweetening the air with their rich fragrance. Only a few flower pots of the once burgeoning patio remained, but my grandparents' shadows were everywhere, hauling water from the well at dusk so as not to shock the plants when the sun shone on their leaves. They were always working, digging, weeding, seeding their garden, the most lavish one in Amendoeiro. Avó sold bouquets to rich homes in Montijo every Saturday; I helped her to carry the filled straw bags with the bouquets. Avó's diabetes was likely already gnawing at her vital organs, then, she always in search of fresh green vegetables in winter in a town without refrigeration. She died two days after her fiftieth birthday. I don't ever remember her laughing.

The dappled sunlight peered through the grapevines and bougainvillea, creating fanciful, muted shapes on the house walls and patio floor, waking memory . . .

I'm sitting on the cement patio on a blanket made of different pieces of flowered and multicoloured cloth, remnants of a fabric left over from dresses going back to Avó's youth. I'm playing with my doll or learning to sew, Avó patiently showing me to thread a needle.

It was also while sitting on the same blanket that I listened to Rafael play the banjo or read his poetry out loud, flipping his brown curls away from his hazel eyes at the end of each stanza, offering me a big smile and a wink, as if to say, aren't I talented? Aren't I handsome?

Now the smile, the wink, the curls, the pomposity and the poems were gone. Rafael turned pensive, seemingly unaware of the cloud-free sky.

"Beautiful day," I say, a remark as wooden as my chair, but I needed to break the stifling silence. Rafael nodded but didn't reply. He rubbed his bony, blue-veined hands, stopped, gazed into the distance, rubbed his hands again. A restrained eagerness emanated from his body as he sat stiffly forward, as if about to say or do something but then changing his mind.

The *andorinhas* chirped in their nests under the bougainvillea and grape canopy serenading us. A large brown spider walked across the patio in front of Rafael. He stretched out his leg and squashed it.

Oh, it's bad luck to kill a spider, I wanted to say, but I didn't.

Rafael got up, picked up the empty wine jug, kicked the dead spider onto the gardenias, and disappeared into the house.

I stared at a clay pot of blood-red carnations by the back entrance. Carnations were my favourite flower as a child, they looked regal and luxurious. As I grew older, I began to favour the modesty of daisies, the simplicity of the single petals bringing me a kind of peace.

Rafael returned, carrying the refilled jug, droplets of red wine staining his grey trousers, like drops of blood. He didn't seem to notice. He refilled our glasses, hands shaking uncontrollably, picked up his glass with both hands and drank it in one fast motion.

He filled his glass again. I placed my hand over mine. It wasn't yet noon!

"I have to tell you something," his words were slurring.

Oh, no, what is he going to confess?

I'd never been easy with confessions, learning that as soon as the confession showed its face, the confessor was sorry and disappointed, expecting *something* from me I couldn't deliver. Just last year, I lost my friend Mattie. Too much wine one evening over dinner and the details of an affair with her priest, the husband who could never imagine she'd do such a thing, came between us like a cancer.

Rafael said, "It was me Milita. Me, who discovered my father."

"What do you mean, *discovered?*"

"I was the one who found him hanging."

"Hanging? But you wrote that he had had a stroke?"

"I didn't want to upset you or your mother, you both so far away in Canada. What could you do? Your mother's heart and nerves so fragile and I knew how close you were to him, how you admired his ambition, his ability, his resolve. You being so much like him."

Rafael waited for my reply but words had left me.

For years I'd been turning my grandfather's drunken episodes into anecdotes at dinner parties miles across the ocean in Toronto. Time muffled fear and sadness and shame, converting the unpalatable into humour, I, the entertainer, the good storyteller, the one whose self-confidence and wit people admired.

"Tell us another story," my friends would beg, laughing before I even started.

I would.

This story was different . . .

"Yap, the son-of-a-bitch got up one day and decided to turn his back on everything he'd worked for," Rafael continued. "Imagine that? The stubborn old fool. I guess the wine had been rotting his brain for a long time. Perhaps his soul too. I'll never know why he did it, all he left was the word *Xega* scrawled in dull pencil on the back of the hardware bill for the rope. He misspelled *chega*. Enough. You know he didn't even complete grade one, school not mandatory in those days, not necessary for a people working that stony soil of Algarve."

Luisa came out of the house. "I need to get parsley and chives for the lamb."

Rafael waited for her to return from the herb garden before speaking, eyes fixed on the ground. She came back carrying small bunches of herbs in one hand, a lettuce and a bunch of radishes in the other, their little red heads shinning in the sun.

"The nightmares continue," he said, voice hardly audible. "Two years and I still wake in the night, that note staring back at me, waiting for days on the kitchen table for someone to read it. *Xega!* You see, I didn't always go visit him, long periods of time passed before I gathered the courage to face him. I hadn't visited him for over two months and the son-of-a-bitch had money for wine but not for a telephone. That afternoon I knocked and knocked. When he didn't answer I asked a neighbour to help me break down the cracked oak door. It was summer. As the door fell backwards, the stench was that of dead cats rotting in the summer sun on the side of the road. I threw up and nearly passed out."

Rafael took another swallow from his wine glass without glancing my way, a drop running down his chin. He wiped it with one swipe of his hand and talked on, as if afraid to stop, afraid the story might leave him, the details might get blurred, the truth forever lost.

"I had to be hospitalized, couldn't sleep for weeks afterwards and haven't been able to work since then or do much of anything. I still wake in the night sometimes, see him hanging from the rope attached to the middle beam on the ceiling, swollen face dangling, skin a deep purple, bulging eyes staring, tongue hanging out three times its size. Only the pink pills the doctor prescribed brought me some sleep afterwards. Imagine, the price tag was still on the rope and his cereal bowl and coffee mug from breakfast were washed and lying on the kitchen counter."

Rafael stopped, took a deep breath.

My head was whirling, images of swollen tongues, bulging eyes, and putrid flesh melding and crashing, appearing and disappearing, like melting celluloid.

He lifted up his glass, then put it down again without drinking. He mumbled *aaahhh*, as he stared straight ahead, as if he'd forgotten I was present.

"The worst was the disappointment in his eyes. It was there all my life. All my life. The son-of-a-bitch so ambitious, so successful and me just a bricklayer, not even a builder like him, all the money spent on that college in Evora that was to make me an architect, remember?

But I wanted to write poetry. It was hard for me to be around him; his anger growing toward me, toward everyone. By the end, no one came to visit him."

I recalled my grandfather never trusting or confiding in anyone, not even Avó, my mother, or Rafael. When life became unbearable, he drank.

Rafael turned to face me. "Remember the *bruxa*? His first cousin, the one we all called the witch? Her mother and father were uncle and niece. Did you know that? It was illegal even then for an uncle to marry his niece. So they lived like hermits—in sin—as people called it then, despised by everyone. The family claimed that that was why the *bruxa* was strange. Bad blood. Even she stopped visiting your grandfather."

"I remember her. How could I forget the *bruxa*?"

Yes, how could I forget the thin wizened face and dark piercing raven eyes I found terrifying as a child. She always wore long black dresses and a black headscarf summer and winter, reminding me of death. "I wear black," she'd say, "not for mourning but for the sorrows of the world." She lived alone by the river in an earthen-floor, one-room house. Avó had taken me there once when I was small and she was looking for ways to stop Rafael from dropping out of the architectural college. The *bruxa* grew herbs to offset many ailments and when in a friendly mood she read your palm, told you your future and how to overcome bad luck. She knew prayers to dispel the evil eye and made up potions and incantations to make you fall in love or appease the dead. Everyone feared her; yet everyone went to see her. "All those suffering and afraid come to me," the *bruxa* would say, something between a grin and a scowl across her face. She was the keeper of the town's secrets.

"They come in the night so they can hide their shame."

"She knew things," Rafael said.

I'd turned nine the summer my grandfather decided to throw a party to celebrate his life, his accomplishments, as he called it, the illiterate farm boy become successful builder. He spared no expenses, unusual for him, considering his parsimonious ways when sober. "Thriftiness, hard work, and sacrifice," he'd say, "means you never have to beg for a meal."

A lamb was to be roasted in an open pit and an accordion player was hired. The dancing was to take place on the terrace. Everyone in town was invited, and the *bruxa*.

I recalled my new white nylon dress with tiny yellow flowers my mother had made for me for the Festa de São Pedro in June. I felt pretty. Virgilio, the boy whose parents were the gate-keepers for a small cork factory across the road, was coming with his parents.

After the lamb was eaten, the accordion player led the party to the rooftop. He limped, his right leg a little shorter than the left one, the sole on that shoe higher than the other. He walked up the terrace stairs, carrying his accordion, one step at a time, one, stop, two, stop . . .

The rest of the party followed. My grandfather carted a case of wine. Avó walked behind with a tray of glasses. Once everyone was on the terrace, the accordion player began playing a waltz. People started dancing, others gathered in small groups, wine glass in hand, my brother, Manuelito, five then, and other boys, running and screaming between the dancers. The accordion-player played tangos and boleros, followed by *El Negro Zumbom*, the baião, a new dance from Brazil. Virgilio was showing me the steps to the baião when suddenly the music stopped. Everyone ran toward the top of the stairs. I ran too, Virgilio ahead of me. A woman screamed. I tried pushing my way through the crowd to see what was happening, but everyone else was pushing the same way. I could hear a loud *thump, thump, thump* mixed with the haphazard notes of the accordion. The woman stopped screaming and started calling for God's help, her pleas filling the air. She was the accordion player's wife. I pushed further into the crowd. It was then I heard my grandfather's drunken voice, the one he saved for hating the world and cursing God.

Virgilio seemed to appear from nowhere and grabbed my arm,

"Your grandfather pushed the accordion player down the stairs." His face was flushed—excited—for being the first one to tell me. "The accordion player didn't know how to play his favourite song. We think the accordion player's leg is broken."

"Oh my God, which one?"

"They don't know; he can't stand up. Someone ran to the Esso station to use the telephone and call for an ambulance."

I looked around not knowing what to say or do, conscious of a new feeling that made me want to hide.

My grandfather was yelling, calling the accordion player *filho da puta*, *velhaco*, son-of-a-bitch, cuckold, this coming from a man who hardly raised his voice, or his eyes, when sober. He was wildly waving his arms up and down, up and down, face a vermillion red, eyes bulging out.

The *bruxa* walked up to him, people quietly parting into two separate groups, creating an opening like the centre aisle of a church, leading from the *bruxa* to my grandfather. She grabbed his hands and held them in hers, everyone watching, fearful of what he might do. He didn't pull back. "Pride," she said, "is the work of the Devil and time is on the Devil's side." Then she hurried down the stairs, long black skirt and shawl swelling in the breeze.

A flock of noisy crows now flew overhead. Dark clouds were moving in, thunder faintly roaring in the distance. A sudden gust of cold wind blew the paper napkins off the patio table.

I shivered, stood up and excused myself. I'd forgotten about the unpredictability of May in this part of the world, showers and storms arriving without warning.

In the kitchen Luisa was busy setting the table. The lamb smelled delicious. I went into the extra bedroom, where I would be sleeping, and grabbed a sweater. I opened my purse and checked my passport and Air Canada ticket, feeling relieved the date of return was an open one. Maybe one week instead of two. I placed the purse back in the armoire.

When I returned to the patio Rafael was gone. I looked around. I could see his head moving above the overgrown weeds back and forth at the back of the garden beyond the well and the cement laundry tub. A gaunt, caged bear. Ha, I thought, the endless yarn of filial guilt.

What about me? Rafael's words jumbled in my mind, making me feel disconnected, lost, like an *andorinha* hovering above a place where its nest used to be.

I was having trouble imagining my grandfather as a suffering figure to whom life had become frightful or unbearable. Where had his stubbornness gone, that dogged determination that led him to turn the arid, rocky soil of Algarve into a verdant orchard? Scorching long summers, cisterns dry, cicadas singing in the night while people sent prayers to *Nossa Senhora da Piedade* up on the hill begging for rain. Several times a day, he'd cart water from a communal well at a crossroads a half-hour distance away, the mule trudging ancient roads made of rocks removed from fields by Celtic or Roman slaves or the Moors who had occupied the area six hundred years ago. The water had been carried in two double-handled red clay containers placed on the harnessed mule, my grandfather walking behind to make sure the mule didn't tumble and spill the water. Avó, a young bride then, helped plough the land until one day she passed out from exhaustion under the unforgiving sun.

I'd grown up hearing of how one morning my grandfather got up, as the sun woke the day, and instead of harnessing the mule, he gathered the family around him: Avó, Rafael, a mere boy then, my mother and father, married only for a year and a half, me only six months.

"Enough of farming. We're moving to Amendoeiro." The trees had dried and turned into food for the locusts.

He'd heard from someone that Amendoeiro offered plenty of water, fresh fish everyday, a highway and railroad running through it, Lisbon just across the river, and plenty of opportunity for those with ambition and ability. He had both.

He'd recount these stories whenever he was talkative. This was often after dinner and a glass or two, adding a few details each time, sitting on his patio in summer and around a brassiere in my parents' house in winter. His words were aimed at me, enlarging his heroism, speaking each word with gleeful pride and seriousness. He turned these stories into proverbs meant to teach me the importance of desire, determination, frugality, and hard work.

Now I wondered if the idea of saying no to life had sprung at him one lonely day the way a flash storm catches you unawares. But how could that happen to a man for whom life was a piece of clay to be shaped at his will by his determined hands? The hired accordion player should've known the song he requested. After all, he was paying him. My grandfather never again mentioned the accordion player or that Sunday afternoon, though we all knew the accordion player had ended up on a wheelchair for a year, my grandfather paying him to keep the case out of court.

But then I had a contrary thought. What if death's mantle had settled on my grandfather's shoulders even as he asked Avó's own parents for her hand in marriage? Or as he carted those clay water containers on the exhausted mule. Or as he built the ornate pink bricked chimney announcing his greatness to the world. Had he been lying to himself and everyone else the whole time? Lying to me?

Rafael returned from the garden and sat down.

"I went to see the *bruxa* after I came home from the hospital," he said. "The pink pills calmed me down but I began to ponder whether suicide runs in families, to ponder whether it's in the blood. The doctor said that sometimes it is. There's no knowing. I began worrying about us all, especially you, you being so much like him."

A swell of nausea began to flood me. Maybe it was the sour wine and the salted sardines. Or, perhaps, the sticky sadness Rafael wore like a talisman, turning the morning into dusk.

Was it a mistake coming here? I found myself wishing Claudio was with me.

"What did the *bruxa* say?" I asked, careful to hide my agitation.

"She wouldn't tell me. We're family, you know. She's your grandfather's first cousin. She just told me to pay heed. For all of us to pay heed."

"Pay heed to what?"

"The bad blood running in our veins."

We couldn't look at each other.

Then Rafael pointed up to the sky. "Look, an *andorinha*. It means it won't rain."

We listened to the *andorinha's* beautiful song. More swallows began circling above the fuchsia, bougainvillea, and grape canopy. Sun rays were breaking through the clouds.

Luisa stuck her head out of the door; a whiff of stewed lamb and potatoes wafted into the air. "Lunch is on the table," she announced.

"C'mon Milita," Rafael said. "Lamb stew was your grandfather's favourite."

My grandfather!

I imagined him getting up one morning, mind made up that he'd had enough of life. *Xega*, today is the day. Enough, he assured himself. Combed his hair, shaved, donned a clean shirt and tie, he always wore a shirt and tie when going out in public, carefully locking the door, walking into town in his usual measured pace, gently putting his feet down so as not to ruin his leather shoes, head bent down, eyes downcast, unsmiling, voice hardly audible when saying hello to a passerby, walking into the hardware store, politely asking for the rope, taking out a bill from the neat roll he always carried and paying the bill with a polite *obrigado*.

No Wire Nor Rope

The pasta fagioli keeps warm on the stove. An offering—pasta fagioli being Claudio's favourite. It's Sunday. We're flying out this afternoon. The two green suitcases wait side by side in the hallway, like two sentinels at a prison door. Inside the *Holiday Now* folder, resting on top of the suitcases, are our passports, air-line tickets, hotel reservations. I've checked the folder three or four times today to make sure all is ready. After dinner yesterday, Claudio drew a black sun on the folder with a felt pen. He did it with the concentration of a heart surgeon working to save a life, boring down at his creation, as though each pen stroke held the key to some mystery. A deliverance of sorts.

He walks through the front door, blue eyes glancing anywhere but at me, a peevish look on his face, like a child who's done something naughty and is unsure what the punishment will be.

At the kitchen table, we sit across from each other, eating the pasta fagioli, heads down, each not wanting to be the one to break the thundering silence. We haven't spoken a dozen words in the last three days. Part of me wants to shake him and talk. Talk and talk until we'll find ourselves in that place before loneliness and pain and doubt and anger and fear knocked at our door. Yet I know—I've known for a while and wonder if he knows too—that the days of tear-filled discussions ending in tussled sweat-soaked sheets have reached the end.

Something in us is spent.

Before Claudio and I married, we went to a New Year's eve party in Muskoka. By the time we left Toronto it was past eight o'clock in the evening. Claudio's old Dodge had no heat and neither of us had thought of bringing a blanket or a scarf, gloves or even boots. Being together was all that mattered, enough to keep us safe. As we turned off onto a country road off the 400, the car swerved onto a ditch. Nothing but blackness surrounded us, not even the beam of a distant cottage to tell us we weren't alone in this black, winter void of snow and cold. This was in the days before cell phones; we couldn't imagine who'd come to save us. Who would know we were here? And how would we dare walk out onto knee-deep snow drifts covering fields and road, Claudio in black patent loafers and me in silver pumps? We held hands and waited, not really knowing what we were waiting for. Our bodies were beginning to tremble uncontrollably, when wavering lights shone in the black horizon like some heavenly visitation. Snowmobilers. Drunken and laughing on the way to another New Year's celebration. They easily lifted the car from the ditch with us in it. Later, at the party, we arriving just before midnight, we told everyone that we were saved by angels who blessed us with their fairy dust and we believed it!

But in time the angels departed; they grew tired of our daily pettiness. We became ordinary. It's a long time since we bragged to anyone, or to ourselves, that our *love* is unique.

Claudio first yelled at me soon after we were married. Before that, there had only been longing in his gaze, tenderness in his words, cotton clouds in his touch.

"Why... why... why did you invite her here without asking me first?"

A heat wave had come early that summer. We finished eating dinner and were too lazy to get up from the table, the air hot and still, as though forgetting it's purpose. The balcony's sliding-door was open in the hope of a breeze wafting in as the sun set. Claudio's roars flew out over the hot asphalt, over the cars in the parking lot, and drowned out Carly Simon who was belting out *You Belong To Me*, on a radio somewhere. A woman sat on a balcony facing ours in the U-shaped low-rise redbrick complex at Lawrence and Keele. The woman lifted her head. She seemed to stare at us for a minute. A baby cried.

Claudio stood up, circled the dining room table, and came to stand by my chair. He grabbed my shoulders with both hands.

"I'm the boss now. You hear? Remember that. You have to check with me before inviting anyone here or doing anything involving me."

"But Liz needs to talk. You know her husband just left her."

"What are you, a do-gooder?" His face was close to mine. The hair on his nose fluttered like tiny banners with his quick inhales. I looked away from this face I didn't recognize.

"But Liz is my friend; she needs to see me and talk," I managed to say.

"I don't care, next time you check with me before doing anything. Okay? Never forget this, I . . . come . . . first." His finger touched my nose, azure eyes moist and deep, cool pools in a vast desert, inviting me to *drown in them* when we first met. Now they'd turned the colour of rage and rage had no place in such blueness.

But something else was there too. Desire? Passion? Love? Shame? I couldn't tell, but it was as boundless as the land of dreams. My anger melted—I couldn't grasp on to its slipperiness.

He walked away, then turned to face me. Waiting . . .

A dozen yellow sweetheart roses arrived the following afternoon. *I'm sorry and I love you* scribbled on the card. Liz came to dinner that evening. Claudio offered her words of comfort and promises of help.

But soon I learned that Claudio couldn't share my affections and time with anyone else. I was his. His love needed to be handled with a velvet hand, uncompromised, submissive. *Think of me, Milita, me, me, me,* eyes begging every time we made love. His image of me needed to remain unbruised—protected—like a priceless artifact in a museum.

In time anger and resentment seemed to kidnap the fairy dust sprinkled on us that New Year's Eve in the snow-covered country road in Muskoka. The silences grew. The cicadas in summer stopped singing only for us. It was always my fault. No consideration for his feelings. Claudio's angry explosions became normal—expected—part of daily living, like washing floors, cooking, and doing laundry. The price of love. But each time he yelled at me, I became a puppet with broken strings, face down in the mud.

"Remember to tip the driver," I now say, as we step onto the *Vidanta* van, taking us to our hotel at Cancun airport. I know my words will annoy him, but I've seen poverty in the driver's eyes, heard it in the rehearsed *Bienvenidos*, smelled it in his frenzied friendliness. "It's obvious he needs the money."

"Don't tell me what to do," Claudio barks back, eyes narrowing into a familiar ferocity. "I hate you when you do this."

By that he means that he's generous enough to do the right thing. But the next time we'll travel—the next airport, next hotel, next restaurant—I'll likely say the same thing for fear he'll forget to be all the things he wants to believe he is and that I expect him to be.

In the van, I close my eyes and pray that the panacea we always find on faraway soil will span its blissful wings over us. A colourful hibiscus or bougainvillea, a resplendent bird, a crimson sunset can invite in the calm and deliver the truce that usually lasts for the remainder of our holiday, until the plane lands us back home.

What is it? I always ask myself. I know Claudio wonders too.

What unseen presence bruises our chance at happiness—our belief in angels—the moment we arrive home? Is it the brick and mortar in our own walls? Do they remind us of our own limitations? Our fears?

We check in at the resort and shed our winter clothes. We move quickly, like prisoners discarding their uniforms upon release from jail. We grasp at the few hours of daylight left.

The sun, the surf, the breeze, the seagulls circling in a noisy mad rush above my head, as I walk the wide, sandy beach, begin to loosen my jaw and lull my mind. Claudio went to the driving-range and will be gone for a couple of hours.

In the distance, I see a crowd of people gathered in front of a large hotel. I keep walking toward them. I have time before Claudio returns.

Whenever he arrives home before I do when I'm out with friends, he's sullen on my return. Being alone disturbs him. "Fear of abandonment," he told me once in an unguarded moment after a shouting, tearful, and make-up episode, languid bodies lying on damp sheets. As a small child, he'd woken once from an afternoon nap in an empty house. A soldier found him crying half naked on the street. His eyes held mine as he told me this, the four-year-old boy without underpants, still lost in the seeking blue eyes of the thirty-year-old man lying next to me.

The crowd facing The Splendido, a resort the size of a small town, is composed of brown-skinned sellers and entertainers, men, women, and children of different ages. They croon, laugh, chat, and call out their wares, filling the air with a festive atmosphere. They stand in a straight row, encompassing the entire front of the large hotel. At first I'm sure a wire or rope is keeping them in that straight line. But when I move closer, I see that there's no wire or rope.

What invisible obstacle, I wonder, is keeping the vendors in such an orderly distance from the tourists?

Habit? Fear? Some unconscious mechanism keeping them where they belong?

The boisterous peddlers sell jewelry, swimsuit cover-ups, t-shirts, sunglasses, wood carvings, fruit, baked goods, excursions, and cruises to the mostly white tourists sprawled on long chairs covered with thick green towels. A tattoo artist flips the pages of his catalogue, displaying an array of designs. A tall, emaciated man in a soiled white t-shirt and white jeans cut high above his too-thin ankles holds onto an equally emaciated mule. He stands apart from the crowd. Every so often he yells, "Rides, rides, forty dollars." Neither man nor mule seem to be of this world. Both are too gaunt, eyes too large and intense, yet distant.

A boy looking to be about eleven or twelve with a black jewelry case hanging from his neck, approaches.

"Buy something, *Senöra? Por favor, por favor.*"

His right hand is missing. I point to my white swimsuit to show him I have no purse, wondering the whole time what could've happened to his hand. "No money," I say. I don't ask about the hand.

"Tomorrow, *Senöra,* you buy tomorrow." He walks away.

In thirty or forty years, I think, he'll likely still be carrying the same jewelry case, his shoulders more hunched, skin, leathery from walking the beaches all day under the torrid sun, eyes duller with the sad resignation of the old and the poor and the disappointed.

I know the look; I've seen it in my own eyes.

The sun begins to hide behind thick clouds, casting long shadows over the beach. It's getting late. The sea is now a dull grey, colouring the sand with sadness and longing. The brown vendors are busy packing up their wares, a lull replaces the laughter and chatter.

I look for the boy with no hand to tell him that I'll buy something tomorrow. But he's nowhere in sight.

Another disappointed one; I'm good at collecting them.

Liz telephoned me one Saturday after she'd settled into her own apartment, inviting me to dinner. She and her husband shared custody of their young son and on that weekend she was free. Claudio circled around me the whole time that I spoke to her on the telephone. He appeared to be looking for something.

The sadness in Liz's voice urged me to say, Of course I'll come. Instead I said, "Claudio doesn't like me going out in the evenings without him, especially Saturdays."

"Okay," she said and hung up. I stared at the ceramic floor, looking for cracks, afraid to consider what I'd just said, just done. I'd known Liz for over five years—we'd worked together for a short while. I stepped backwards, bumped into Claudio, and sent the receiver crashing onto the floor. I was not aware he was behind me. "I love you," he whispered in my ear, lips soft, tender. He led me up the stairs to the bedroom, undressed me, but Liz's sorrowful *okay* echoed throughout his hungry panting. It's still with me today.

She never called me again; I never called her, either. Not in the twenty years since.

I walk into the sea and let it embrace me.

The waves are now higher, hungrier, repossessing the beach. I look around. Almost everyone is gone, even the seagulls are likely asleep on some quiet sandy patch. A rough wave pushes me back but I keep walking forward. I seem to be alone in this grey world where the sky and the sea are melded.

The water is surprisingly warm, welcoming. *Bienvenida*, it says. I ought to start walking back, Claudio is likely back from the driving range. But the water is alluring; it's as though an invisible hand is pulling me in. There's a sort of freedom in this grey, violent chasm.

A high wave rolls over my head. I inhale water, the saltiness making me cough. Then another wave surprises me, whirling me around. I can't touch bottom; my heart is racing.

"God help me, please!" A voice screams.

Was that me?

My arms and legs scramble against the engulfing greyness, my head barely above the water. My sons' faces appear for a second but the next wave washes them away. Then another wave swirls me back to shore.

As I walk back to our resort, heartbeat slowing down, I see Claudio in the distance, a tiny figure half wrapped in the folding darkness. The beach is now completely empty; all is quiet. It's as though the world has shut down in preparation for another day.

As I get closer, I wave to Claudio but he doesn't seem to recognize me. Folded arms, long legs apart, face hard, he looks like some angry god.

"Where the hell have you been?" he says, once he realizes it's me and I'm within hearing distance. "I checked the apartment, the shops, the restaurants, the pools. You don't care about my feelings, do you? I mean nothing to you."

His blue eyes shine through the gloomy mist. I circle his firm body with my arms. He hesitates, pulls back a little, then holds me tight, as though he might never let me go.

The thin man in the soiled white shirt and jeans, cut high above his thin ankles, emerges from the descending dusk. He's riding his emaciated mule, "Rides, rides, forty dollars," he calls out to the emptiness.

I pull Claudio's body closer to mine.

Night falls.

Even the Lowly Squirrel Cares For Its Young

"Hello!"
"Luisa, here."
"Aunt Luisa?"
"Why do you sound so startled?"
"It's the middle of the night in Toronto."
"Oh, I forgot about the time difference. It's morning in Amendoeiro."

Aunt Luisa's call surprised me. Since my grandparents (my mother's parents) died years ago, the only communication from Portugal had been from my uncle Rafael, my mother's younger brother and Luisa's husband. A Christmas card arrived in early November thanking me for the money I'd sent the year before. Sometimes I wondered if the gift was all that mattered.

"I'm calling to say we buried your uncle last week."
"Oh, I'm so sad to hear that."
"He was sick for a while. At the end, the doctors and medicines wiped out every penny."

I recalled Luisa's life-long struggle with money. The musty bar she and Rafael once owned in the dusty outskirts of Amendoeiro, never generating enough money to pay the bills. Paolo, their only son, consumed every escudo and breath, having to be medicated to control his permanent rage. His wife had left him shortly after they were married and their daughter was born. They were young. She went on to join her sister and mother, who were the town's whores. He'd set fire to her house one night after nightly surveilling her door and watching men walk out. The house was built with brick and mortar and so the fire didn't spread quickly and she managed to escape. But the barbarity of his act never escaped the town's memory, sticking to Aunt Luisa, Rafael, and Paolo like poisoned burrs. They hardly left their house.

Still, I was taken aback by her mention of money at this time, Rafael's flesh, surely, not yet a meal for worms.

"Your mother, God bless her," Luisa continued, "sent money for cakes and port for a celebration after the funeral. It being September, we set up outside on the patio. It was lovely."

I remained silent at the mention of my mother.

"She telephones us sometimes, you know. Your mother does. She's so kind."

Had Aunt Luisa forgotten how my mother hadn't spoken to me in twenty-five years? Forgotten how she forced me to marry that idiot Eduardo when I was only fifteen? I'd hated everything about him, his short bowlegs and the way he showered those near him with spit when he spoke and laughed, and he laughed at everything. Terrified of my mother's ailing heart, shadows of its fragility hanging over me ever since I was a child and recalling the spectre of a glistening knife at my throat at thirteen when I told her I hated him, I signed the proxy-marriage and immigration papers. He'd arrived just before Christmas. A gift, my mother called him.

The five of us had all lived together under my mother's watch, my brother Manuelito still at home until I left. Proper behaviour was expected, of course. The right thing had to be done, which meant that my mother would *always* be part of my life and I part of hers. What I didn't know—she never said—was that my presence was only needed as a means to keep Eduardo near her. After I escaped from my mother's stronghold, the ex-son-in-law never left her side.

It was never about me.

Luisa was no stranger to this story, no stranger to the wound that thirty years later still refused to heal. Did she not think a mother shutting her child from her life was an act against God and against nature? Ought a mother not love and accept her child's life choices? the freedom to carve her own future? Had I been just the wrong daughter?

I'd sat in Luisa's kitchen on my first visit back to Portugal, ten years or so after departing. In those days, she, Rafael, and Paolo lived in the small quarters behind the bar.

It was May but the air was still dank from winter; winters I remembered well, when dampness streamed down cement walls like tears, mildew growing at every corner of the house.

The robust May sun had filtered through the cobweb-covered small window of the living room, revealing a layer of dust on the meagre furnishings, but failing to warm up the room.

I shivered in my white silk shirt; I'd expected Portugal to be warmer at this time of year. I sat across from Aunt Luisa and Rafael, trying hard not to stare at their rumpled clothes and the maps of the hard travelled roads on their faces. Luisa had kept smoothing her soiled apron and pushing back her straggly thin hair from her bloated face. I ought to have written to let them know I was coming. But I thought the surprise would bring them joy. She smiled the whole time, her welcoming smile, the only remnant of the pretty girl of her youth.

Paolo sat to my right. His pumped-up body spread over the sides of the plastic chair he sat on. He never uttered a word. Whenever I glanced his way, he seemed to be staring at me. I began to wonder if visitors were a rarity in this house and, perhaps, I was a mere interference in the normalcy of his day. Or was it my voice piercing through the lethargy imprisoning him? I was nearly sixteen and he five or six when I emigrated to Canada. I'd loved him.

I talked and talked and talked that afternoon determined to get Rafael and Aunt Luisa to understand my side of the story, understand that I was not the guilty one. I coveted their sympathy, their support, confirmation that to walk away from Eduardo and my family was the only path open for me. Yes, yes, turning my back on my mother was the only option for my life to be lived, the door to my future to be opened.

Aunt Luisa made coffee.

As she poured it into three chipped cups, one with a missing handle, she said, "Your mother, God bless her, writes often, you know. Sometimes she sends me a bit of money."

I drank the bitter, hot black liquid and announced I was flying out early in the morning and couldn't stay for dinner. They'd mentioned dinner when I first walked in.

They didn't argue.

I handed Paolo some money and left.

There was silence now at the other end of the line. I could hear Aunt Luisa breathing.

"There's something else," she finally said.

"*Sim . . .*"

"It's about a piece of land in Algarve left to your mother and Rafael by your grandparents. Your mother—God bless her—said I could have her share because she never plans to return to Portugal. By giving me her part, the lot becomes a decent size."

I waited, not sure why she was telling me this. What did I have to do with my mother?

"For the land to be mine, the law requires your approval. You and your brother are the natural inheritors of anything your mother owns. Your mother said so."

"My mother said what?"

"She said, you need to call Milita in order to get her approval. Your brother said I could have the land. He's not interested in it."

My mother uttered my name?

"*Puta*," she'd hollered from the top of the stairs, the night I ran away, the burning red marks from her choking hands still imprinted on my throat. "Your name will never again be uttered in this house. I have no daughter. May the devil take your soul, *puta*."

Aunt Luisa chatted on. I could hardly decipher what she was saying. Was it a faulty connection or my stale Portuguese?

"I don't understand. You need my approval for what?"

"I need your approval for the land to be mine."

She spoke with the conviction of a sales pro, explaining that the land was a worthless piece of wilderness, a wasteland on top of a craggy hill without water, not good for cultivation or anything else. "If you say no, the land will have to be divided into two even smaller pieces worth shit. Just shit."

Sim, sim, Aunt Luisa. Yes, yes, you can have the land. It's yours.

There! A few simple words and the good deed would be done. But words had left me. I couldn't say, *the land is yours.*

What was it? What did I fear by giving her the land?

Something I could not name was stopping me from severing that link to my place of origin, that ancient soil named by the Moors long before the nation of Portugal was even imagined. Yes, that place where those who came before me and shared my blood, died toiling the dry, red earth, flesh and bones failing to nourish those infertile mystical hills of brush and rock.

I heard myself saying in a voice that sounded as though it was coming from some hidden interloper, "If the land is no good, why do you want it?"

"Ah, for your uncle's sake. His memory. Rafael was never happy in Amendoeiro. It was never home for him or your grandparents. Their souls remained in Algarve."

A long time had passed since I'd thought of my grandparents or their lives.

I looked across at the bay window of my dining room and there they were, gazing at me from a photograph I'd placed on the bottom of the window years ago. They're standing side by side in the middle of their garden in Amendoeiro, where they'd been living for over a decade by then. It must've been spring, blossoming freesia and sweet pea encircle them, spilling out of the picture frame. My grandfather looks stern, a man for whom life was a serious matter. He'd tried turning the patches of that rocky, dry soil of Algarve he'd inherited from his father, who'd inherited it from his father, going back generations, into an orchard, until one day, after the droughts turned the fruit trees into fodder for locusts, he gathered the family and said, "*Chega*." Enough. My mother, father, me as a baby, Avó, and Rafael ten or eleven by then had joined other *Algarvios*, whose small farms no longer sustained them, in the adhoc town called Amendoeiro. There was work in the cork factories, where my father was hired, and for those with ambition like my grandfather, entrepreneurial opportunities, like building houses. Yet, at the mention of Algarve, my grandfather would go silent, a furtive tear once escaping from his coal-black eyes. Avó too is unsmiling in the photograph. There's a no-nonsense quality in the way her arms fold over her belly, as if responsibility and work are waiting for her just beyond the freesia and the sweet pea and her memories of home.

I told Aunt Luisa I needed to wait. Needed to speak to my father first and understand why my mother required my authorization to give away land that was hers.

Silence fell at the other end of the line.

Before saying goodbye I asked her who'd given her my telephone number.

"Your mother."

As a child I was certain that, once childhood departed, so would my fears and mystifications about adulthood. Why did grownups do the things they did? Their actions didn't always make sense. When I was eight or nine I asked my mother why she punished me for not making my bed when she often didn't make hers. She said, "Do as I say and don't do as I do." Then she slapped me hard across the face for impudence.

My mother was always right.

I visited her only once in two years since leaving home, after my divorce from Eduardo, then my new marriage to Claudio, and the birth of our first son. It was a visit that wasn't a visit.

It was up to me, I'd thought, the child who'd broken all the rules, the *enfant terrible*—falling in love with Claudio while still married to Eduardo. Yes, yes, it was up to me to reach out and make peace. "One look at her first grandchild," Claudio insisted, "and she'll forgive you. What grandmother doesn't love her first grandchild?"

Salvation in an infant.

I, the spurned child, the one kicked out of my own house by my mother, like a rabid dog, needed healing, needed to close the invisible wound that kept festering.

It was April, the day still cold, snowflakes mingling with rain, reminding Toronto that winter was still in charge.

Claudio parked the green Dodge in front of my mother's house, a tiny bungalow in a street of other tiny bungalows and broken littered sidewalks close to Dufferin and Eglinton. My parents, Manuelito, and Eduardo had moved there soon after I left; without my wages, Eduardo had been unable to keep up the payments on the back split in Mississauga we'd bought.

Claudio waited in the car, fearing the reception he might receive. I feared it too.

I walked up the slippery front steps terrified of falling and dropping the two-month infant wrapped in a blue blanket. My hand shook as I rang the bell.

Why had I listened to Claudio? What did he know about my family?

The door opened; my mother stood before me.

A few moments passed before she recognized me. I'd grown thinner, hair longer, straighter, a new black liner framing my eyes. My mother looked shorter, shoulders more hunched, brown eyes duller, smaller, sunken. This face, a face I knew so well, a face that had always spoken of iron-fist discipline and terror, now appeared weak, frightened, apologetic.

"Come in," she said, her voice laced with a sadness that seemed to cling to her clothes, her thinning hair, the empty walls, me. "Come, I'll make you something to eat."

Was this an admission of sorts?

As I stepped into the hall, she blurted out, "Not the baby. Oh, no, no. Never, never. Not in this house. He's got the wrong father. The baby ought to be Eduardo's not that man's." She pointed toward the green Dodge parked in front. "You can come in, but not them. No, no, never, never them." She shook her head violently from side to side.

I turned around and walked down the same slippery steps, hardly seeing the slush-covered sidewalk for the tears.

I stayed home from work today. An unfamiliar exhaustion seemed to have taken possession of my body after Luisa's phone call. It was as though the weight of the *wanting* of all the years was depleting me of oxygen. Claudio would dial my father in the evening.

All day I practiced what I'd say to my father. I was convinced that if no one else understood my need to keep a piece of that mystical place called Algarve, my father would.

After Aunt Luisa's call, the crippling fear lasting through the years of anything to do with my mother began to soften. I reminded myself all day that Claudio would now be able to dial my parents' house and openly ask to speak to my father. Why not? Hadn't my mother given Aunt Luisa my telephone number? *She had, she had.* Now the need for games and lies had ended. It was always Claudio calling my father the few times we'd contacted him in the past. If my mother or Manuelito (when he still lived at home) or Eduardo (who'd continued living with my parents) picked up the telephone, Claudio pretended he was calling from the Compensation Board. My father had fallen down a ladder at work years earlier, permanently injuring his shoulder. There were times, I wondered, if my mother or Eduardo knew who was at the other end of the line. But I never asked; my father never said.

Wasn't forgiveness flying over me like a white dove? A baptismal of sorts?

Yet...

A sinking feeling kept me sitting all day on a long chair in my back garden. I tried to keep my mind from shattering into a million fragments of confusion, panic, disdain, regret, by concentrating on the busy sounds of fall. Squirrels scampered all afternoon in the soft October sunlight up and down the neighbour's walnut tree storing food for winter to ensure the survival of their young.

Even the lowly squirrel cares for its young...

The moment Claudio arrived home from the salon he dialled my father. He handed me the receiver and I quickly explained the reason for my call. My hands were trembling. After all, this was the first time that I'd spoken to my father on his home telephone with my family and Eduardo within earshot, I assumed.

"But Milita, what are you going to do with that useless piece of wilderness?"

I detected a touch of annoyance in his habitual meek voice.

"Nostalgia," I said. "Something in me wishes to be connected to a bit of that exotic land. Maybe it's the Moorish blood still coursing through my veins."

"Moorish blood! The Moors have been gone for six hundred years. You're imagining things, Milita. You were always good at making up stories. There's nothing exotic about Algarve. Only hunger and toil, growing up. Figs and almonds didn't satisfy a growing man's hunger."

"Why did you never tell me this?"

"What would be the point?"

"The point? You're my father. I want to know all about you, know where I come from."

"Romance, Milita, you want romance. The past is gone. Gone, puff, like smoke, you understand? Accept it. Just give Luisa that useless piece of brush and rock. She really wants it."

"But I want it too and I'm your daughter. Don't I have more right to it than she does?"

"What will you do with it?"

What would I do with it? I'd never given it much thought. All I knew was that I *wanted* the land, *needed* to have it, *had* to have it, in my keeping.

I felt like a child hogging all the toys.

"Now you're spoiling everything. Your mother is listening to this conversation and getting extremely upset. You know she has a bad heart. Had three attacks already."

"But she gave Aunt Luisa my telephone number?"

"Your mother's mind is gone."

My mother's mind is gone?

"Many times she doesn't know what she does or says or even remembers her own name. It's too late, Milita. Too late. Sometimes your mother talks about you as a child, things you did and said, how you used to spank the papier-mâché doll we bought you one Christmas the way your mother spanked you. She laughs. Other times she tells people she has no daughter. Did you hear that? She tells people she has no daughter."

I said nothing.

"It hasn't been easy for me either, you know, lying to your mother all these years, keeping our telephone calls and visits a secret. But I think your mother knew, somehow. She knew it was Claudio pretending to be calling from the Compensation Board all along. She'd be agitated for days after those calls. Come to think of it, it's best you don't call here ever again."

Pause.

"Now your mother is crying and walking the hall—her weak heart won't take this. Do me and yourself a favour. Forget you have a family? Okay? Throw away our phone number."

I said nothing.

"Remember, it was you who walked out on us."

I had.

He hung up.

I remained standing on the patio, receiver in hand. Evening had descended, bringing with it a fall chill.

Claudio stood close by listening, watching, waiting, not understanding a word of Portuguese. He was always there, always in reach when I most needed him. He put his warm, strong arms around my shoulders and held me tight.

The idea of inviting my father and mother over for dinner had crossed my mind earlier in the day. Manuelito, too, with his wife and son. Sunday, I'd do it Sunday. I'd cook something Portuguese—stewed *bacalhau* with potatoes, tomatoes, onions, parsley, and black olives.

I could smell the rich aroma of the fish stewing as I imagined the meal, all of us sitting around the kitchen table laughing, lifting our glasses and sharing silly stories from our past.

What Do We Know About Anyone?

I'm surprised at the starkness of the place. I expected the feeling of two warm arms hugging me. No paintings or sculptures, no tablecloths or flowers adorn Frank's, the restaurant in the newly renovated AGO. I mention this to the handsome waiter dressed in black, fashionable mohawk, small gold earring on his left ear. "Simplicity is best," he says. "It's a counter-balance to our busy and stressful lives." He gives me a smile that feels too familiar, a knowing smile. What is he seeing? He's young. A life not yet lived. What can he know of life's blisters?

Stop it!

What do we know about anyone? The pain behind the smiles, the laughter, the masks of the everyday? I repeat this mantra, silently, trying not to move my lips, as I smile at the mohawked waiter filling my water glass. He lingers a bit, looking as though he's about to say something. Share a secret? But he seems to change his mind and walks away with an open smile.

It's two pm, the restaurant is empty for a Thursday. Except for a table with two women in front of me, there's no one else.

From the upper section of Frank's, where I'm sitting, I can see the bar below. The bartender, also dressed in black, hair pomaded back from his forehead, dries wine glasses, holds them close to his face, then gently places them on the rack above his head. I like the way he inspects each glass, as though nothing else matters to him at this moment, nothing else is on his mind. A clean conscience. I keep staring.

A pamphlet handed out by the priest at the Portuguese church at Bathurst and Queen streets years ago and still in my keeping reminds us that a clean conscience comes from God's gift of forgiveness.

Forgiveness.

The pamphlet has yellowed through time and the edges tattered with handling.

I was still married to Eduardo then, my parents and Manuelito living with us in the old house on Euclid Avenue, before we moved to Mississauga. Church on Sundays provided an escape from my mother's watch, the feeling of the walls closing in. Sundays were noisy and long with nowhere to hide, especially after Claudio came into my life and filled every inch of my being. Sometimes I'd catch my mother gazing at me, eyes intense, the way she did when threading a needle. She'd quickly avert her gaze when she saw me looking.

Did she sense a change in me? Did my love for Claudio show?

Later, after I divorced Eduardo, married Claudio, and gave birth to my two sons, I found myself rereading the words on the tattered pamphlet, whenever my past reappeared like some fiendish ghost in a dark tale. Claudio's love, my new life, my children, had failed to padlock the doors to those inner mining fields. But mining fields of what? Sadness? Resentment? Loss? The desire that my life ought to have begun differently? That my father had once—once—stopped her from raking us all into the quagmire of disillusionment, self-pity, and anger that was her life?

Forgiveness! the pamphlet read. Forgiveness to all those who have done us harm.

Simple words. Redemption made simple so all those stumbling pilgrims on that Sunday long ago could understand.

But how is it done? How do we forgive the anger and the hurt oozing out in our soul like a festering abscess?

It's not true that time heals.

"You're too judgemental," my older son, Michael, the sensitive and creative one, once said. He was sixteen. I'd commented on the lack of ambition his long-haired guitar-playing friends had, a comment he likely extended to himself. He knew that *I knew* he was missing that ingredient called ambition required for the soup of success. And I wanted success. Oh, yes, yes, for my sons, my husband, me. Me, me, me . . . Success, like a tidal wave, so it could wipe out the past. But Michael paid no attention to my needs. Playing his guitar, he let life be. Later, I asked my younger son, Jeffrey, if he also saw me as being judgemental. "Yes," he said, without a trace of hesitation. Claudio, of course, would easily agree. "Stop judging me," was his habitual accusation, the source of most of our arguments that sometimes even sprinkled the word divorce over our heads.

But how are we not to judge those we love? Or those who betray us? Those who toss us out from their lives like putrid flesh?

As my mother did.

The two women sitting across from me, stand up, having finished their meal. The younger one, her back to me, slim, shiny black long hair, embraces the older one, whose hair is also long but peppered with strands of grey. "Thanks, Ma," the younger one says. "We'll do this again soon."

They walk out, my eyes stuck to their backs, their chatter and laughter filling the empty restaurant, filling the blanks in my life. My mushroom omelet arrives; it gets cold before I take the first bite.

Three years or so after Eduardo arrived from Portugal, we'd all gone to Sibbald Point Park on Lake Simcoe, as we often did in summer. The beach, though rocky, reminded us of the beaches in Portugal. By then Eduardo and I had bought the new yellow Ford, enabling us to join other Portuguese immigrants on Sunday outings. My parents and

Manuelito always came along. My mother couldn't fathom being left behind from anything Eduardo and I did. These Sundays never varied. The same fifteen, twenty people, same games, same conversations about the loneliness of immigrant life, the *saudades* of home, how much better things were back then. So much better...

I had no *saudades* of home. I did not miss Salazar's deadly regime, the disappearing men never heard of again, the mistrust of all—anyone could be an informer—the petty gossip of a small town, the patriarchal rules keeping women and children in perpetual servitude to fathers and husbands, the traditional respect and obeisance of children to parents, even to detached fathers and unsound-of-mind mothers like mine. I loved this new country, its promised freedom, the new language, the possibility of anything one chose to be. Wide open. Welcoming. Judgement-free. I was nineteen, bored, frustrated, repelled by a marriage forced on me by my mother, a husband I despised, a life I was living without *being* in it.

The afternoon was waning, dark clouds blanketing the sun. Feelings of escape into a future with me at its centre burst through me like a geyser.

I lay down on the grass, face upwards, arms wide open, silently screaming at the darkening clouds above. Even the heavens were conspiring to keep me down, down, down... Above me a lone seagull screeched. I watched it until it was lost into the misty distance over the lake. I closed my eyes, hung on to its wings. My hair blew backwards with the strong lake breeze up high, where the air was moist and fresh on my face.

"Milita!"

My eyes jolted open. My mother was bent over me. She'd been busy laying out supper on the red checkered tablecloth covering the picnic table. She'd made *pataniscas* the day before—fritters made with boiled cod and potatoes, egg, onion and parsley. Eduardo had helped her.

"What are you doing?" Her right hand lay over her heart, "I thought you were dead! Are you trying to kill me? You know I have a bad heart..."

Everyone gathered around me, puzzled faces staring down. I sat up and searched for the seagull but it was lost behind the dark clouds. Crows perched on a nearby pine, cawing loudly.

"*Má sorte*," my mother said, pointing up. "Bad luck, crows are bad luck."

Then she walked to the picnic table and sat at the edge of it, saying nothing more. The crows flew away.

We all chewed the *pataniscas* in stifling silence. Even our friends were quiet; I prayed for the return of the crows. Today, the *pataniscas* tasted greasy but I ate three, my mother watching me. Any rejection of her cooking or anything else she did was seen as a criticism of her, a devaluation of her value as a mother, a wife. She didn't eat any; she wasn't hungry.

The first drops of rain fell before the meal was ended; everyone scattered to their cars.

Days passed before my mother said anything around the house more than was necessary. To friends and acquaintances, she referred to the events of Sunday as a "A nasty joke. Nasty, nasty." It became her story, her only story for a long time. "Milita knows I'd die—I'd simply die—if something were ever to happen to her. She knows I couldn't live without her."

She didn't die.

The prodigal daughter, the *puta*, was easily replaced by Eduardo, the one she'd *always* wanted near, anyway. The one still living with her and my father today.

She never did come after me, as I was sure she'd do, feared she'd do, some filial archetypal urge in me, hoped she'd do, her wrath preferable to the *nothingness* of all the years.

One day—I was sure of this—maternal instincts would carry my mother to my door. Did birds not care for their offspring? cats? dogs? squirrels? worms feed their skin to their young to ensure their survival?

My mother lived. She lived without ever again laying eyes on me, the seed growing in her womb for nine months.

But what did I care now? I found myself asking on those nights when sleep's diaphanous wings flew over me on the way to more deserving souls. I had Claudio, my sons, friends. I'd repeat this, over and over, a mantra against the naked reality that my mother did manage to live without me.

Once out of Frank's, I walk through the gift shop. No browsing. The jewellery and china seem more like clutter today. I have enough clutter.

I look out the gift shop's large windows; rain is pelting the glass. It's as though the clouds, tired of the burden in their bellies, have opened up in angry revolt.

All seems to be in revolt.

I shake my head. Tell myself there's no room for unpleasant thoughts in this place of art, beauty, this peaceful lair without contrariness. But I can't seem to stop the dark churning of my mind. I walk out of the gift shop. Pause. Wonder if I should return upstairs to the Canadiana room for one last look at the white-haired woman. *My friend.* She sits on a chair dressed in mourning black, a shawl covering her shoulders, holding a small black book (appearing to be a bible) in her knobbly hands. Pale complexion, eyes tired, face wrinkled, a mirror of her life's sufferings. Yet her tiredness is not weary. Something about her soothes me, makes me feel less alone. Peace in mock companionship. Her faded smile speaks of a negotiated peace, an acceptance of all that has been thrown her way.

The clock at the Welcome Desk shows 4:30.

It's getting late. I decide to leave *her* for another day.

I sit on the long bench in the lobby, head leaning against the back wall, waiting for the storm to pass. I have no umbrella and no protection against the rain. I watch art lovers passing by; no one looks my way. What would they see, anyway? A middle-aged woman, fashionably dressed, comfort and assertiveness framing her every move. Yes, someone able to clutch her problems in the palm of her hand and discard them into the nearest garbage container. Easy.

The long-haired mother and daughter from Frank's appear from the galleries behind the lobby. I find myself wondering what art they've viewed. Modern, I think. Something light, inspiring. Futuristic.

They're still chatting and laughing as they pass me. The mother throws a smile my way, as though I'm an old acquaintance, a smile that says, I have it, I'm the one. They walk down the two steps and turn left, toward the coat check. I wait for them to reemerge. In a few minutes they appear, wearing matching red shawls. They soon disappear through the revolving doors.

I turn to look at the man sitting to my left. Tall, dressed in jeans and a sports jacket, handsome, a bit of grey showing on his sleek, longish hair. Likely in his fifties. An artist, definitely an artist. Sensitive, interesting, knows what he wants out of life, a man with clear convictions.

Life can be so simple for some, simple for those born in swaddling silk from loving mothers.

There you go again . . .

He catches my eye and offers me a smile. *Is he pitying me?*

I close my eyes. I'm disappointed in the tall man dressed in jeans. What did I expect from him? What do I expect from Claudio, my sons, my friends? What does this tenebrous yearning, thrusting through me like a growing nerve, want from others? Admiration? Love? Belonging?

Years of accumulation of things, comfort, golden mountains of pleasure, rivulets of laughter, yet . . .

Yet.

A few years ago when I visited the Hindu temple in Etobicoke and the *pujari* dribbled holy water on my head to demonstrate a blessing ritual, I couldn't stop crying. Sobs rose up from some untapped ghostly well within me, my legs trembling so badly, my friend Lucy had to hold me. The *pujari* gently sat me down, whispering something over me I didn't understand. Was it a prayer? A supplication? Later, over coffee, Lucy asked me what was wrong.

"I don't know," I said.

I meant it.

Winds whip the rain, night is approaching, my shoes and feet are wet and cold. I touch my face, run my hands over my body. My clothes are drenched. I run looking for shelter but the streets are deserted, the doors of buildings and houses, padlocked. There's no place to hide. I run, shivering. Cold, cold . . . I'm so cold. Then I see that I'm naked. Someone stole my clothes but I don't see anyone. Yet I hear voices . . .

The gallery is now closed.

I wake with a start.

I sit up. Look to my right, left. The handsome man in jeans and sports jacket is gone. The bookstore is dark. A young black woman, hair in a mountain of braids, stands before me.

"Excuse me, are you alright? Is there someone you want me to call?"

"No, no. I'm fine, thank you. I just fell asleep."

"You were talking, so I thought you were awake."

A shiver runs through me, "What was I saying?"

"I couldn't understand; it sounded like a foreign language."

She watches me as I stand up. Smiles, the kind of smile I've seen on the faces of nurses and caregivers of the old and meek that says it's okay but hurry up.

I straighten my back; she returns to the Welcome Desk and turns off the lights.

The rain has stopped; I walk out. The still distant April sun is now breaking through the heavy dark clouds. Patches of blue make the sky look checkered, like a tablecloth. The Sunday at Sibbald Park comes to mind. I push the thought away.

Claudio will be home soon. I'll cook him pasta fagioli, his favourite.

He likes coming home from work to a home-cooked meal on the days when I'm off.

Walking along Dundas Street, through Chinatown, toward Spadina, I jostle through crowds of mostly Asian shoppers and pedestrians. They all look busy.

I raise my face to the sun, feeling the soothing warmth, and take another step, then another. The Spadina streetcar rattles past me; I decide to walk up to Bloor.

At the corner of Wilcox a woman sits on the sidewalk, hand stretched out. I stop. Make sure our eyes meet. She must see that I see her. She looks to be about my age. Her eyes are brown and round like mine, but empty-looking, like a wine glass that's used and forgotten. Her clothes are filthy, her hair tangled, two large, equally filthy green plastic bags stand by her side, likely the sum total of her possessions. I think of home, the comfort, the security, and feel, what? Guilt? Pity? Fear?

The pungent smell of her unwashed body and clothes wafts up toward me.

I step back.

"Would you like something to eat?" I ask.

"Oh, yes, please, I'm very hungry." Her voice is clear, self-assured. "I've missed lunch."

"Okay. Don't go away."

"I live here."

I hurry toward a coffee shop, a block up, wondering the whole time why someone so lucid is out on the streets.

Was she thrown out?

I buy a chicken salad sandwich on brown bread and a bottle of orange juice. Nutritious. As I approach her and get close, she looks up at me, as though she's never seen me before.

"Here," I say. "I bought you a chicken salad sandwich and an orange juice."

"Oh, no, no, no, I don't eat meat. Meat is not good for you." She violently pushes the bag with the sandwich and drink toward me with her soiled hand.

I place the sandwich and juice in my bag and walk away.

I begin to tremble, my whole body like a twig in a wind storm. I walk as though in a daze. When I reach Bloor, I sit on the ledge of the massive oblong cement flower container at the corner. A tear falls on my cheek. Then another and another.

What did I think buying the homeless woman the sandwich and juice would do?

As I dry my tears, I gaze at the hasty feet of passersby. All seem to have a destination they're hurrying to, as though someone is waiting for them.

I stand up and cross Bloor. The sun is setting but the early evening is warm.

Claudio is waiting for me.

Before walking out through the revolving doors of the AGO, four or five waiters, young, slim, dressed in black, had walked by me. They came up the basement stairs, carrying planters of flower arrangements, white tulle, and long ribbons. I recognized the mohawked waiter from lunch. He waved, then turned to face me. He arched his eyebrows, shrugged his shoulders and said, "Another wedding!"

He's so young but seems to already know so much. Knows that the journey isn't easy.

But it's okay.

Okay . . .

Okay . . .

He knows he's not alone—I'm not alone.

River Crossings

I stand at the mouth of the Tejo, the vast Atlantic lost beyond the dull horizon, the bustling city behind me. Car horns, guitars, drums, chatter, fill the air. It begins to drizzle. A sudden gust of wind ruffles the wide, restless river. Out of the mist, a chrysalis of grey river and overcast sky, a skinny girl, brown eyes open wide, emerges, mollusks on her hair. She beckons me, skeletal arm reaching, reaching . . . I see her tears. They meld with the raindrops, the river, the mist. I wipe my eyes. Gulls cry angrily above my head. Deafening. Disarming. Haunting.

For whom are they crying?

I have no umbrella. But I remain fixed on a drama only I can see.

A massive white screen has been erected next to the equestrian statue of King José I in the monumental square facing the river. This is where the king's residence used to be before the devastation of 1755. The statue celebrates the rebuilding of the city after the earthquake. This screen, too, must be a celebration. Then I remember: the 2018 World Cup. Portugal vs. Uruguay. Later today. Cristiano Ronaldo comes to mind. Our modern hero. Other names follow, those who navigated these waters long ago. Vasco da Gama, Alvares Cabral, Magalhães, who set out in discovery of sea routes, lands, spices, riches, power. Later, fishermen followed. They salted cod on the shores of Newfoundland. Their faces and names are not known, not remembered or recorded. But they opened the doors to future immigrants, men and women ready to confront the unknown. Begin anew. Ha, the new-found-land on the other side of these turbulent waters, where I have lived, trying to forget the very land I'm standing on. Yes, yes, trying to forget a childhood spilling over with brutality masqueraded as love from a mother whose insanity was never diagnosed. Never, it was never she who had a problem. Four decades spent at the smithy of life trying to cobble a new me.

Yet...

You stand on the upper deck of the ferryboat crossing the Tejo from Montijo to Lisboa. The wide river is tempestuous on this grey November morning. The waters are angry. It'll take an hour to cross. You shiver, pull your green woollen scarf tighter around your neck. You look behind you. There's no one. *Good.* You want to be alone in this long-awaited farewell. This departure from everything you've known up to now. You glance back at Montijo. The bullring in the distance, the black mountains of garbage at the river's entrance, Lisbonites sending their refuse across on barges. In summer, stench and flies undo good intentions. The black mountains of garbage darken the sky, like monolithic guards at a Stygian passage to a subterranean kingdom. Behind Montijo lies Amendoeiro, where you lived, that ad hoc town of unpaved streets, whirling dust, stray cats and dogs, whores, drunkards, beggars, gossip, the lingering terror of Salazar's regime, the sweaty hands of your grandfather's greasy-haired tenant next door on those parts of your body that made you feel ashamed when you were only eight! You never told anyone. Left behind the swells vomited by the ferry too is the dread of your mother's anger, her beatings, the savagery of her exactitude—you were always deficient. But you're turning fifteen next month; soon you'll be too old to be beaten into submission. Behind too are the shameful piss pots under the beds, the manure pile of shit and food leftovers at the back of the garden, and Eduardo, the buck-toothed idiot your mother chose as your boyfriend. He's in the ferry's bar at this moment drinking coffee with her, planning your future. Soon he'll be left standing at Lisbon Airport with you waving goodbye. Forever goodbye. You've imagined this scene a thousand times. In a few hours, your mother, Manuelito, and you, will be in a Canadian Pacific plane away to Toronto to join your father. A new larger world is waiting for you.

The Tejo girdles the ancient white city, whose foundation pre-dates history, eternally watching it. It begins to ebb, unveiling its black muddy bottom. There's something disarming, disappointing, forlorn in the nakedness of the river. Waves of dread run through me making me feel vulnerable. Afraid. I can't speak. Claudio fears my silence, he fears being left out of my world but he says nothing. Draws me close. The drizzle persists. We buy an umbrella from a Chinese vendor. She says *obigado* instead of *obrigado*.

We walk the old city, Alfama, Chiado, Bairro-Alto, Belem, a maze of cobblestoned streets with shops, restaurants, crowds, laughter, a hymn to the dark past—smashed bones and screams of terror in the night— and a cheer to this bustling EU present. Newcomers now fill the city for whom Portugal's past has no meaning. These changes dissolve the familiar, warping my earlier memories of Lisbon. Now people of different colours and ethnicities stand at establishment doors, calling us in. Indians hawk the traditional *pasteis-de-nata*; an Angolan sells us the port wine we'll take to my cousin Margarita tonight for a family dinner. A reunion of sorts. Lisbon's doors are open; the world descends on this native soil. A new aurora heralds from every corner.

Before dinner, my cousins ask me about my mother. They know that it's been years since we've spoken, know too that my first marriage to Eduardo was her idea. "Last week I called my parents," I say to my cousins in Portuguese with a chuckle, meant to entertain, to amuse these relatives I haven't seen in years. They sit around me, forward, intense, showing interest. "After four decades," I say, "I was sure my mother had forgiven me . . . " I start to cry, softly at first, then sobs roll over me like a bulldozer storming this safe space. Claudio comes closer.

"Stop," he says.

My cousins are all silent; I've frightened them. A fifty-year-old woman sobbing like a child isn't pretty.

Time morphs.

The rain pounding the windows of the CP plane seems angry, as though determined to destroy it. The Tejo below looks black, menacing. *Cristo Rei*, colossal, across the river, blesses the city and the river crossings, those departing or arriving, as destiny decrees. You pray *Cristo Rei* is blessing you.

Your mother sits behind you with Manuelito. You hear her sighs and wonder if the other passengers are hearing her too. Her promise to Eduardo, as they embraced, still rings loud in your ears. Both were crying like two broken-hearted lovers in some melodrama. "Don't worry," she said. "I'll call for you as soon as possible." You hurried past the gate.

In Montreal, two men in uniform ask you questions. You don't understand what they're saying; they don't seem to understand you. But you're not frightened. They smile, voices soft, blue gazes welcoming, assuaging the strangeness, the disarming sense of dislocation running through you. They are different from the terrifying authoritativeness of Portuguese officials using the vocabulary of threat and intimidation.

You feel this new world is opening wide—*wide* . . . It's calling you. *There, there . . . You can almost touch it.*

You're told by a clerk speaking Portuguese that the flight from Montreal to Toronto is a short one. An hour. But the plane is small, claustrophobic, wobbling in the vacuum of the skies, as though trying to duck some unseen enemy. The pilot announces that there's a snowstorm. FASTEN YOUR SEATBELTS, the lit-up signs say.

Your mother now sits next to you; Manuelito is across the aisle. She's crying, "I'll never forgive your father."

It's late when the plane arrives. The airport feels ghostly. Your father is waiting with a man and a woman and a girl your age. You don't know them. The girl is dressed in a Cinderella-like long dress, blue lace, and tulle, as though at a costume party. You have a strange feeling that you are travelling back in time, that the new world is receding into something unrecognizable.

A trial. It feels like a trial, this last supper. I'm surrounded by a jury of cousins sitting around the dinner table. It's behind their smiles, in their eyes. I catch them. Suspended knives and forks in midair when they least expect. They stare at me, wanting to know, figure things out, reach a verdict that will satisfy them because my mother was loved by them too. A favourite with her kindness and open-arm generosity. They want to make a choice. Decide which one of us is guilty. Then they can go forward with their lives, pick sides, stop the arguments.

But it's a tale not for the pure of heart, or to be told to children. The thirty-year-old mother and the sixteen-year-old daughter's boyfriend. The journey is paved with thorns and thistles of shame, gossip, and my father's silence. Perhaps his shame too; he's never said. How much does he know? My mother's promise to Eduardo was fulfilled— he arrived in Toronto within a year. My proxy marriage to him, at sixteen, only needed one signature. Simple. I stayed for over six years in a marriage so unwanted, I pretended I was single for a year while dreaming of escape and love's ambrosia. I stayed until I walked out at twenty-two, never to return. Cupid offered me his golden cup in the rapturous gaze of Claudio's blue eyes.

But I say nothing of this to my cousins. I let them think I'm the hero, the winner, in this tawdry contest. I don't speak of freedom's price, the debt exacted by the cosmos. There's always a price.

My father's visits and telephone calls ebbed to a stop through the years; I never again saw Manuelito. And when I least expect, just when laughter drowns out all other senses, the skinny girl with mollusks in her hair reemerges from the muddy depths of memory's river.

But tomorrow I'm flying back to Toronto; the Tejo left behind.

For now.

Acknowledgements

An armful of gratitude to Mawenzi House for publishing *Yellow Watch*. I truly appreciate the guidance and caring offered by Nurjehan Aziz and Crystal Shi, and the editing precision provided by MG Vassanji.

Eternal hugs to Mark Anthony Jarman whose patience and help gave shape to these stories. I am also grateful to all those who early on my writing journey offered me instruction and encouragement. To name a few: Christine Pountney, Alyssa York, Heather Birrell, and Nino Ricci.

Also, I offer a long embrace to the original Writing Group who, tirelessly, read and edited many of these stories, encouraged and shared a glass of wine together: Hege Jakobsen Lepri, Ian Mallov, Afarin Hosseini, Babak Lakghomi, Kate Blair, and Medhi M Kashani.

My husband and sons for their faith in me. Always.

The following stories have previously been published as follows:

"Strays" in *Belletrist Magazine*; "A Black Kitten" in *Antigonish Review*; "River Crossings" in *The Hong Kong Review*; "Pumpkin Seeds, My Mother and Other Dangers" in *The Magnolia Review*, 2021; "The Bêbeda" in *Blue Mesa Review*, 2021 (Issue 43); "Lucinda's Bouquet" in *The Maine Review*, 2021 (Issue 7.2); "The Disappeared" in *The Fiddlehead*, 2020 (no. 282);

"Warlocks, Spells and My Mother" in *San Antonio Review*, 2020; "Casa do Relogio" in *Prairie Fire*, 2019 (Volume 40, Number 3); "And Still I Said Nothing" in *Litro Magazine*, 2018.

Carmelinda Scian emigrated to Canada from Portugal as a teenager in the late 1960s with her parents. After marriage and two children, she obtained a BA and an English MA from the University of Toronto on a part time basis while operating a hair salon. Her works have appeared in several literary magazines across Canada, the USA, and Britain and have won several prizes, including the *Malahat Review*'s Open Season Short Fiction Writing Contest, and the *Toronto Star* Short Story Contest. The story "Yellow Watch" was nominated for Canada's Journey Prize, and the story "River Crossing" has been selected for the 2022 edition of Best Canadian Stories. She lives in Toronto.